PENGUIN BOOKS
DO IT AGAIN

Martyn Harris was born in Swansea in 1952 and educated at the universities of Keele and Kent. He now lives in north London. He has written regularly for a number of magazines, including the *New Statesman* and *New Society*, and now writes the 'Odd Man Out' column in the *Daily Telegraph*. He is currently working on his second novel.

DO IT AGAIN

MARTYN HARRIS

PENGUIN BOOKS

For Sarah and Tom

I would like to thank Cathy Meeus, Paul Fisher,
John Phillips and Joceline Bury — but especially Max Hastings,
who was generous with encouragement, and time.

PENGUIN BOOKS

Published by the Penguin Group
Penguin Books Ltd, 27 Wrights Lane, London w8 5tz, England
Viking Penguin, a division of Penguin Books USA Inc.
375 Hudson Street, New York, New York 10014, USA
Penguin Books Australia Ltd, Ringwood, Victoria, Australia
Penguin Books Canada Ltd, 2801 John Street, Markham, Ontario, Canada l3r 1b4
Penguin Books (NZ) Ltd, 182–190 Wairau Road, Auckland 10, New Zealand

Penguin Books Ltd, Registered Offices: Harmondsworth, Middlesex, England

First published by Viking 1989
Published in Penguin Books 1990
1 3 5 7 9 10 8 6 4 2

For permission to reproduce copyright material, grateful acknowledgement is made to the
following: Olwyn Hughes for lines from Ted Hughes's poem on the eighty-fifth birthday of
the Queen Mother (copyright © 1985); Century Hutchinson Limited for the extracts from *100
Years of Royal Style* by Colin McDowell and *Dreams about HM the Queen and Other Members of
the Royal Family* by Brian Masters; Chatto & Windus for the excerpt from *Lies, Damned Lies
and Some Exclusives* by Henry Porter; Rondor Music Ltd for lines from 'Do It Again'
(Wilson/Love), copyright © Irving Music Inc., 1968; and Anthony Sheil Associates for the
extract from *Hotel de Dream*, by Emma Tennant, copyright © 1976, first published by
Gollancz.

Printed in England by Clays Ltd, St Ives plc

CHAPTER ONE

From *The Republican Reader*:

> If Royalty is absurd, then we are even more so, because it is we who invent them.

Alec Smith, millionaire socialist, decided to leave London on 1 April, his thirty-ninth birthday. It was May before Susan, his wife, agreed to join him. 'I don't want to go to Uplands,' she told him. 'We've lived there before. Done all those things. It's going backwards.'

But Alec was nursing gloomy thoughts, of half his life already past, and he felt that things had gone forwards far enough already. Alec had the practical man's faith that you could fix anything if you tried hard enough. He could strip a car engine, lay bricks, rewire a house. He had built his own publishing company from nothing and sold it for a lot of money. He had got fat, then made himself thin again. He had even given up smoking. What was so hard about going backwards?

And he was a millionaire socialist. A newspaper had called him one the other day, and it was probably true, if you threw in house, shares, car and kitchen sink. Millionaire socialists should be able to do whatever they wanted, and so Alec argued with Susan:

'We were always happiest when we lived at Uplands. Things have never been the same since then.'

'We were young then,' she said crossly. 'We were at university. We didn't have children. We didn't have jobs.'

'We're not old, the children are at school and I haven't got a job now,' said Alec, all of which was true.

He was fixing the kitchen drawer when they had this conversation, at three o'clock on a Monday afternoon. Susan liked to save carrier bags from Sainsbury's and stuff them in the drawer until they came in useful. Over the weeks they would mysteriously fill with air, and balloon up, spill over the sides and back of the drawer and jam in the runners.

Alec pulled the drawer clear of its carcass, set it down on the floor and examined the mechanism of the runners. Susan watched, with mingled guilt and irritation. Alec was good at things like this – determined, patient, resourceful. He was also good at making them a matter of reproach.

The nylon bearings and retaining clips of the drawer runner were clogged with fluffy shreds of plastic carrier bag. The steel angle strip on the side of the cabinet where the drawer rested had been wrenched loose by Susan's forcing it in and out against the pressure of the plastic debris. Alec sucked his teeth irritably and began unscrewing it.

'You could easily get somebody to come and do that for you,' said Susan defensively.

And, of course, she was right. He could have got somebody in from the fitted-kitchen company with a new runner, a new drawer – fuck it, why not a new kitchen? They could afford one. But then Alec would have been denied the pleasure of this silent but eloquent demonstration of masculine competence and of the evils of hoarding plastic carrier bags. And in any case, he had absolutely nothing else to do.

Alec's business, Prometheus Press, had made a lot of money in the 1970s, when it published self-sufficiency handbooks and jokey, illustrated guides to serious subjects like Marxism. Then, when political fashion changed, it had lost a lot of money and Alec had thought about getting a job in marketing with a bigger company.

Then Prometheus produced *The Republican Reader* and

made more money than anyone would have thought possible. It made so much money that an Australian publisher with a helicopter flew Alec from Battersea heliport to lunch at the Quat' Saisons, near Oxford, and asked him to name his price. Which he did.

So now Alec had a seat on the board of the Australian's company, though he didn't expect that to last for long. They had produced spin-off books from the *Reader*: a diary called *The Republican Roster* and a children's pop-up book called *The Right Royal Rip-Off*. They had sold a series of morning readings to Radio Four and there were plans for a TV puppet series. Not that Alec had much to do with these things. When his friends asked what he actually *did* with himself nowadays, he blushed and told them that he went to bullshit marketing meetings twice a month. He also swam long distances in empty public baths and cooked a lot and fixed things around the house. But no, he didn't have a job any more.

He wasn't proud of his idleness. *The Republican Reader* had drawn up lists of jobs once for the idle Royals:

In a republican future, it would, of course, be necessary to find work for the Royal Family. The Princess of Wales, for instance, because of her looks and rather dim academic record, would have to be a check-out girl – but in a rather superior supermarket like Waitrose or Sainsbury's. Prince Charles, agonizedly dutiful and sober, could be a social worker, perhaps a probation officer. Princess Margaret might find a role behind the cosmetics counter at Dickins & Jones. Princess Anne – a farmer's wife. Prince Andrew – a bingo caller.

The Duke of Edinburgh, with his vehement opinions, mechanical aptitude and short fuse, could be a taxi driver. The Queen's steely demeanour and renowned efficiency would make her a first-rate sub-postmistress. The Queen Mother might become the wife of a successful publican or bookmaker and fulfil much the same social role as she does today, albeit on a more local scale. Princess Michael of Kent would rise, indeed *has* risen, whatever her social background. In a republican Britain she might be married to a rock star.

'Well, *I've* got a job,' said Susan, 'though I know that doesn't count any more.'

Susan had been a designer when they got married. She created the covers for the early Prometheus books and for *The Reader* itself. Even now, when they didn't need the money, she still took on the odd commission, and she taught two days a week at a south London art college.

'Of course it counts, my love,' said Alec, dishonestly. 'And you must keep on doing it. You could work more from home. Perhaps you could use one of those new Macintosh computers with all the graphics. Anyway, it's only an hour from Uplands to Waterloo, door to door. And we'd keep on this place in London, of course, if you wanted to spend the odd night here.'

He pulled the metal strip free of the side of the cabinet and frowned at the dusting of wood fibres that came with it. It was an expensive German fitted-kitchen with sleek, post-formed worktops, cool pools of concealed light and magnetic catches that just *kissed* shut when you pushed the doors to. But the cabinet carcasses were made of shredded wood fibre, mixed with epoxy resins and compressed into slabs between the sleek, grey, melamine panels. It would take a self-tapping screw once but not twice in the same place.

'Well, it's nice of you to let us keep *my* house,' said Susan.

It *was* her house, the deposit paid for by Susan's father as a magnificent wedding present fifteen years ago. Their friends had still been living in basement flats in Kentish Town and squats in Kilburn. But Alec and Susan had a flat-fronted Georgian house in Islington, with purple wisteria trained over curly wrought-iron balconies. It had cost £30,000 then, and was now worth ten times as much. 'Daddy is still a bit alarmed about you,' Susan had explained to Alec when they moved in, 'and this is his way of saying that he isn't.'

The house was in Susan's name, though it was Alec who had paid off the mortgage. At first, in front of their friends, loyal Susan always called it 'our house'. But then it became hers again, along with certain of the things in it.

— 4 —

The German kitchen, with its doors that were beginning to chip and drawers that had started to jam, for instance, was Alec's. So were the video and stereo and matching suites of furniture and the fitted carpets. Susan said she didn't know why they had ever got these stupid things in the first place. Suites of furniture were really rather common and so were fitted carpets and videos and stereos and mixer taps. What they should have had, apparently, was polished wood floors, rugs and proper furniture.

Alec thought they had bought all these things together in the early years of their marriage, browsing through *Which?* magazines and wandering companionably around Habitat. But apparently not. These were all Alec's things which he had bought himself and was welcome to. Susan's things were the pictures, the good pieces of furniture from the old house in Holland Park and the walnut box with the baize-lined drawers which lived in the bank. Susan had already divided the spoils of their marriage mentally and Alec was beginning to worry that it might become actual.

'I liked the kitchen the way it was when we moved in,' Susan told Alec now. 'Those quarry tiles on the floor and the old stone sink and that lovely old painted dresser you knocked down.'

'It had woodworm,' said Alec, through a mouthful of screws. 'And it was the only place the central heating boiler could go.'

He blew the residue of dust out of the empty screw holes and squirted a blob of wood glue into each. Plastic rawlplugs would be no good in these holes. They would just twist with the screws and gouge even bigger cavities. He groped in his pocket for matches.

'You know, I used to think they made these panels from bits of leftover timber from the saw mills, but they don't. They grind up whole trees. Perfectly good wood. The fibres are easier for machines to process into panels than sheet timber. It never warps and there's no wastage.'

Susan had once rather enjoyed Alec's little lectures: the

arbitrary chunks of information which he retained so effortlessly. How mayonnaise emulsified; why Americans had primary elections; what carburetters were for. The remark about wood fibre might once have led to a conversation about the environment, the rapacity of industry, the tackiness of industrial products and the gullibility of consumers. But nowadays Susan found the lectures irritating. Why were men so interested in all these bits and pieces that didn't matter to anybody and which they could do nothing about? All this *junk*.

'I never understood when we moved in here why you were so determined to buy all these *units*,' she told him. Alec noted that she gave the word the special topspin that she could also give to *beer*, *William*, *Republican Reader* and *television*, and most of the other things which Alec bought or sold or liked.

'We bought this kitchen together,' said Alec.

'Oh no, we didn't. You saw it in the *Sunday Times* Magazine in 1975, the year after Dora was born, and decided you wanted it. And then you dragged me to that awful showroom on the North Circular Road with the Chinese furniture salesman with bad breath. And then you just went on and on about labour saving and hygiene until I gave in.'

How did women do that trick? Alec could not remember what he had been doing yesterday evening, much less what he had said. The whole span of years between about twenty-five and thirty-nine had become a vagueness, punctuated by new jobs and holidays and childbirth. Counting carefully backwards he could just about work out the year this child had been born or that car replaced.

But women. Women could play back verbatim a conversation you had had in a launderette ten years ago about whether you liked carrots chopped or sliced. They knew what your mother thought of your second cousin, and what the second cousin had worn to your sister's wedding. The *Sunday Times*, 1975 and Chinese halitosis were too detailed for Alec to dispute and he went on with his repair. The stubs of the matchsticks, wedged into the screw holes, should give enough grip with the help of the glue.

He searched for an opening to return the conversation to its proper course.

'The kitchen at Uplands still has all the old stuff, you know. Cold stone floor, knackered old furniture, smoking Aga, Scotch airer. You should like all that.'

'We haven't got any friends down there any more,' said Susan. 'Everyone's moved away.'

And that was another thing about women. They always changed the subject. The subject was kitchens, not friends.

'There's Malcolm . . . and Vivien . . .'

'*Your* friends,' said Susan. The topspin again.

They used to be *their* friends, like the furniture, but now they were his. Who were Susan's friends? Someone at the office called Lizzie. One of the mothers at the children's dancing class. The silly bitch she was at boarding school with who worked for the BBC and whom Susan met for lunch once a month. Alec didn't know Susan's friends. He registered, uneasily, that they were all after Alec, before Alec or in spite of Alec.

After fifteen years together he still loved her. That was the thing which had surprised him most when things began to fall apart. She could be such a cow, and he still loved her. He looked at her now, leaning back against the kitchen table, watching him crouched inside the cabinet.

She was the same height as Alec, who was five foot eight, and in her heels she was two and a half inches taller. Her face was round and pale beneath an untidy brown fringe. Slightly bruised-looking beneath the eyes and around the mouth, like a thumbed peach. It had been a perfect sixties face, a Biba face. Childlike but a little *used*. Up all night but still dewy.

She was wearing a tight red cashmere pullover that showed the ponderousness of her breasts and a full, black skirt he didn't recognize that came down to mid-calf. She had become embarrassed about her legs. The Englishwoman's bum had crept up behind her in her twenties; crept up behind and clamped itself to her hips, turning her boxy teenage buttocks into something deep and welling and womanly.

Steatopygous was the word for it. All Englishwomen became steatopygous in time, and embarrassed about it. Susan waged war on her bum with an exercise wheel and a rowing machine. But Alec liked the Englishwoman's bum. He would even have liked to go to bed with her now, in spite of the chilliness in the air between them. To undress each other slowly, kneeling face to face on the big pine bed, and then, with one half of the creamy, steatopygous, English-woman's bum clasped in each of his hands . . .

Wouldn't work though. It never did seem to work any more. Half-way through, something would fly away. She didn't resist him or anything. He would just discover, mysteri-ously, that he was on his own in the bed, and something would fly away.

Then he would get angry with her. Why didn't she want him any more? And she would say it wasn't her fault he couldn't do it, and how could he expect her to relax if he always got angry? And he would say that she started being like this long before he ever got angry. Then she would say that on 12 October 1977 he, Alec, had got angry. No, he didn't. Yes, he did. No, he didn't.

And Alec knew perfectly well that if he did ask her now, it would be too late, or too early, or too sudden, or too silly. When they first met they had done it all night in two-foot-six college beds. They had done it out on the croquet lawn at Uplands after a party. They had done it swimming in the ice-cold gravel pits near the university. Once, on the train down to Wykeham, he and Susan had fucked each other standing up, giggling in the lavatory, with a ticket collector rattling the doorknob. But now they could not find the time and space to make love in an empty house, on a six-foot bed, with children at school, at three o'clock on a Monday after-noon.

Of course sex got dull after years and years together; that was expected. Once a week, once a month. You don't mind if I sleep in the spare room tonight, do you? It could even stop for months at a time. After making cautious inquiries amongst his friends, over pints in pubs, Alec was able to reassure himself that he and Susan were not alone.

You didn't just *ask* your men friends, of course. For all the calculated candour and comic brutality of male tough talk, it was women who were the direct sex.

'When are you and Susan going to have another kid, then?' William asked him once in The Ferryman.

'When the Archangel Gabriel takes a hand in it,' said Alec.

And then they had another beer and William told a funny story about his Dutch cleaning lady coming in while William was having a wank, which was William's way of repaying the confidence. And so you got the idea. Even William didn't do it that much any more. Malcolm hadn't done it for months. Vivien hadn't done it for years. Perhaps nobody did it any more.

When Alec was at school he had thought he was the only teenager in the world who wasn't doing it. The only celibate adolescent in the 1960s. This boy was doing it in an air-raid shelter with a girl from the fairground; another was doing it with his sister; a third with the gym mistress.

When Alec returned home from blameless evenings of playing table tennis in the youth club Harry, his father, would wink and nudge him in the ribs. 'Don't do anything I wouldn't do,' he would say, and 'You're only young once.'

Harry ran a small clothing wholesalers, but when people asked what he did he still liked to say that he 'travelled in ladies' underwear'. He hadn't been on the road in twenty years but he still had a dash of Jack the Laddery about him. A smack of Old Spice, a gob of Brylcreem and a smear of soap down the inside of his trouser creases.

Harry was the son of a labourer from Edgware and had left school at fourteen, but the Second World War had made him classless. He had entered as an aircraftman and left as a warrant officer, with a waxed moustache and improbable accent. He married, in uniform, a plump girl from a Methodist family in Watford and, so far as official family history went, she was the only girl he had ever had.

But Harry liked to suggest to his only son an unfathomable sexual experience.

'I'm not too old to remember what it was like,' he would tell the adolescent Alec. 'There's not a lot you could tell me,' and 'if you can't be good, be careful.' And Alec would wink back and blush.

Alec believed it all for a while, and then he didn't believe any of it. If it was so difficult for him, then it must be so for everyone else. None of his friends were doing it. Probably his parents had only done it once in order to produce Alec.

Alec and his friends existed, so sex too must have existed at one time – in the years after the war, like dried eggs and rationed bananas – but it had clearly gone out of fashion. Nobody was doing it now. Not until they went to university and confessed, like Alec, in a narrow college bed, that this was their first time too.

That was to Susan, and of course, she had done it lots and lots. There was William and the lecturer with the Land Rover and the wanker who had gone to Sandhurst. And even bloody Malcolm. She wasn't worried that Alec couldn't manage it at first. She didn't even mind that he cried. Susan took Alec in hand, and he tried hard not to make his gratitude too pathetic.

'We could always have a party,' he told Susan now. 'At Midsummer. Even if we don't move there, it would be fun to have a party.'

'Who's going to drive seventy miles from London to a party in a crumbling old slum somewhere in the middle of Kent?'

'All the old Uplands people,' said Alec stubbornly. 'There's Vivien, Malcolm, William, Geoff Bright, Ralph, Daisy Dee . . .'

'Six people,' said Susan.

'Someone told me Daisy was married to a judge now,' said Alec.

He tightened the screws and they fitted satisfactorily, spreading the matchsticks firmly into the woodpulp and clenching the metal angle tightly against the wall of the drawer unit.

She watched him crouched, half inside the cabinet, like a busy monkey, his narrow, hairy hands clenched around the handle of the pump-action screwdriver. He was good with his hands, but he didn't look as if he should be. With his moist, dark curls and fragile, pudgy body. Her own father grew up in a world where you called a servant to change a lightbulb, and Alec's father, Harry, was too recently escaped from the labouring classes to see any virtue in getting his hands dirty.

When Alec was fixing up the house in Islington Harry would drop by and wring his hands over the digging of the garden, the plastering of the walls and the glazing of the windows. 'Look, son, if you want some bricklaying done, you should pay some Mick to do it. You really want to dig up your garden, then you get some black geezer from Brixton. You don't go to university for five years so you can go breaking your fingernails on a shovel.'

Harry would appeal to her for support: 'You tell him, Susie. He won't listen to me. Go to your office. Earn some money. Pay a man who knows what he's doing for a proper job.'

But Alec always knew what he was doing. He laid bricks from an article in a book, and they ran true as water, with pointing crisp as marzipan. He changed nappies deftly, without screams and without smearing sticky tapes with cold cream. He even learned to cook better than Susan, unflappable Alec, with hollandaise that never curdled and lamb that was always delicately rose. And Harry came and ate and marvelled at his son. New father. New man.

Female friends envied her Alec, and male friends grew sheepish at tales of the Alec–Susan equality. He was everything the new feminist agendas required, so why did he get on her nerves so much? Because he *was* so bloody omni-present and omnicompetent, that's why.

She lived in an Alec climate, swam in an Alec soup. Alec fixed the house. Alec chose the cars. Alec cooked the dinner. So fucking *busy*. His busy little hands on his tools, on his driving wheel, in his pockets and down her knickers. Sod off, Alec.

He lectured her about politics, literature, cooking and art (Christ, *she* was the Fine Arts graduate). Alec made all the money, chose all the furniture, scolded her for being untidy in *her* house and now Alec was telling her where to live. Sod off, Alec. Go and get fucked, Alec. And not with me.

The repair job was finished. Alec swept out the shards of matchstick and wood fibre from the cabinet and dumped them in the pedal bin. He collected up his tools, snapped them into clips in his tool chest and stowed it on its shelf beneath the stairs. Susan had left the kitchen and was talking crossly on the phone to Lizzie or Debbie or Poppy or somebody.

He had saved the best bit until last, as a small present for himself. He knew what would happen, but it was still satisfying. Picking the repaired drawer off the floor, Alec pushed it into place with hardly a finger's pressure. It slid home with a pleasing *ssschup* of its nylon bearings and kissed the rear of its housing with a barely perceptible click. It wouldn't last for ever, of course. A year or so with careful use and not too many bloody carrier bags. And in any case, they wouldn't be living here in a year, would they?

CHAPTER TWO

From *The Republican Reader*:

The Queen has eight palaces: Buckingham
Palace, Kensington Palace, Hampton Court
Palace, Windsor Castle, the Palace of Westmins-
ter, the Palace of Holyrood House, Sandringham
and Balmoral. Of these, all but the last two are
maintained by the State, though from sources
other than the Civil List.

Malcolm read his invitation to Alec's party with satisfaction,
entered it in the diary file of his I B M computer and then
dropped the card into the empty waste-paper bin beside his
desk. There was no need to hang on to bits of paper these
days. A week before the party the machine would remind
him with a message on its screen, and again on the day itself.

Not that Malcolm would forget. Since moving back to the
university town of Wykeham he had been just a little bit
lonely, which was an uncomfortable sensation for someone
as self-contained as Malcolm.

He had left London a year ago, announcing to his friends
that new technology now made it unnecessary to work in the
city any more, to pay outrageous mortgages and to spend
half your days in tube trains and taxis. He had sold the
studio flat in Belsize Park and spent the money on a tiny
cottage near the cathedral, a computer, a fax machine and a
photocopier. He wrote pieces for newspapers and magazines,
and transmitted them to London with his modem; he began

work on a book called *Out of Their Heads*, about the inspirational effect of the major narcotics on famous literary figures; and he waited confidently for others to follow in his footsteps.

He was still waiting. He wrote to his friends in London, and lectured them on his occasional visits to the city, about the cheapness of the countryside; about the high quality of productions at the Jonson Theatre; about the ease of communications with the capital; about the benefits of word processors, modems and fax machines. But the stubborn way in which his friends continued to ride on tubes, to spend outrageous sums on mortgages and to pay inflated prices for films, theatres and restaurants had begun to inspire in him a mild misgiving. And Malcolm rarely suffered from misgivings about anything.

Amongst his friends Malcolm was famous for his lacks: of misgivings, of embarrassment and of compunction. It was his greatest charm. When he had lived with Alec and Susan at Uplands, he had painted his whole room silver: walls, ceiling, floor, furniture, everything. For his finals philosophy paper he had worn purple lipstick and a leather mini-skirt, and had dropped a tab of acid as he entered the examination hall. He passed as well. Just.

After that Malcolm became a rock and roll journalist, a pub landlord, a talent scout for a porn-video maker in St John's Wood, a stringer for the News Association in Managua and a disc jockey on a pirate radio station in Croydon. He had written the scandalous account of the cocaine addiction of Prince George, Duke of Kent and brother of King George VI, for *The Republican Reader*. When other things failed Malcolm dealt drugs himself, in a small but profitable way, from a briefcase which he replenished with occasional trips to a mysterious house in Coldharbour Lane, Brixton.

It was a career which for anybody else but Malcolm would have been judged erratic. Someone going off the rails fast. A real fuck-up. But Malcolm had the knack of endowing everything he did with a certain unflappable rightness. He even made some money, and it was money that seemed to go further than other people's. It was everyone else who felt slightly wrong, slightly dull.

He had always looked right as well. His hair, which was very long and gorgeously curly in university days, had fallen out, which was a pity, but there it was. Malcolm resisted the temptation to wind the remains around his scalp or to grow a moustache. He had dealt with the loss by shaving it all off, buying a sun-ray lamp and wearing baggy black suits from Japanese designer shops.

When people asked other people over dinner what Malcolm was doing these days, they liked to recite these facts about him. 'Oh, he *hasn't*. You're *kidding*,' they used to say. 'He is *amazing*, isn't he?' Malcolm's friends, the ones who had succumbed to jobs and children and mortgages, liked to be amazed by Malcolm, but Malcolm was entirely unamazed by himself. He was the least sentimental of all the people he knew. He had the same awareness of past and future as a pussy cat, which is to say, none at all, and like a cat, Malcolm was always warm, comfortable and well fed.

At five to one the computer beeped softly and he padded across the room in his socks to switch on a row of radio cassette recorders. Each radio was tuned to a different local station and after lunch Malcolm would listen to the recorded news broadcasts in turn, picking out stories that could be sold to the diary columns of national newspapers.

The newspapers liked local colour in their diary columns. It gave them an air of solidity and breadth; provided ballast to their shrill campaigns and misinformed opinions. If there were no sufficiently interesting titbits in the radio news, then Malcolm would make some up. The newspapers never minded so long as the stories were sufficiently amusing, malicious and legally fireproof. But Alec's invitation had given him an idea, and he sat down again at his keyboard.

'I am told that left-wing publisher Alec Smith is to abandon the revolutionary struggles of the Groucho Club and the Harrods sale for the rural fastnesses of Kent,' he wrote.

'The "socialist" Smith, who has two children in private school and is married to Gloucestershire heiress Susan Price, was once a defendant in the infamous Soho Seven trial, but is now better known as producer of the scurrilous *Republican Reader*, which . . .'

Malcolm's fingers pattered happily over the keyboard of his IBM for the next thirty minutes, until he was satisfied. He still considered that he'd never been paid properly for that *Republican Reader* stuff and this would be a perfect filler for the *Standard* or the *Mail*, or both. £60 at least. It was surprising what people would buy.

Crouched busily over his computer keyboard, with his narrow hands flickering and the glow of the screen lighting the regular planes of his bronzed, angular skull, Malcolm looked more than ever like a pretty cat. He had slept with Susan once, but they were still friends, because, as Alec liked to say, you didn't make many new friends once you were over thirty. He looked forward to the party.

William stuffed his party invitation into a dog-eared and bulging wallet which also contained the following things: £200; 150 Dutch guilders; five credit cards; two 'perhaps you have overlooked' letters from his bank; two condoms in crushed foil wrappers; an expired driving licence; three sticks of Wrigley's chewing gum; a plastic sachet of marijuana, mostly stems; nine addresses on a Ritmeester cigar packet; and an erotic postcard from a girl called Rachel he had met in Amsterdam.

The wallet, freed from his jeans pocket, took on its natural shape, which was that of the roof of a cartoon dog kennel. His wallet was his office, and William had never been able to close it completely, even in the days when he had no money and no credit cards at all, and the Wykeham Midland Bank had confiscated his chequebook and rationed him to £4 a week. He had never been able to keep his shirt tail inside his trousers either, or his pullover label from sticking up over his collar, or his blond fringe from flopping in his eyes.

He still wore the uniform of cowboy boots, flying jacket, jeans and t-shirt he had worn at university, though the t-shirts were from Hamnett rather than Millets, and the flying jacket from Schott rather than Kensington Market. There were still many women who found William's dishevelment charming, and there were still neater men, like Malcolm, who suspected him of affectation. In the antique trade, where William made his living, nobody ever noticed.

Absentmindedly he unwrapped a stick of chewing gum, discovered it was a condom, and threw it on the floor of the Jaguar. He was sitting in the car because it had a telephone: one of the new radio things from Connections, the company that seemed to have replaced British Telecom since he was last in England. He found a stick of gum and started chewing it.

Why did they want a phone company to sound like one of those prolesmart cocktail bars, he wondered. All the new names for things in England sounded like cocktail bars. Fizzers and Sizzers; Rumours and Bloomers. They would have hospitals soon called Tumours, and undertakers called Doomers.

Connections could have been a single parent group, an electricians, a travel agents, a knocking shop ... Unless calling a phone company Connections actually persuaded people to buy more telephones, which seemed unlikely, what on earth was the point of it? Why not just call it the Phone Company?

The phone in his new flat, above a launderette in Finsbury Park, had been stolen. In the week between William and the previous tenant, thieves had broken in and stolen the telephone, the cooker, the kitchen units, the carpets, the light switches and the cat flap.

Nobody had broken into William's car yet, but only because it was a fifteen-year-old Jaguar XJ12 covered in patches of red oxide paint. The car was actually lovingly restored and expensive. The oxide paint was urban camouflage, randomly applied by William over faultless coachwork, but he did not expect it to work for ever. William was a hardened city dweller with two years in New York, three in Paris and four in Amsterdam behind him, but the rapacity of Finsbury Park had begun to alarm him. What sort of a place was it where people stole cat flaps?

England had changed in ten years. The streets were much dirtier, as dirty as New York, but there were far more new cars. People blew their horns in traffic jams and pushed in front of you in queues. They gave bigger tips. Telephones and postal services did not work. People communicated by fax machines, radio phones and motorcycle couriers. Newspapers arrived free, and were full of stories about rapes and sponsored walks and hospital cuts.

Television ads had once been about dim but friendly housewives who recommended detergents to each other over the garden wall. They were still about detergent, but now they showed tough businessmen in shirtsleeves and braces trampling on less tough businessmen with grubbier shirtsleeves. When William had left England his friends had all talked about books and relationships. Now they all talked about schools, left-wing councils and property prices.

In Amsterdam William had lived in an enormous flat on the Vondelpark with twelve-foot windows and concertina radiators thick with chalky emulsion. In London he found his friends living in strange new areas he had never heard of, which they described in a special, apologetic way: 'North Hampstead, actually,' 'Highgate East, as a matter of fact,' 'Sort of Muswell Hill South, you could say.' They all told him he had to get on to the property ladder, and William found he had just enough for a short lease on a rung in Finsbury Park. The estate agent called it North Highbury.

Alec, of course, had two houses, one in London and one in Wykeham, and he could hardly live in both at the same time, could he? And Rachel Thingy was at Wykeham. Her address was on the Ritmeester packet. William retrieved the party invitation from his wallet. He picked his Connections telephone from the litter on the floor of the Jaguar, gingerly plucked the condom from its stubby rubber aerial, and punched buttons.

Alec and Susan lived in the same banana-shaped area of north London as everybody else they knew. Its pointed ends were in Hackney to the east and Kilburn to the west, and its thickest part was around Hampstead and Highgate. As people became older and richer they tended to migrate from the thin ends to the fat centre.

None of them ever reflected on the gentle but irresistible social pressures which had achieved this remarkable symmetry, any more than they reflected on the millennia of environmental nudges and Darwinian selections which had gone into the shaping of their toenails or the patterns of their beard growth. Alec and Susan did not know anybody in the vastness of London who lived outside this small, sickle-shaped area, but they considered this no more odd than the fact that they did not have tails or compound eyes.

'That was William,' said Alec, 'telephoning from his car.'

'How do you know it was from his car?' asked Susan.

'Because he mentioned it. People always manage to mention it when they telephone from cars. He said he had to go because his parking meter had run out.'

'I didn't think there were any parking meters in Finsbury Park.'

'You see what I mean?'

Alec ticked off William's name from the party list on the kitchen pinboard. That was fifteen coming, for certain. He had lovingly created this board ten years ago, from cork wall tiles and hardboard, five-feet square, smartly covered in crimson felt. There were to be family photographs, funny postcards, odd newspaper cuttings, children's drawings. It would be an interesting, witty, ever-changing kaleidoscope of the evolution of the Smith family.

The deal was that in return for the labour of creating the board, Susan would empty it every so often. She would in addition promise faithfully to keep the kitchen walls and doors and refrigerator free of those flapping pieces of Jonathan's and Dora's infant artwork, stuck with milk bottle tops, lentils, dried pasta and fragments of polystyrene packaging, which their primary school produced in massive quantities, on some kind of production line basis.

Susan hadn't kept her side of the bargain, naturally. The smart crimson felt had disappeared rapidly beneath short shopping lists, written out on long sheets of expensive cartridge paper, which she invariably forgot to take to the shops with her. The shopping lists disappeared under infant artwork, which disappeared under more shopping lists. The pinboard bulged with bunches of yellowing paper, which fell off whenever you slammed the kitchen door, showering dried pasta and lentils into the works of the central heating boiler below.

In defiance Alec had cordoned off a quarter of the board with white tape, like an unexploded bomb site, and labelled it 'Alec's Corner' in menacing headline typefaces, snipped blackmail-style from the *Guardian*. In Alec's Corner, neatly and symmetrically pinned, were the party list, a doctored sepia portrait of Victoria and Albert with his hand down her frock, a *Sunday Telegraph* review of *The Republican Reader*, headlined 'An Affront to Basic Morality', a photograph of Dora and Jonathan, taken last year in Lesbos, and an invitation to a Royal Garden Party. It was on the thickest board Alec had ever seen in an invitation, and it read:

The Lord Chamberlain is commanded by Her Majesty to invite Mr and Mrs Alec Smith to a Garden Party at Buckingham Palace on Wednesday, 20 July, from 4 to 6 p.m.

In the lower, left-hand corner were the words 'Morning dress, uniform, or lounge suit', below which Jonathan had written in red biro, 'Very fucking democratic, har, har.'

'I wish he hadn't done that,' said Alec.

'Why on earth not?' said Susan. 'It's not as if you intend going to the bloody thing, is it?'

'No, of course not.'

Alec was pouring himself a large gin and tonic, his second of the evening.

'You know, I can't see much point in all this swimming and dieting you do, if you're tipping gin down yourself all the time,' said Susan.

'No,' said Alec, which seemed like the shortest way of terminating that particular avenue of conversation.

'I was wondering whether you had thought any more about seeing a doctor about . . . your sex problem, and so on.'

'I don't think it's a medical problem,' said Alec. 'And I don't think it's *my* problem.'

'That isn't what you were saying the other week.'

'No,' said Alec again. End of avenue.

'Have you seen William's new flat?' Susan asked him later.

'I don't think he's exactly moved in yet,' said Alec. 'In fact he was asking on the phone whether I minded if he stayed at Uplands for a time. While we were doing it up.'

'So you said no.'

'I said he should come down with me next weekend and see what sort of state it's in.'

'Oh, Alec, he'll be putting his socks in the dishwasher.'

'And draping batik scarves over the lamps.'

'And decoking engines on the hall carpet.'

'And telling policemen his name is Kemo Sabe.'

Regretfully, they ran out of William memories.

'He's actually quite good at decorating and things like that,' said Alec. 'And he could organize the plumbers and electricians and so on. I can't be down there all the time. And there's some girl at the university he wants to see.'

'Another one of William's floozies?' said Susan.

'Dunno,' said Alec. 'You're the expert.'

CHAPTER THREE

From *The Republican Reader*:

King George VI believed the word 'highbrow' to be spelt 'eyebrow' and since no one had the boldness to correct him, he remained baffled by its meaning all his life.

Summer term at Wykeham University began warm and dry. Lawns that had been greasy clay at Easter steamed in the sunshine and grew firm underfoot. Damp stains dwindled to brownish ghosts on the concrete walls of the colleges. Plastic carrier bags of butter and milk, the makeshift refrigerators of student life, blossomed upon the windowsills of college bedrooms. The birchwoods around the hilltop campus became misty green and the tender nubs of bluebell shoots unfurled cautiously in the leaf mould.

In his college garden the Master of Marcuse noted with satisfaction that his new *Clematis jackmanii* had survived the winter and was curling fresh tendrils around the first-storey windows. On the south side of the college Virginia creeper had already climbed to the second storey, while the catering block was almost submerged in jasmine and old roses. The Master of Marcuse had spent five years of the Senior Common Room's catering budget on climbing shrubs, and he was well pleased with his works. A few more years, he told himself, and you wouldn't be able to see the horrible place at all.

The colleges of Wykeham University had been built in a confident age. They were boldly abstract geometric statements, flung down upon the bare hillside above the ancient cathedral town. They were brilliant, playful assertions of the new way, challenging the old in poured concrete, smoked glass and pre-cast panels; arrogantly cantilevered over thin air; daringly naked in their purposefulness.

The new university had teased the pretensions of the ancient institutions of learning, organizing itself along Oxbridge lines with colleges named after twentieth-century luminaries: Marcuse College in the shape of an M; Saussure as a giant figure S, cascading down the hillside towards the cathedral; Galbraith as a five-pointed American star. Ten or fifteen more were envisaged for the years to come, embracing and integrating with the old town; a new centre of learning for a new intellectual era.

Wykeham had been greatly admired in its early days. The *Architect's Journal* had featured Marcuse College on its front cover. *New Society* had written respectfully about the 'serpentine glass umbilicus of Saussure College, symbolizing the new unity of academic and secular, drawing town beneath the folds of gown'. In its early years it turned down nine in ten undergraduate applicants, who had heard that Wykeham had the best weekend parties and the most freely available drugs in the world of higher education. It had taken its pick of academic talent from among the PhDs of Oxbridge and Ivy League. And then, quite suddenly, it had not been admired any more.

Concrete had become grubby, prefabricated panels had leaked water, an arrogant cantilever had subsided abruptly. Academics complained about the freezing, windswept distances between the scattered colleges. Undergraduates grumbled about the lack of a Student Union for proper rock concerts.

No more colleges had been built. The Senate had debated and narrowly defeated a motion from Business Studies to rename the existing ones in less explicitly 'political' and controversial style: Marcuse to become Milton, for instance, and Saussure to become Shaw. The building programme had petered out in an overspill to demountable sheds. Abstract geometric statements had become embarrassing. Boldness, playfulness and arrogance were *passé*.

The colleges began, absentmindedly, to plant shrubs and creepers around their walls. The stark outlines of the campus on the hill became softer and more blurred, and the people of the town, who had never taken to it much, learned to ignore it completely. The age of confidence was over and people began to drift off to London at weekends.

Vivien read her invitation to Alec and Susan's party with a sniff and slipped it into the middle of a shallow pile on her mantelpiece.

Vivien, at thirty-eight, was middle class enough to know you did not wedge invitations into the side of your looking glass. You did not set them out in rows like Christmas cards either. You put them in a pile, with the best on top.

The best was for a party in Amwell Street, from the oldest and nastiest of the small periodicals. The literary reviews which Vivien wrote for its arts pages paid practically nothing, but the parties were good. Alec and Susan's invitation found its way, by some process of natural selection, between the Master of Marcuse's sherry party, which he held at the beginning of each new term, and a card announcing the opening of a ski shop in the High Street.

'I'm sorry,' she said, as she realized that her student had stopped reading. 'Would you mind starting that bit again. The bit about reality.'

Rachel sighed, and snuggled herself deeper into a corner of her tutor's sofa. It was *all* about reality. Her essay title was 'Discuss the role of reality in Alain-Fournier's *Le Grand Meaulnes*.'

'Can I have another one of your chocolates?'

'They're macadamia nuts,' said Vivien. 'From America. Very expensive.'

'They're very nice,' said Rachel, taking two from the bowl on the coffee table. She resumed reading in the piping monotone of one who encounters a meaningless text for the first time. A nine-year-old reading from the Old Testament at school assembly.

'Every work of art is an exploration of reality by the artist, just as every work of art is an experience to the person who fully grasps it. What, then, we have to ask is, of what reality, of what realms of experience, is this book an exploration?'

It was a deplorably long-winded way of asking what a book was about, thought Vivien, and who was this 'we' anyway? Legions of clubby chaps with briar pipes and thornproof tweeds and cast-iron opinions. The great Edwardian mahogany 'we' of Hours in a Library and *Times* leaders.

What did *they* have to do with this nineteen-year-old girl in Doc Martens, a perfect brown navel peeping from beneath her t-shirt and a palm tree of blonde hair on top of her head? Why did a woman student have to recruit the massed ranks of male, middle-class critical authority in the first person plural to support her not-very-controversial and not-very-original views? What the hell was wrong with a bald, straightforward, up yours 'I think'?

Vivien, at the age of nineteen, had not been middle class enough to say 'looking glass' instead of mirror or 'sawlt' instead of salt or 'what' instead of pardon. But she had said 'I think', and said it quite a lot. She had arrived at the new university of Wykeham in 1968 with a fibre-board suitcase, a Wolverhampton accent and a brand-new prescription for contraceptive pills. She graduated with a first in English, a cockney accent, and chronic vaginal thrush, which she blamed (incorrectly) on unhygienic lovers and (correctly) on nylon tights.

Once upon a time, Vivien had slept with five different men in a week, two in one day. What disciplined abandonment, she marvelled now, to wake up with one man, to write your – rather good – essay on *The Waste Land* and go to bed with another. He said, Marie, Marie, hold on tight. And down they went.

The modern Vivien taught English at the university. This

term her course was 'The Lost Domain: The Literature of Longing'. She wore expensive but wholesome cotton knickers from Sloggi. Her copper hair, once long and teased, after Lizzie Siddal, was now a shining geometric bob. Her slender brown legs were waxed and stripped monthly of their tough reddish stubble. No more tights, no more thrush, no more men, thank God. Modern Vivien had slept with nobody for five years, not even Rachel. Ah yes, Rachel.

'And further, we can ask not only what may be found in this realm but what adventure within it are we asked to share? The realm, to put it briefly' – Thank God, thought Vivien again – 'is that of the impulses and sensations, the intuitions and idealisms of that period in life which lies between adolescence and manhood, a fleeting period which Fournier felt to be so infinitely precious that he wished to fix it . . .'

Manhood, she had said, and without a flicker of disapproval or hint of irony. What was wrong with 'adulthood' or 'womanhood'? Why was an intelligent young woman in the 1980s swallowing stuff about the 'intuitions and idealisms', the 'infinitely precious' 'fleeting period' of *men* growing up, or rather, of men not growing up? Wasn't that what the Lost Domain was all about? The freezing of adolescence in perpetuity? The evasion of maturity and sexuality?

Vivien forced her attention back to Rachel's essay, which had entered a thicket of subordinate clauses and literary allusions.

'For Rivière, we might guess, the reality of Fournier was his attempt to come to terms with life, as revealed by the immense appreciation they shared in common of the French poetry of the nineteenth century, from Mallarmé and Baudelaire and Rimbaud to Francis Jammes and Paul Claudel. For Péguy, we can suppose, the reality lay in Fournier's very refusal to come to terms with life, the insistence that what we call actuality is only a clumsy rendition of what, in essence, really is . . .'

Who the fuck was Francis Jammes? Vivien had never heard of him. She doubted if Rachel had ever heard of him either, or of most of the others, before she mugged them up in the library the day before. Once, when Vivien was a student, she had pretended, in a seminar, to have read Richardson's *Pamela*.

'What did you think of Northrop's death in the penultimate chapter?' her tutor, old Professor Barlow, had asked her.

'Very finely drawn,' Vivien had replied, safely, she thought.

'Funny,' said Barlow. 'No such character as Northrop in *Pamela*.'

The old bastard had probably never finished *Pamela* himself either. Who had? But Barlow's bullshit detector was unerring. Should she subject Rachel to the Northrop test?

She had finished reading her essay. 'I don't think you were listening at all,' she said reproachfully. 'You were looking at your mail. And who was that invitation from that you were trying to hide away?' She uncurled herself from the sofa and began rifling among the pile on the mantelpiece. When Vivien was an undergraduate she had been too frightened to speak to professors like Barlow. Now they went through your mail. Now they made passes at you.

It was only last week. Rachel had invited her tutor to dinner at the house she shared with her boyfriend on Faversham Road. Not unusual. The next night she had invited her to see a film at the Castle, which was more unusual. Then she offered Vivien a peck on the cheek when they said goodnight, which had somehow turned into a kiss on the lips, with Rachel's tongue in Vivien's mouth. Which had been most unusual, but not unpleasant.

'You know you're fairly bright,' said Viven, 'and you know that sort of tosh will get you a 2 : 1 any day, so I won't waste your time being polite about it. I'll just say three things.'

Rachel reached again for the bowl of chocolate-coated nuts.

'First of all, stop reading second-rate lit crits. I don't mind Matthiessen or Eagleton or even Leavis if you have to. But for God's sake don't waste your time with reheated doctoral theses. Most of them are written by thick blokes who got tenure in the 1960s, when the grass was greener, and haven't got anything better to do with their time. We are both here, being paid by the state, to cultivate your powers of analysis and discrimination, not to copy other people's.'

She was bright, Vivien knew. Rachel had turned down a place at Oxford to come to Wykeham, though God knew why. Vivien's cottage, a converted oast house, looked across the valley of the Stour, over the spikes of the cathedral, to the university on the far side. It was a pleasant enough prospect in spring, when the orchards were in bloom and the birches screened the bleak Lego-land of the campus. But the back of the house, where they sat now, looked out on the real Wykeham of council estate and ring road and tannery, with the dreary vistas of pylons and hop poles of the Kentish Weald beyond.

In 1968 you had made a statement about yourself by coming to Wykeham: you had rejected dreaming spires for plate glass; discarded Mill for Marcuse; *Beowulf* for Bellow; sniggering homosexual dons for butch Trotskyist lecturers on motorbikes. For three, four years, places like Wykeham were *where it was at*, just as now they were, unarguably, where it was not. Money had run out; concrete had grown streaky; Trots had become Tories. The only statement you made about yourself by coming to Wykeham these days had to do with the shakiness of your A-level results.

'Secondly,' she was saying, 'you must read the *text* more closely.' Your mind could wander while you delivered this rigmarole, since it was the same for every student worth expending the breath upon. Most of them, of course, were not. 'You must observe your own reactions to it and try to explain them. If you feel there is a connection between Alain-Fournier and the symbolist poets, ask why? It's an interesting question, but you mustn't just chuck the names in for decoration. They don't impress me, and the cumulative effect of over-citation is to obscure your argument.'

Rachel was eating another macadamia nut. There were only three or four left in the bowl now. Vivien really didn't know how she did it. The child lived on Mars Bars and nougat and liquorice. She had munched popcorn all the way through *The Battle of Algiers*. Yet she had skin like damp sand and had to bore extra holes in the belt that held up her baggy Levis.

'You told me there were three things,' said Rachel.

'The third thing is to stop trying to sound like Henry James after a heavy lunch.'

'It's from your friend Alec, the publisher,' said Rachel, removing the invitation from the pile. She wandered back over to Vivien and popped a macadamia nut into her surprised mouth. 'Was he your lover or something – when the grass was greener?'

'My friend Alec the ex-publisher,' said Vivien, indistinctly, through oily fragments of nut. 'Who seems to have decided to move back to the country with Susan, his wife. My friend.'

'I liked *The Republican Reader*,' said Rachel. 'They're doing a puppet version on BBC2 in the autumn.'

'I wrote some of it,' said Vivien modestly.

'Did you really?'

'So did lots of other people, of course. I just did a little bit about literature.'

'It was funny.'

'The only person who didn't think so was Alec,' said Vivien. 'He thought he was publishing a left-wing assault on the monarchy, and instead the right wing all fell about laughing and made him rich.'

'You don't seem very pleased about them coming to live here.'

Vivien's small, pointed tongue searched her soft palate for macadamia crumbs while she framed an aphorism.

'The first thing couples do when their marriage is breaking up is to have children. The second is to move to the country.'

Rachel was becoming impressed by Vivien's talent for tabulating her thoughts into threes.

'And what is the third thing?'

'The third thing is that they invite their old friends to reunion parties.'

CHAPTER FOUR

From *The Republican Reader*:

The Lutyens doll's house designed for Queen Mary and on show at Windsor is the most remarkable of its kind ever made. There are tiny shotguns which can be broken to take microscopic cartridges, a library containing 200 volumes the size of postage stamps, each written by a contemporary author in his own hand, real water coming from the taps, bed-linen which took 1,500 hours to weave, fingernail-sized bottles of real vintage wine in the cellars and a gramophone in the children's nursery which plays 'God Save the Queen'. It is the country house, anti-industrial, anti-modern England of 1923, for ever shrunk to the scale of a baby's dream.

On the first Saturday in May Alec and William drove down to Wykeham in the oxide-spotted Jaguar. It was going to be a hot day. Michael Fish told them so on the radio, but outside London there was mist still clinging to the folds of ground in the orchards and a smell of apple blossom and tar wash in the air.

'Why are you driving around in this old shed?' asked Alec, poking the debris on the floor with his shoe, and so William put his foot down.

Apple orchards turned for a time into a pinkish blur and motorway bridges shuttled sickeningly overhead. German coaches and French TIR trucks leapt hugely at the windscreen, then swerved aside at the last instant, great cliffs of rust and chromium that brushed past Alec's flinching cheekbones with a honk of air horn and hot stink of diesel.

'All right, all right,' Alec said eventually, and then they dawdled the rest of the way. They turned off the motorway before Maidstone, and stopped in Marden to buy newspapers and sausages at a butcher which Alec said was the best in Kent. Alec enjoyed the rituals of these small expeditions together: William driving, he reading out passages from the papers and rolling single-skin joints on his lap. It reminded him of other, younger expeditions, in packed-out vans and clapped-out Minis: going to see Pink Floyd at the Rainbow, or to score some dope at the squat in Brixton, or to buy junk for William's stall at some country auction.

There was a companionable male frowsiness about sitting in a smoky car, giggling over tabloids and looking forward to a beery lunch later on, with no particular urgency about getting anywhere.

'"Bish! Bosh! Loadsa dosh!"' he was reading. '"How the nation's grafters are cashing in on Boom Boom Britain, by Charles Rae and Vaughan Freeman".'

'I like that one,' said William. 'Bish, bosh. I wonder how you get a job writing headlines like that?'

'A First in Classics, at least, I should think,' said Alec. 'And the right sort of background. Charles and Vaughan would have to come in to Wapping every morning on bicycles with wicker baskets, wearing step collars and gaiters.'

If Susan had been here, she'd have been wincing at the way William juddered around corners in fourth gear, with one hand on the wheel, and she would have fretted over getting lost. But William navigated on mysterious principles, which involved keeping the Thames estuary to the left and the Channel to the right, and which generally led him to the university.

'What's the house like these days?' he asked Alec.

'I don't really know. I haven't been down here for seven

or eight years. You know we rented it out to students after we moved to London, but I left all that to an estate agent in Ashford. They pay some old bloke called Mr Truss to do the odd bit of decorating and to cut the grass.'

'He can't really be called Truss,' said William. 'What's he like?'

'Never met him,' said Alec. 'Anyway the rent was so cheap there was never any problem filling it up. Then last year the agents said the roof was getting bad, so I'm afraid I just let it stay empty.'

It was a curious thing, but he didn't much like thinking about the house. Over the years since university it had become a mythical zone rather than a thing of bricks and mortar and rates. When we were at Uplands . . . Do you remember at Uplands? . . . He was an Uplands person . . . That was a very Uplands thing to do . . . It was hard to say what was so special about it; why it had become so powerful. It was just a house where some people had lived for a few years in cheerful chaos. Friendships, affairs, parties, rows. It was just that it had been, for the only time in his life, the right place, at the right time, where you did not, for once, wish that you were somewhere else.

Uplands was Susan's house officially, but he, Alec, had taken charge of things when they moved to London. They had decided not to sell it. They might come back one day; the rent would help pay the London mortgage, and of course it would appreciate faster than any other sort of investment. Alec could keep an eye on the tenants and make sure everything was looked after. But then Prometheus Press had taken over all his time, and the children had come along. God, Dora was only six when he last came down and Jonathan hadn't even started school. So it must be ten years at least.

'It sounds to me like you could do with somebody living there to look after things properly,' said William hopefully.

'Ummm,' said Alec.

They stopped for lunch at a pub on the River Beult near

Sissinghurst. Alec remembered it as a pleasantly run-down place with eggy mild and cheese and pickle doorsteps. But a new gravel car park was full of salesmen's Sierras with coat hangers in the back window, and a plastic illuminated board advertised traditional fayre in gothic script.

In the lounge bar the stone floors had been covered in a migraine-patterned carpet. A row of video games machines throbbed and chattered nervously in the corner, while traditional fayre of chilli con carne and turkey provençale simmered sullenly under brass warming lamps on a smeared glass counter.

'My round if you can guess what the music is,' said William.

Alec concentrated. It was pitched to the precise level of irritation that lies between inaudible and not-ignorable, and it was heavily dubbed. 'Oh, I dunno. "Brown Sugar" by the Swingle Singers?'

'Not bad,' said William. 'But I think I'm right in saying that it's "Jumping Jack Flash". Do you feel that we should give the food a try or shall we just start smashing the place up straight away?'

After waving a £10 note at the empty bar for five minutes a barman in a pink bow tie and black shirt approached and examined William's flying jacket and Club Dead vest. 'I'm afraid our policy requires a jacket and tie in the restaurant area, sir.'

So they went into the public bar, where a cover version of 'Michelle' crooned at the sub-audible level against a background of chugging and moaning from another set of games machines.

'You wouldn't think someone like that could have a *policy*, would you?' said William. 'You could understand him having reflexes, like an amoeba, or a simple set of customs, like a honey bee. But a *policy* seems a bit high on the evolutionary scale.'

After another few minutes of tenner-waving the same barman appeared.

'We'd like some food.'

'I'm afraid we don't serve food in the public bar, sir.'

'Oh, come on,' said Alec. 'We can find somewhere else.'

'No, hang on,' said William. 'Regard it as a challenge. We'll *force* them to take our money.'

'Where *can* we eat in this place?' he asked the barman.

'We have some tables in the riverside garden, sir.'

'You mean you'll let us eat in the car park?'

'William, we can find a pub in Wykeham,' said Alec.

'Okay,' said William, ignoring the interruption. 'We'll eat in the car park. I'll have two pints of bitter, two large gin and tonics for the girls and four lemonade shandies for the children. To eat we'll have two chillis, two turkeys, four gammon and chips and four bags of crisps.'

While the barman began to prepare the food, they carried the beer and crisps outside, climbed into the car and drove away.

'I've never seen that one before,' said Alec admiringly, as he tried to prevent the bitter from slopping over his knees.

'Got it from a Jack Nicholson film,' said William.

William telephoned Vivien.

'Where are you?' she said. 'Susan said to expect you for lunch.'

He told her about the traditional fayre and the amoeba in the pink bow tie.

'We just drove past your twee little oast house actually.'

'So why didn't you call in and say hello?'

'We wanted to impress you with the car phone.'

'Idiots,' said Vivien. 'I'll expect you for dinner.'

Rachel was picking the stalks off a pile of mangetout and dropping them in the waste disposal unit.

'Is he funny, this Alec person, like *The Republican Reader*?'

'I think William did most of the good jokes for that,' said Vivien. 'All the recipes and things.'

'Ten economical ways with leftover corgi,' said Rachel.

'That's right. Alec was more the organizer. When we were at Uplands it was Alec who was always drawing up rotas and organizing kitties, and buying everyone mugs with their own names on so he didn't get hepatitis off Malcolm or William. He's very sweet, though, in a gloomy sort of way.'

'Did you ever sleep with him?'

'Yes. But sleep was the operative word.'

Rachel studied the pile of decapitated pea cases critically.

'Do you think I'd better invite Toby to this dinner tonight?'

'If you must,' said Vivien.

They parked the spotted Jaguar in the bursar's space outside Marcuse College.

'It's got very furry, hasn't it?' said William, studying the climbing shrubs on the college walls.

'According to Vivien they've been drinking British sherry for five years to pay for this lot,' said Alec.

The whole campus was softer and more blurred than he remembered it, which was all wrong, because it was memories that were supposed to be blurred. It seemed smaller too, and that was wrong as well, because it was childhood places that got smaller. His stomach was becoming absurdly knotted as they set off down the hill through the apple orchards. The house, a mile or so away, was invisible behind a belt of beech trees which were much taller than he remembered.

'We could have just driven around the front way to Uplands and parked in the drive,' William complained.

'I thought we'd walk the way we used to go, through the woods,' said Alec. 'Just an old man's fancy.'

It was the way he had first come to Uplands, though it had been at night then, and on a motorcycle, with Vivien on the pillion. 'We're having a party at the house tonight,' she had told him. 'I'd better show you the way.'

It was obviously a pretty big deal, this house, from the

way she always referred to it as just 'the house'. Everyone else in the first year lived in G-Plan college rooms or digs in town. Alec was sharing with Malcolm in a damp house by the station that smelled of mothballs and bacon. But Vivien, who was only a first year herself, lived in 'the house', with 'a few friends'. It was all so *casual*.

So he had borrowed the motorcycle from Malcolm. A Royal Enfield 350, it had been, which was pretty cool for a first year too. He picked her up outside the library at nine. No helmets of course. You didn't need them in those days, but even if you had –

'What's *that* for?' she had said.

'It's for impressing girls with,' he said honestly.

'But the house is only about a mile away.'

'So we can test the acceleration,' said Alec.

But he drove the Enfield slowly down the dark orchard track, careful Alec, with Vivien's arms hot across his stomach and her nipples, sensed rather than felt, lasering through his thick leather jacket. He had hardly known her then. She was just someone from his seminar group who went along to Socialist Society meetings. He was a bit frightened of her, to be honest, this fierce Brummie redhead, who seemed to have read everything on the course before it began. But Alec was still the last virgin student on the campus, so far as he could tell, and the most casual touch of a girl, any girl, had been enough to scald.

They turned down the rutted path she pointed out through the woods. The engine grunted and snarled in the echoing beeches, and the cone of light from the headlamp bounced wildly, picking out a broken gate, an ivy-covered stump, a rusting harrow. A largish bird exploded from cover and went rattling through the leafless branches. A pheasant perhaps? Urban Alec knew nothing of birds or trees or flowers. Could have been a Christmas turkey for all he knew. His arms ached from the strain of holding the heavy machine with its two passengers upright over the pitted ground and polished roots of the path.

Then they were passing a laurel hedge, eight or nine feet high, with twigs plucking at his sleeve, and there were coloured lights shining through the branches and snatches of music over the snarl of the engine.

Well I've been thinkin' 'bout all the places we surfed and danced,
And all the faces we've missed,
So let's get back together and
Do it again

The Beach Boys, it had been. Absurdly bathetic in a Kentish woodland. Rhythmically crude and lyrically banal, but the sound of it could still make him thrill. Vivien tapped his left shoulder and he swung obediently left, along another arm of the hedge, with the engine throttled back to a thud.

And there it was. A tall, square house in tiny, soft, red bricks from a local kiln. A doll's house design with a central door and two windows either side; five above and another five set in the mansard roof. Light streamed from every window and the open door, on to the lawn and borders, where coloured paper lanterns hung in the trees.

It was late eighteenth or early nineteenth century. The house of a deacon or a local builder. He never did find out in all the years he was to live there. You didn't wonder about things like that in those days. It was just a bloody big house with a bloody big party going on and you were nineteen years old on a motorbike and with a girl on the back. So he had skidded, unnecessarily, to a halt on the gravel – God, the crunch of private gravel – turned off the engine and begun the rest of his life.

'The track was around here somewhere,' he told William, twenty years later. They were casting about along the fringe of trees below the university. But half the apple orchards seemed to have disappeared to make way for winter wheat, and some of the hedges too. A new tarmac path, lined with concrete lamp posts, cut across the fields at a different angle. Geography had shifted subtly.

'I thought it was further along to the right,' said William.

'It can't be. The house is only just beyond those trees.'

They found a likely-looking gap and followed a path which led them only to a small electricity sub-station, humming to itself in a clearing.

'That didn't used to be here,' said Alec.

'If we turn right through the trees, we're bound to cut across the proper path,' said William.

'Unless it was left.'

It was warm, but in the woods the sun had not yet hardened the ground after the April rain and the going was sticky. After a hundred yards of brambles they found themselves by a pond in a clearing among tall birches that neither recognized.

'This whole wood can't be more than ten acres,' said Alec. 'I lived in the middle of it for five years. It's just not possible to get lost.'

'Unless you happen to be lost,' said William.

'Keep the Thames estuary to your left and the Channel to your right.'

In the distance they heard the unmistakable coughing snarl of a petrol chainsaw.

'It's the local psychopath on a yuppie hunt.'

Ten minutes later, after William had plunged to his knee in a ditch and Alec had torn his suit jacket, the chainsaw sounded nearer, but they could no longer tell in which direction.

'Heads left, tails right,' said William, and heads it was.

It was only when he noticed the laurel leaves he was clutching that Alec realized he was forcing his way through his own garden hedge, grown to a height of twelve to fourteen feet. As they burst through into the sunlight, with twigs and brambles clinging to their clothes and hair, the noise of the chainsaw stopped. An old man whom Alec did not recognize had stopped sawing down one of Alec's cherry trees, in his, Alec's, garden, and was staring at them warily.

'Hello,' said William, advancing towards him, his hands outstretched in a gesture of peace. 'Can you tell us if the Second World War is over yet?'

William phoned Vivien.

'He's actually called Mr Truss. No, really. And he's cut down everything in the garden to make it more tidy. The whole garage is full of paraquat and flamethrowers and chainsaws. And he keeps tugging his forelock at Alec and calling him "Zorr".'

'Are you phoning from your silly car again?'

'No, from the house. The phone is the only thing that's still working. Mr Truss needs it to call in air strikes against the dahlias. The gas is off, and the electricity. There are mushrooms on the carpets and a dead pigeon in the bath, and probably bats in the belfry.'

'I'm cooking pheasant for dinner.'

'Wonderful. What shall we get to drink?'

'Some '82 Margaux from Oddbins, if there's any left. Or the '76 Barolo.'

'Aren't we grand. I meant red or white. Or would you prefer a crate of Woodpecker, so you can puke it all up like in the good old days?'

'Fuck off, William,' said Vivien affectionately, and hung up.

Alec was inspecting the garden with Mr Truss. All the large trees had gone, and the honeysuckle, and the Virginia creeper that had covered the south wall of the house. Formerly curving lawns had been dug straight, with edges sharp as cut cheese, and mown into jailhouse stripes. Of the peonies, Chinese poppies, hellebores and hostas that had once filled the herbaceous borders there was nothing to be seen. Only savage rectangles of turned earth, like fresh graves, with clods of yellow clay subsoil on the surface, to attest to the vigour of Mr Truss's shovel.

Beyond the towering hedge which surrounded the garden,

the jungle might have encroached, but here in Uplands Mr Truss had created his own demilitarized zone.

'There used to be raspberry canes behind the kitchen,' said Alec.

'Those brambles?' said Mr Truss. 'They get everywhere if you don't root them out.'

'What about the clematis that used to grow over the summer house?'

'Those creeper things will just weaken the structure of your buildings if you don't keep them down.'

The only new plants were three standard roses, staked in a line like gibbeted miscreants, in a new rectangular bed cut into the centre of the croquet lawn. 'Nice tidy plants,' said Mr Truss, 'and they'll give you a bit of colour right through the summer.'

'You could get one of those mop-head hydrangeas to cheer things up,' said William, when Mr Truss had left, 'with the nice flowers like the Queen Mother's hats.'

'And a few floribunda roses,' said Alec sadly, 'like tarts' tea cosies.'

'And a circular bed of annuals shaped like a clock face.'

'And a gnome with a fishing rod for the lily pond.'

'If he hadn't already filled it in.'

The house was much worse. Rain had flooded the attic rooms and ruined much of the plaster down as far as the first floor. Dry rot had flowered in the cellar and scorched a dozen joists with its hot breath. One corner of the kitchen extension had subsided and was sagging badly.

And where nature had not devastated, Mr Truss had gone before, with woodchip wallpaper and non-drip gloss paint and polystyrene ceiling tiles.

'He's covered all the plaster mouldings with that porridgy textured paint,' said William.

'It's all over the tiles in the bathrooms and kitchen as well.'

'I think he's painted the window frames with emulsion.'

'And most of the glass too.'

Alec still had photographs somewhere of that first party, or it may have been a later one. They did tend to merge a bit now. There was one of Vivien, sitting on the staircase with Drummond, the philosophy lecturer she had got off with, and showing a lot of knicker. There was Malcolm, picking his nose to camera, with a joint the size of a parsnip in his hand. There was another of Geoff Bright doing his party piece of scratching his ear with his wooden leg. There was one of William, whom he hadn't known then, looking incredibly young and beautiful and wearing a Jerry Rubin headband. William hated that picture.

The clothes were a mess actually. People now remembered sixties clothes as much more homogeneous than they really were. In recollection at least everybody wore mini-skirts and kinky boots and Loons and tie-dye vests and beads and Afghan coats. That was what people wore nowadays to fancy dress parties and nostalgia nights. The actual pictures showed horn-rim schoolboy specs under Afro haircuts; black lace-up policemen's shoes with kaftans; and Marks and Spencer jumpers over chintz bell-bottoms.

Alec had wandered about, not knowing anybody, and drinking too quickly. A fat American who worked at the Ben Jonson Theatre had given him a snort of cocaine, his first ever, which had made his ears ring and his eyes fill with tears. He had shouted excitedly about Gramsci to a drunk New Zealand history lecturer. He had kissed a girl from Grimsby who didn't seem to have any teeth.

He had danced with Vivien and later he had been sick in the garden, had fallen asleep on someone's bed and woken to a room full of people smoking more dope and arguing about astrology. He had driven up the motorway at dawn with a dozen other people and, feeling ridiculously well, had eaten bacon and eggs in a transport café. And somewhere along the way he had met Susan.

There was a blurred photograph of her, looking pale and drunk and beautiful, her eyes stained red by the flashlight. Here in the kitchen, it had been, where now the Scotch airer hung awry from its hoist and green furred teabags clogged the sink and curling linoleum crackled underfoot. The now paralytic New Zealand historian was swaying over her with a bottle of red dangling from his hand and she was scanning the room over his shoulder.

What had he said to her then? Something fairly cloddish, which she had made clever.

'This man's an historian who's never heard of Gramsci.'

'When everyone knows he invented the gramophone,' said Susan.

'He's probably never even heard of Pascal.'

'Who developed the fruitgum.'

'Or of Chateaubriand.'

'The famous talking steak.'

Susan said she couldn't remember meeting him then. It had been later, at the Marcuse Guy Fawkes party. But that was when it had been.

When the New Zealander had ambled away she asked Alec his name, filled his glass and introduced him to someone else, who turned out to be William.

'Carries on like she owns the place,' said Alec, disappointed she had left so soon after his act of gallantry.

'She does,' said William.

'Nobody owns a house like this.'

'Her name's Susan Price,' William said, 'and she's my landlady. Twelve quid in a brown envelope on the first of the month.'

'My landlady wears cornplasters. She's got knitted covers on the toilet rolls.'

'Well, at least you've got toilet rolls,' said William.

'I'll swap you,' said Alec.

Which, as it turned out, was more or less what they did.

It was William again, clumping up the stairs from the cellar, who drove the twenty-year-old ghosts from the kitchen.

'There's quite a lot of room down there, you know, once

you've got rid of all the rubbish. I could use some storage space near Dover if I'm going to start shipping stuff over to France.'

'I wasn't really thinking of turning this place into a furniture warehouse, William. I was planning to live here.'

'It would only be temporary, until I got a proper place nearer the docks. And I could stay and keep an eye on the house. Organize the builders and all that sort of thing. Some of the rooms are fairly habitable.'

'Let's go and see Vivien,' said Alec.

CHAPTER FIVE

From *The Republican Reader*:

Even in his twenties Edward VII had a passion for very large amounts of very rich food, and age only increased his appetite and his waistline. Tum-Tum ate anything and everything and he ate it very quickly. 'The King Emperor', as his official biographer, Sir Sidney Lee, tactfully recorded, 'did not toy with his food.'

Alec was drunk. They had finished the two Barolos with the pâté and the two clarets with the pheasant. With the cheese they had made do with a couple of bottles of undated Safeway's plonk, and then polished off Vivien's half-bottle of white port with the Bakewell tart.

He was glad that the cuisine poseur phase of dinner party cookery seemed to have passed and that roast meat and pudding were back. He was fed up with fiddling about with goujons of plaice and wafers of raw duck in puddles of pretty sauce. You could drink more with proper food.

They were smoking now, and drinking a fierce grappa, which tasted of almonds and bonfires. 'Last year's duty-free from Tuscany,' said Vivien, 'but it's the only thing left, I'm afraid.'

With cunning courtesy Alec topped up everyone's glass, and then filled his own empty one. He knew that as long as you could remember exactly how much you had drunk you were never in danger of becoming a serious alcoholic. Alec might be falling-over drunk, fighting drunk or pissing-in-the-corner-of-the-bedroom drunk, but he always knew how many drinks it had taken to get him there.

Vivien was wearing a cream jersey dress with apparently nothing underneath, and no sign of the Englishwoman's bum either. Malcolm was wearing one of his enormous Japanese suits that made him look like a crashed hang-glider. Neither was drinking anything to speak of. Alec didn't understand how someone could chew through the whole main course without touching the glass in front of them while you were itching to fill up your own for the fourth time, but there it was. They'd had two glasses of red each and Vivien was still playing with her first of port.

Wossname, the student, Toby, in the paisley bow tie and Sebastian Flyte haircut, had drunk even less. A glass and a half perhaps. The girl – Rachel . . . Wilson? – about four glasses, and half a box of Bendick's Bittermints. Wonderful body, by the way. Real torpedo tits. His eyes stole looks at them as his face smiled and nodded elsewhere. Was she actually *with* the Toby person? Poor taste if she was.

That still left almost four bottles between himself and William. Only proper drinkers in the place. Two bottles each, not counting the port and grappa. Or the gin and tonics when they had arrived at Vivien's. Surely it couldn't be that much? Frowning, Alec began his sums again.

The others were talking about education cuts. If you ate with doctors they talked about NHS cuts; with actors it was Arts Council cuts; with soldiers it was defence cuts; and with social workers, local government cuts. Alec wished he had some cuts of his own to contribute, but the only ones he knew anything about were tax cuts, which were presumably the cause of everyone else's cuts. So he kept quiet and poured himself another glass of the oily grappa. It had, he noticed, a small black skull and crossbones on the label.

Toby Wossname was saying: 'But of course, if you look at the figures, higher education spending simply *has not* fallen in real terms . . .'

'Well, I don't know what these real terms are,' said Vivien, 'but I do know I was the youngest lecturer in the literature faculty when I was appointed ten years ago, *and I still am.* We haven't even been able to afford a new research assistant for five years.'

'But I'm afraid this country did not become the workshop of the world,' said Toby, 'by funding research assistants for English departments.'

William snorted. 'And you seriously think we're on the way back to being "workshop of the world" now, do you? Screwdriver of the world would be more like it.'

'The gross national product . . .' Toby Wossname began.

'Oh, do shut up,' said Rachel.

'Education has absolutely fuck all to do with the gross national product,' said William. 'Education is an end in itself, an aspect of civilization. But then, all education apart from mere training is seen as subversive by a totalitarian government like this one.'

Toby studied William's flying jacket and Club Dead vest. 'I think that's an extremely jejune remark,' he said.

'And that's an extremely odd use of the word jejune,' replied William promptly, 'which when I last looked in a dictionary was a synonym for meagre rather than a posh word for prattish.'

Toby flushed, began to say something and then stopped. There was an embarrassed pause. God, thought Alec, I must be pissed. Had this been going on all evening? William's usual conversational style was combative but amiable. What had a nineteen-year-old prig with a Brideshead haircut said to annoy him that much?

Vivien, whose job as hostess was to sort out this sort of thing, was just looking amused. The girl, Rachel, sat, head down, sawing a mint in half with her butter knife. Her hair was silky blonde, clasped into a sort of vertical pony tail on top of her head. Completely amazing tits actually, or perhaps it was just the narrowness of her back.

'William got that from *It Pays to Increase Your Word-*

power,' said Alec into the silence. 'He was always a great student of the *Reader's Digest* at university: *Quotable Quotes*, *College Capers*, *I Am John's Left Testicle*. Do you know that he once wrote a 5,000-word essay on the *Reader's Digest*'s 4,000-word version of *The Great Gatsby*?'

William smiled happily at this. Twenty years had given each the licence to be as rude as he pleased about the other, without risk of offence.

'By the way,' Alec went on, 'have you ever played *Reader's Digest*? All you have to do is imagine you are a distinguished author of the past submitting a fifty-word plot synopsis to a modern publisher.'

'Give us an example,' said Rachel gratefully, and with a dazzling smile. It was definitely the tits, not the back.

'All right,' said Alec. 'This is Shakespeare selling *Macbeth* to Virago: "A Scottish housewife oppressed by domesticity and child-rearing seeks fulfilment through ancient magic sisterhood. Her husband is swept along by her new ambitions and abandons bourgeois conventions for self-expression and adventure. But middle-class male hegemony reasserts itself in the shape of stolid Malcolm. A tragedy for our times."'

'My turn now, then,' said William. 'This is *Madame Bovary* for Mills and Boon.'

'Too easy,' said Vivien. 'Do a difficult one, like *Moby Dick*.'

William ignored the interruption.

'Emma is nursing her beloved father when she falls for shy and brilliant young surgeon Charles Bovary. Emma is no easy catch, and the shallow charms of aristocratic Rodolphe and the cleverness of student Léon threaten the course of true love. But when the sun breaks through at last Emma has found lasting peace with her beloved Charles.'

'I thought she took strychnine at the end,' said Rachel.

'No market for suicide,' said William.

Then Vivien did *As I Lay Dying* for Ladybird, Malcolm did *The Naked Lunch* for Bloomsbury, Rachel did *Brideshead Revisited* for Lawrence and Wishart and Alec went to the lavatory.

It had a mahogany seat which matched the mahogany of the vanity unit and the towel rail in the bathroom, where he washed his hands and splashed water on his face. It was flushed and puffy when he examined it in the mirror, and he waited for it to cool down. There was an Indian copper bowl filled with crushed cinnamon bark on a marble washstand and a giant kentia palm in the corner. A short row of austere Clinique bottles filled a single shelf of the medicine cabinet. A bachelor bathroom.

Vivien was waiting outside the half-landing.

'That was nice of you, Alec.'

'Well, I usually try not to pee at the dining table or down the stairs.'

'I mean it was kind of you to rescue Toby from William.'

'Oh, I didn't do that for his sake,' said Alec. 'I think he's a prick. But I didn't want your friend Rachel to fall on her butter knife.'

'I think she's very fond of him. But they're both much too young to be living together like mums and dads.'

'Same age as Susan and I when we met.'

'Much too young,' said Vivien.

Alec found Rachel in the kitchen, making coffee. Her small, muscular, oval buttocks in black jersey ski-pants were even more spectacular than her breasts.

'Your *Brideshead Revisited* was rather good,' he told her.

'It's one of our Lost Domain books.'

'What? Oh, yes. Vivien's course. I never really thought of Brideshead as a lost domain. It was the sort of place that was better off lost when I was at university. We'd probably have done it as a study of rentier capitalism in decline, and good riddance.'

'You were very lucky to have gone to university then, you know,' said Rachel. 'When I hear people like Vivien and Malcolm talk, I can't help feeling I've missed out a bit. University is very serious nowadays.'

'Well, at least you won't be sodden with nostalgia for the rest of your life,' said Alec.

'Was everyone really so *political* in those days?'

'Not really. It was more a general feeling that you could do what the hell you wanted. People played at politics. Your parents were Labour and your lecturers were Liberal or Communist, so you became a revolutionary Trotskyist just to annoy as many of them as you possibly could. Now students like your mate Toby play at being Sebastian Flyte to wind up old farts like William and me.'

'Well, my father's a Conservative, so I suppose I should be an anarchist or something.'

'The only respectable political position these days,' said Alec.

He recited:

> Lady Dynamite, let's dance fast,
> Let's dance and sing and then let's blast!

'What's that? A 1960s song or something?'

'More like 1860s,' said Alec. 'It was a thing that the French Proudhonite anarchists used to sing. "La Dame Dynamite".'

'I shall recite it to my father.'

'What does he do?'

'I told you, he's a Conservative. A government minister.'

Alec smote his forehead. 'Your father is Ronald Wilson, the Education Minister.'

'Yes, it's awful, isn't it? Where are you going?'

'I'm going to tell William, and then we're going to kidnap you and hold you hostage until your father gives Vivien a new research assistant.'

'How about a round of tennis-elbow-foot?' said William later.

They were sitting around the log fire in Vivien's drawing room with William and Malcolm rolling joints and Alec smoking them. Vivien and Rachel had taken a toke on the first one, while Toby had refused.

'How do you play that?' asked Rachel. She was sitting beside Alec on the sofa, and he was enjoying the infinitesimal pressure of her hip on his own. Not that she would be aware of it.

'Just word associations,' he told her. 'The only rules are that you must irritate Malcolm and that William must win.'

'In the pure form of tennis-elbow-foot,' said William, 'you have to take off an item of clothing every time you miss a word, but in deference to Toby we'll play the junior version tonight. Vivien can start.'

He began to beat out a waltz rhythm with a teaspoon on the arm of his chair.

'If you don't get your word on the third beat then you're out. Ready? Right. One, two, three . . .'

Vivien: 'Tennis.'

Malcolm: 'Ball.'

Rachel: 'Wool.'

Toby: 'Knit.'

Alec: 'Malcolm.'

William: 'Campbell.'

Vivien: 'Soup.'

Malcolm: 'Spoon.'

Rachel: 'Fork.'

Toby: 'Bent.'

Alec: 'Malcolm.'

William: 'Umm . . .'

'Gotcha,' said Alec. 'You're out.'

'Just a warm-up round,' said William. 'Now we start properly.'

They played the game eight times, with William winning five, Alec one and Rachel two. Malcolm would not play in the last game and they gave up.

'Why do we have to irritate Malcolm?' Rachel asked curiously at the end.

'Ancient Uplands tradition,' said Alec, 'because he has

such a monstrous ego. And because he makes up stories about me in the newspaper.'

And Malcolm blushed.

William led Rachel up the garden path. It was cold after the indoor fug; their breath smoked and his steel-shod cowboy boots grated on the stone flags. Above them the sky was very clear and banners of stars were streaming endlessly by. He lifted the flap of his flying jacket and wrapped it around her shoulders. Her warm body fitted neatly under his arm and they fell into step with each other.

'I didn't expect you to bring someone else along,' he said.

'Toby's just a friend, not "someone else",' said Rachel. 'Anyway, I haven't even seen you since Amsterdam. You didn't answer my postcard.'

'I've got it in my wallet. I've been moving about a lot.'

'And besides, Vivien doesn't even know that I know you.'

'What's that got to do with it?'

'I don't think she approves of you much.'

'Don't be ridiculous. I've been friends with Vivien for half my life. Anyway, she's your tutor, not your bloody mother.'

'I'm fond of her. We've become very close. She's offered me a room in her house this term. What was it you wanted to show me, anyway?'

'Over here.'

Vivien's cottage stood on the crest of the valley slope opposite the university. From the top of her steeply terraced garden they could look down over the cones of the oast house, across the town and cathedral to the wooded slope beyond. William glanced surreptitiously at his watch.

'You see that white shape over there, among the trees?'

'That's the radio telescope on the hill below Marcuse.'

'If you kiss me now it will pick up the vibrations and look our way.'

'Don't be ridiculous, William. It always looks this way at midnight. It's when Sirius rises over the horizon.'

'Yes,' said William, crestfallen.

'I'm going inside. It's too cold here.'

He watched the delectable buttocks scampering down the path through the starlight and blew them a regretful kiss. Across the valley the radio telescope slowly swung its pale and mournful face towards him.

'You never let me down before,' said William.

When they finished coffee Malcolm opened his magic brief-case and Alec went to help Rachel with the washing-up.

'Aren't you going to have any of Malcolm's coke?' she asked him. 'It's very nice.'

'How do you know? You haven't had any either.'

'Oh, I'm one of Malcolm's regulars.'

He lifted her chin with one carefully chaste finger and studied her face. Caramel eyes with flecks of amber gazed solemnly back at him. 'Well, you've still got two nostrils at any rate,' he said. 'And you were the one who was telling me how serious everyone was at university these days.'

'Perhaps I'm some kind of a throwback.'

Alec tucked one of Vivien's tea towels around his waist and rolled up his sleeves. 'I don't particularly want any favours from Malcolm at the moment,' he told her. 'He wrote this nasty thing about me and Susan in the newspaper. He says he didn't, but it must have been him.' He began stacking dishes in the sink.

'Vivien says you're thinking of moving back here to Wyke-ham, but your wife doesn't want to come.'

'I suppose she must have been talking to Susan,' he said. 'They still see each other quite a bit. We're a very incestuous lot, as you can see. We've all known each other such a long time. Susan, William, Vivien, Malcolm. I've known them nearly twenty years. And practically everyone has been to bed with everyone else at some time or other.'

'You and Vivien too?' Rachel asked him.

'In the sense that we have both been unconscious together in the same bed. Yes.'

'I don't know why you sound so gloomy about it all. It sounds rather nice to me.'

'I don't know. Perhaps it's really just a kind of arrested adolescence. I know Susan thinks we would have been better off if we'd met each other later. Or perhaps we should have been like the Victorians, when the man of thirty-five married the girl of twenty.'

'So the man could sow his oats and still marry a sweet little virgin.'

'Not many virgins of twenty around,' said Alec.

'Oh, I don't know,' said Rachel.

'You're not telling me that you're a virgin?'

'In *Light in August* Lena Grove is nine months pregnant with an illegitimate child, but Faulkner said he still thought of her as a virgin.'

Alec turned to look at her. 'So your virginity is literary rather than literal?'

'These glasses are still covered in soap,' said Rachel.

It might just be his imagination, but the conversation seemed to have taken a rather steamy turn. He could feel that his face was hot and red again, though that was partly the heat of the washing-up water. A vein in his forehead was throbbing, and chilly curdlings in his bowels threatened repercussions from all the wine the next morning. But his mind felt brisk and elated; that sunlit plateau of clarity which sometimes emerges above the clouds of a long evening's drinking.

He was very conscious of the closeness of Rachel's body to his own as she cleared dishes from the drainer. Now and again her elbow or knee brushed against his as they worked, with what seemed like deliberate emphasis. When he said something that made her laugh she even leaned against him for a moment, her upper arm hot through the limp cotton of his shirt.

He chattered nervously, not really listening to what he was saying. 'You'll notice the way we've adopted our classic male–female roles. Even in a modern marriage with a more-or-less equal division of labour it has been observed that the man will grab all the pivotal, directional tasks for himself, while the woman carries out all the marginal ones. I wash and you dry.'

'My father always used to do the Hoovering before he was in the Cabinet,' said Rachel.

Alec allowed himself to enjoy for a moment the picture of the Secretary of State for Education in a pinafore, wielding an Electrolux.

'But I bet he never put the Hoover away afterwards, or did the dusting. Men will load washing machines but never hang out the smalls. They dig the garden but don't prune the shrubs. They make beds but don't change the sheets.'

Rachel's hand, rummaging in the soapy water for a missing fork, slid briefly but firmly along Alec's. No doubt about that. But some women were always touching you, weren't they? It was something they did when they fancied you a lot, or when they didn't fancy you at all; when they were scarcely aware of you sexually. Alec never had worked out how you told the difference.

He glanced surreptitiously down at the foreshortened Rachel. All he could see of her from this angle was some wisps of hair and the damp brown skin of her neck. The skin vanished under the thin white cotton of her t-shirt, then reappeared briefly at her navel, then again at the ankles of the black ski-pants. Her bare feet were brown, with the white V-stripe of a sandal thong and tiny, sweetcorn toes, clenched for purchase on the damp linoleum.

From the next room he could hear William's voice, arguing with Malcolm, and Vivien asking if anyone wanted more coffee, meaning please bugger off home, I'm tired. Rachel's hand slid over Alec's once again under the blanket of soap-suds. The things that hands could get up to underwater. 'I think that's about it,' she said.

'What a shame,' said Alec.

He offered her a hand towel from one of the mahogany pegs beside the drainer. She took it and, looking full in his face, began to pat his hands dry, pressing them between her own. She was standing very close to him and her breasts were brushing his shirt. The base of his throat had gone tight and the vein in his temple was throbbing harder. What did he need? A printed invitation? Do something, he told himself. Do it now.

'I'd like to come and see this famous house some time,' said Rachel.

'Next weekend,' said Alec, and in a sudden fit of decision rested each of his now-dry hands on the delicious curves of her hips.

'I didn't mean . . .' said Rachel.

'Never mind,' said Alec, pulling her towards him.

'I was just trying to tell you . . .'

'Tell me afterwards.'

Rachel's head fell back with a sigh, her lips parted. Alec leaned forward greedily to take them and Rachel, with a short jerk of her neck, nutted him briskly on the bridge of the nose.

'What's all the blood on this tea towel?' said Vivien, the next day, as she fished it from the washing basket.

'Your friend Alec cut his finger when we were washing up,' said Rachel.

CHAPTER SIX

From *The Republican Reader*:

Between 1958 and 1972 the Queen was pregnant
92 times, had 149 accidents and nine miscarriages
and took the pill 11 times. She abdicated 63 times
and was on the point of breaking up with Prince
Philip 73 times.

– Henry Porter, *Lies, Damned Lies and Some*
Exclusives

Malcolm's fingers pattered over the keyboard of his word processor.

Education Secretary Ronald Wilson's daughter Rachel was at the
centre of a campus row herself this week after throwing a punch at
a drunken groper.

Pretty, nineteen-year-old Rachel, who is a student at Wykeham
University, was forced to defend herself at a wild weekend party
where drink flowed freely and drugs were taken. Among the students and academics at the all-night rave-up were leather-jacketed
Hell's Angels, and Alec Smith, disreputable left-wing publisher of
the notorious *Republican Reader*.

A friend of Rachel's tells me, 'She was minding her own business
in the kitchen when this middle-aged drunk started pawing her.
Fortunately Rachel knows how to look after herself, and left him
on the floor with a bloody nose.'

Wykeham is a 'plate-glass' sixties university and a one-time
centre of student sit-ins where local residents would regularly be
outraged by the sight of students sunbathing naked on the lawns,
and even wandering topless into nearby shops.

Education Minister Wilson, who has initiated the recent debate on falling standards and lack of relevance at the high-spending 'modern' universities, is known to be seriously concerned by the latest incident, and will be asking university authorities for a full report.

William read the story to Alec in the Jaguar as they drove back to London on the Monday morning. They had spent Sunday recovering from their hangovers at Vivien's and then drawing up lists of building works at Uplands. William was to move in the following weekend.

'I suppose I must be the Hell's Angels,' said William when he had finished reading. 'You know, Malcolm is really getting quite good at this sort of thing.'

'I think I'm going to thump the bastard next time I see him,' said Alec.

William studied the diary paragraph again for a moment. 'I should think he's much stronger than you, Alec. Anyway, he doesn't actually say it was you that made a pass at her.'

'No, but I'm the only other person who's mentioned by name, so it's pretty obvious.'

'I suppose the "friend of Rachel's" is that little shit Toby.'

'Well, Malcolm's definitely not coming to my housewarming party now,' said Alec.

The Right Honourable Ronald Wilson, MP, found the story among the sheaf of press clippings that was prepared for him each morning by his Private Secretary. As a man with some sensitivity to the English language, a minor poet in his own right, the Secretary of State for Education tried to avoid reading the newspapers as much as he could.

Execrable style apart, he found them mildly embarrassing, like the attentions of an over-enthusiastic springer spaniel. 'PM Thumps Opposition Again', crowed the headline on one. 'Government Triumph Over Loony Council', gloated another. Wilson sometimes suspected the jaded left-wing journalists who wrote these things of sending up their own organs and the administration they ostensibly supported. Perhaps they were transmitting coded messages to the British public, for surely nobody could believe such nonsense?

He was, nevertheless, concerned about his daughter and instructed the PPS to telephone her at once. He had been relieved when Rachel had decided not to take up her place at Oxford. The minister had taken his own degree, a first in Classics, at a peaceful Scottish university. He disliked what he had heard of the fleshpots of Cowley, whence the children of his Cabinet colleagues regularly emerged addicted to heroin, pregnant or socialist. Wykeham sounded rural and harmless and was, he had been told, much favoured these days by the dimmer sons of the merchant classes, with one of whom Rachel might well strike up an attachment.

She was the eldest of his three daughters and a source of anxiety to him since it had become plain that she had scooped the beauty and intelligence which might have been more fairly distributed among all three sisters. Hattie and Michaela had developed the teeth, legs and charm of the snappish ponies they constantly rode. Bashful young bankers with thinning hair already looked languorously upon Hattie and Michaela as they thundered over brushwood jumps and splashed about the puddles of point-to-points. But for Rachel her father could uneasily envisage a future of unsuitable lovers, difficult novels and Islington bedsits.

His telephone rang.

'I've got your daughter on the line, Minister.'

Then Rachel's voice, sounding sleepy and puzzled. He realized that it was still only 8 a.m. You had to be at your desk by 7. There was rarely anything to do but read newspapers and listen to the *Today* programme, but there was always the possibility that She might phone you up.

'Daddy. What's wrong? Is Mummy all right?'

'Of course she's all right, darling. I'm sorry if I woke you up. It was just this thing in the paper about someone attacking you.'

'Attacking me?'

He read out the first two paragraphs.

'Oh, I suppose that must be Toby.'

'Someone called Toby attacked you.'

'No, Daddy. Nobody attacked me. I mean, it must have been Toby who sent them the story.'

Toby? Was he the chap she had met in Amsterdam that her mother had mentioned? The one who was in antiques? No, that was Wilhelm or something. She was rattling on about some dinner she had had with her tutor and a man with a telescope. An astronomer? She was obviously fine in any case.

'Look, darling, I'm going to have to go now, I've got Cabinet this morning. Perhaps Mummy and I will be able to pop down one weekend soon. I can tell her there's no truth in the story, can I?'

'Oh, of course it isn't true, Daddy. It's in the newspaper.'

Melanie had taken all her clothes off and was sitting facing Alec, with her knees crossed and her chin propped in her hands. Two brown nipples peeped from behind her forearms. They were always called Melanie wherever you went: strip club, massage parlour, peep show, escort agency. A whole world of Melanies.

'Shall I tell you what I will do for you?' she asked.

'Yes, please,' said a croaky voice, very far away. Quite like Alec's.

'I will masturbate myself and you can masturbate yourself at the same time. That will cost you £20.'

'Oh,' said the Alec voice, feebly.

'What's the matter? Too much money?'

Melanie explained some of the other options. For £5, she said, she would spread her legs and show Alec her cunt. For another £5 she would stick her fingers up her cunt. And so forth. She did not actually say 'cunt'. She said 'myself', as if acknowledging the bleak economic fact that herself and her cunt were, to all intents and purposes, the same thing. The plastic bench she was sitting on gave a little fart every time she shifted her buttocks. For £25, she told Alec, she would put a dildo up herself. She took the dildo from a Safeway's carrier bag on the floor beside her to show him. It was chrome-coloured and ribbed like a giant lipstick. He noticed a shrink-wrapped packet of butcher's mince in the carrier bag.

Everything seemed to have a price, except for actually touching each other, because there was a half-inch sheet of plate glass between them. The sign outside in the street had read 'Nude Encounter Parlour' and Alec had imagined a dimly lit, sybaritic salon of divans and tasselled drapes, with candlelight gilding naked bodies. But the parlour had turned out to be only a plasterboard cubicle in the cellar, a little larger than a lavatory, with a door at each end, and two of the farting benches, each completely sealed off from the other by the six-foot sheet of smeary glass.

He had come in through a narrow passageway off Greek Street. A pink-cheeked girl with the cheerful smile of a Woolwich advert explained the protocol to him. It was £10 for ten minutes, £15 for twenty minutes and so on. 'The girl will strip off completely and talk to you for ten minutes,' said Woolwich, in a level, matter-of-fact voice. 'Anything else you want' – her voice lingered briefly – 'is arranged between you.' Someone's fingers, nimble as bananas, found the money in his wallet. Someone's feet tramped solidly, resignedly downstairs, carrying his body with them, to the basement cubicle where Melanie was waiting.

He must have passed the doorway a hundred times on his way to Prometheus Press. He had passed it this morning with scarcely a sideways flicker of the eye, then marched purposefully on, briefcase swinging, to the tall, narrow house behind the Regent Palace Hotel.

The Australian had spent money on Prometheus Press: filling the foyer with rented pot plants; carpeting the editorial offices in battleship grey; installing sleek dove-grey computer terminals on every desk. Jim the doorman, a retired police sergeant, had disappeared from the foyer, together with his desk and kettle and Page Three pin-ups. You poked a plastic card now into a slot beside the door, the same card that operated the lift and coffee machine.

'Our lost leader,' said Ralph, when Alec stepped from the lift on to the fourth floor. A few hands were raised casually in greeting; a few faces looked up from their terminals. Most of them he did not recognize. He sidled sheepishly to the tiny glass box that was his office and examined the small stack of mail and messages in his in-tray. After a minute his intercom buzzed.

'Mr Smith.'

'Yes.'

'It's Josie speaking. We haven't met but I'm the MD's new PA. I'm so sorry. We tried to reach you at home, but you'd left. This morning's meeting has been cancelled.'

'Oh, right.'

'I'll notify you of the new date.'

'Thank you.'

He stuffed the messages and envelopes into his wallet and sidled out again, past the ranks of grey terminals.

'Hard day at the office, dear?' said Ralph.

He had created a small, defiant island of disorder around himself: boxes of Bic biros with the tops chewed to shreds testified to his attempts to give up smoking; crowded ashtrays testified to his failures. Collapsing piles of galley proofs were shuffling themselves into collapsing stacks of unopened circulars; yellow Post-It notes curled around the edge of his computer screen, like a ragged wig. 'Remember taramasalata,' said one; 'Tell D K to fuck off if they ring again,' said another.

Ralph was managing editor of Prometheus Press, Alec's partner once and his friend, though they embarrassed each other now.

'Meeting's been cancelled,' he said.

Ralph poked a Craven A between his curtains of greasy blond hair and lit it from a giant box of kitchen matches.

'I know. He'll be planning the synchronized swimming version of *The Republican Reader*, I should think. Or the ice dance spectacular.'

'What's happened to Jim?' said Alec.

'Tin handshake,' said Ralph. He adopted the flattened vowels of the Australian's bluff and comradely style. 'Efter all, who needs a flaming retired plod setting downstairs looking et dirty pictures end pulling his plonker on the company's time.'

'You know Jim's wife was ill?'

'Yes.'

'He is a shit, isn't he?' said Alec.

'And we've won the Battle of Waterloo,' said Ralph.

Alec began sidling again towards the lift.

'We must have a drink soon.'

'Where are you off to now?'

'Go home, I suppose,' said Alec. 'Have a wank.'

'Have one on me,' said Ralph.

'I will,' said Alec, but he didn't.

In the cellar Melanie's body was tallowy and crumpled-looking in the fluorescent light, with little handles of flesh above the hips. Her breasts were small and rather saggy. Her face was pale and wary, with a bob of dark hair. Alec thought she must be about thirty. In the cubicle next door somebody had chosen the £25 option to judge by the rhythmical gasps and groans drifting over the partition. 'Go on, please. Oh, please, go on, go on.'

'That will cost you another £20,' said a girl's level voice.

Melanie said it would be another £10 if Alec wanted to talk to her.

'I thought I'd paid to talk to you upstairs,' he said.

'I don't get any of that money,' said Melanie. 'I only gets what the punters give down here.'

'That seems unfair.'

'P'raps I should write to the Trading Standards Officer.'

The tiny spark of animation which Melanie had managed to fan alive for what was probably her tenth customer of the day was beginning to fade. Alec poked the extra £20 through a slot in the top of the glass. She reached up to take it, exposing her body fully for the first time. There was a puckered, horizontal Caesarean scar above the dark puff of her pubic hair, like a stitched mouth. She sat down quickly, tucking the money in a shoe and recrossing her arms and legs. The bench gave another fart.

'Well, what do you want to talk about?'

Well, what did he want to talk about? He had wanted a tart with a heart, he supposed; a bosomy blonde with a lamp tan and a gold ankle chain whom he could tell about Susan, who wouldn't fuck him any more, and about his cock, which didn't seem to want to fuck anybody any more. Then the tart-with-the-heart would have laughed kindly at his foolishness and inspired him to an instant 45-degree erection with some simple trick of her trade.

Then Alec and the TWH would have bounced away the afternoon on peach satin sheets, the TWH exclaiming over his skill, stamina and powers of recuperation, and vowing that he, Alec, was the first man to give her an orgasm since Reggie Kray. He would have become a TWH regular after that, with no charge of course, and been introduced to, and embraced by, a galaxy of raffish Soho characters like Fat Mort, the barman who served Dylan Thomas his last whisky before he embarked for America, and Sally Patchouli, the flower child turned porn novelist, and Dan Rasher, the alcoholic sports writer who had once been a painter.

Instead, what he actually had was a stripped-off shopgirl, erotic as a peeled parsnip, who obviously couldn't wait to get away to meet her kid – Darren? – from school.

'How did you get into, er, this?' asked Alec, conversationally.

'I've always done it, haven't I? I like it, don't I?'

A silence.

'Do you ever touch people? Have sex with them?'

Melanie tapped her foot impatiently. 'Snot allowed, is it? Sa notice onna wall over there, isn't there?'

A longer silence.

'Look,' she said at last, 'are you sure you don't want to do anything?'

Alec introspected obediently. But his libido, and his penis, were as cold and inert as clay.

'Really . . . thank you . . . not.'

'You shouldn't be embarrassed. There's nothing wrong with it, you know. It's quite *natural*,' she told him loftily.

'Yes.'

The thick sense of excitement and panic that had made him walk past the Greek Street doorway three times had evaporated. It was like visiting some remote relative in hospital. They sat looking at each other through the glass. Alec's mind empty. Melanie faintly hostile, as well she might be. She'd be a lot more comfortable if he would just be decent enough to do something to make the degradation mutual.

'Do you mind if I get dressed?' she said eventually. It had only been about five minutes, but there didn't seem much point hanging around in this smelly cubicle any longer. She dressed with the speed and precision of twenty times a day and led the way upstairs.

'He didn't do *anything*,' she told Woolwich.

Outside in the street there was someone cutting bread in the window of a sandwich shop; a tourist with a backpack looking at an A–Z; a man fiddling helplessly with the wheel-clamp on his car; a Chinese waiter in a miniature apron sluicing down the pavement.

There were many sleepwalkers too. Men like Alec, with suits and briefcases and fixed expressions, avoiding eye contact. They plodded purposefully along, off to buy coffee in Old Compton Street or some cheese at Camisa Fratelli. But then, as some invisible magnetic points switched in the pavement, they would wheel suddenly into a porn cinema or a peep show or a sex shop.

They had all just come from offices with pot plants or business lunches or shopping for presents for children in

Gloucester, and now their feet were carrying them to dark cellars where they would masturbate or be masturbated. Their hands would reach, banana-fingered, for their wallets. Their voices, sounding thick and strange in their ears, would ask for pleasures they could not ask of their wives.

He used to think he was a freak, an oddity, but he knew now that he was normal. All men were like this. They were. Some dared to do it and some didn't, but they all wanted to at some time or other. He just had more desperation, or less shame, or more foolishness. But his lusts, he knew now, were just ordinary.

It was worse when he had thought he was mad, or going mad. When he thought it was just him who walked past the massage parlour, three and four times, his throat constricted with dull desire, and then climbed into his car to drive back home, sour with victory . . . over what?

Was it only him who would slow his car by the tarts under the street lights, then accelerate viciously past? Only him who bought the cheap magazines with their mad picture captions and made-up letters and Melanies splayed out like Smithfield turkeys? Only him who hid them in the space behind drawers, beneath corners of carpet and tucked inside books?

Perhaps no one except Alec bought the Victorian maid confessions at station bookstalls and wanked himself to sleep with them in the bedrooms of provincial hotels. Nobody else ever selected the eighth channel on the hotel TV to watch, on stained sheets, *The Sweet Sins of Sexy Susan* and *Swedish Scheherazade* and *Blue Mink Bikinis* into the small hours of grey, Midlands mornings.

The boys in the video studios in Wardour Street and the editorial offices in Camden Town, just laid it all on for Alec. Alec's off to Newcastle, they would tell each other, we'd better plug some smut into the hotel TV for when he gets there. He's browsing outside W. H. Smith today. Fill the top shelf with some real filth for him, can you? That perv

Alec is going to be horny next week. Fake up another edition of *Walter's Secret Life* or *Delta of Venus IV*, can you, chaps?

It was around that time that Alec had begun to fear he really was going off the rails, down the river, over the top, into out-of-control, onanistic crazyville. He'd be exposing himself soon. Feeling up his daughter. Rubbing himself against women in trains.

He watched TV reports of railway rapists and screwdriver sex fiends and newspaper boy nabbers. And though Alec had never hit anyone in his life, though the idea of rape was technically as well as emotionally inconceivable to him, though he had never had the smallest stirring of paedophilia, or necrophilia, or coprophilia, or any serious philia, phagia or phobia in his life, they weren't so very far away any more. They weren't so remote and unimaginable, all those fiends and freaks and fuck-ups, with their screwdrivers and garottes and rubber masks and martial arts shit and probably a mummified mother back home in a rocking chair. If a nice Watford boy with a sexy wife, a university degree and a liberated sixties background could get a kick out of *Hustler* and a buzz from *Blue Mink Bikinis*, then the fucked-up freaks were only just out of sight, massing over the horizon.

It was his bank manager who had saved him in the end. He walked into the newsagent's in Upper Street one day, not even buying a *Hustler* this time, and there was the bank manager. Right there in the middle of the row of dreamers. The stargazers who stand with their hands behind their backs – I'm looking, not buying – and whose gaze skips so nimbly from motoring mag and angling paper to *Hustler* and *Rascal* and *Rake*.

It was the bank manager, and he was a regular, you could tell. He waited for a lull at the cash desk first. You had to do this or you ended up standing next to some good-looking girl, or, even worse, a bad-looking girl. The bank manager pulled down his *Rascal* and flipped it double (booze ad facing outwards) with the skill of the habitué. He tucked it inside his *Financial Times*, dropped the exact change at the cash desk and was out of the shop without even noticing Alec. A real pro. He was probably home, wanked off and washing his hands before the girl finished counting his money.

So that settled it. They all did it. Bank managers beat their meat. Probably policemen pulled their plonkers, judges definitely doodled with their dongs and Alec had, in any case, never doubted that teachers abused their beef bayonets. They were all wankers, from puberty to pension. It wouldn't have made any difference to Alec, he knew now, if he had been married to Kim Basinger and slipping it to Diane Keaton on the side. He'd still be off to the bog every few days for a good wank over a paper turkey with her feet behind her ears.

Susan phoned Vivien.

'He's been even moodier since he came back from last weekend. I thought all this nonsense about doing up the house might cheer him up. Give him something to do. But he's more miserable than he was before. And he's drinking all the time.'

'He did drink a lot,' said Vivien. 'What's he doing now?'

'He had to go to a meeting at Prometheus. Then he said he was going swimming at the Oasis.'

'My mother says it's always a bad sign when middle-aged men start trying to keep fit,' said Vivien.

'What are the good signs in your mother's life?'

'Funerals always cheer her up,' said Vivien, 'and a lingering disease in one of her closer friends can be a source of great satisfaction. Actually,' she went on, 'I was thinking of coming up to London next weekend. There's this summer party at the *Bystander* that I've been invited to.'

'Aren't they terribly fascist on that?'

'More sort of Tory anarchist really. Anyway, they don't mind me being rude about all the dreary writers they read, like Anthony Powell and Barbara Pym and Patrick Leigh-Fermor.'

'Come and stay with us,' said Susan. 'Alec is going down

to Wykeham again with William. We could go shopping. Go to your fascist party together.'

'I'd like that.'

'That story I heard,' said Susan after a while, 'about Alec getting hit by some girl. It wasn't true, was it?'

'Of course it wasn't true,' said Vivien. 'It was in the newspaper.'

CHAPTER SEVEN

From *The Republican Reader*:

> The defenders of monarchy typically maintain two contradictory positions. One is that the monarchy is everything: the embodiment of all those values of tradition, continuity, family life and political moderation which are the soul of the nation. The other is that the monarchy does not matter, has no real power, and so to attack it is to be humourless, eccentric and unfair.

In times of trouble, some people buy doughnuts and others new clothes. Alec Smith found solace in hardware, and Meakins in Wykeham was his favourite hardware shop in the world. It was 112 years old and staffed by ancient, withered men in brown cotton shop-coats who treated their customers with weary contempt, who weighed everything in tiny brass scales and wrapped each purchase laboriously and individually in brown paper and string.

Meakins was lined from floor to ceiling with tiny, polished mahogany drawers filled with rare and curious items that were smelted and cast and turned to order in backstreet workshops in the Midlands: tiny screws; enormous bolts; hinges for doll's houses; lion's head door knockers with tongues that went in and out; and flushed brass handles for eighteenth-century sea chests.

Alec had bought many of the fittings for Uplands here, and for the house in Islington, and he came equipped with careful lists and sets of sketches. The Meakins countermen had served their apprenticeships in the age of the professional builder and decorator: monosyllabic and authoritative men, with folding rules and square carpenter's pencils tucked behind orange-peel ears. But the customers now were the DIY Blackandeckermen, strong on their dignity as consumers but weak on terminology, and the Meakins men despised them.

In the front of Alec's queue was a man in a leather blouson jacket and trainers, drawing wild diagrams in the air. 'I want some of those, erm, some of those little nails for, fixing the leather to chair seats, sort of like drawing pins, only bigger . . .'

'You mean some *chair nails*, sir,' said the counterman smugly.

Further along the counter another Blackandeckerman was miming the opening of an invisible sash window. 'Some of those little curved brass things you fix on the bottom of sliding windows, for, erm, sliding them with . . .'

'Sir would like some *sash lifts*,' said a second counterman.

The trick, Alec had learned over the years, was the *obviousness* of the names of these obscure pieces of hardware. A brass corner piece for protecting the corner of a military chest, for instance, was known as a *military chest corner*. A sliding bolt for a lavatory door, which indicated whether there was anybody in the lavatory or not, was a *lavatory indicator bolt*. The cast-iron ends of old-fashioned wooden ceiling airers were called *airer ends*. And just in case a regular like Alec ever got cocky, the countermen could throw in a name as unguessable as Rumpelstiltskin. Alec had once asked firmly for a 'Brass swivel match' for a kitchen cupboard, only to be told, loftily, that what he required was *a button-on-a-plate*.

His father, Harry, hated this sort of place, of course. Harry had made his money in the wholesale clothing business. He disliked retail establishments on principle, but hated DIY and tools and hardware even more. He could have hated Meakins just for its olde worlde name, or for the dusty pyramid of Polyfilla packets that was its hopeless window display, or its complete lack of commercial acuity. He would have loathed its queues and its sluggish, condescending service; raged at its cruel little courtesies and its finnicky nomenclature; despised its total lack of interest in selling merchandise and making money in preference to irritating and baffling its customers.

Alec Smith was an ordinary man who had begun to feel his life sliding inexorably towards oddness. He had grown up in Watford, had supported Arsenal, collected Robertson's gollies and constructed Airfix models of British fighter planes. He had eight O levels, three A levels and a 2:1 in Political Science from an ordinary university. The book jacket of *The Republican Reader* stated that 'Alec Smith is married with two children, and lives in north London' – and what could be more ordinary than that?

He was ordinary, but Susan, Rachel and now Melanie had, successively, made Alec begin to feel very odd indeed. He had begun to fear that he was on the verge of making some impatient, dramatic, self-revealing gesture that might ruin everything for ever. Some terrible and shameful act which would change him in an instant from wealthy, successful, affable, family-man Alec to a freak-outcast-pervert Alec, fit only to be stoned in the cathedral precincts by brown-coated shop assistants, Scots Presbyterian Education Secretaries and students with Sebastian Flyte haircuts.

So he came to Meakins in search of the finely graded inefficiency and fractionally modulated rudeness which are the indices of ordinary English life. He came for the stoicism, the flinty reserve and the fanatical attention to meaningless detail which, for Alec, were quintessentially English, and to which he quite naturally responded, and which reassured him, therefore, of his essential Watfordian, Battle of Britain, Robertson-gollyish dullness. And he needed to buy some hardware.

'I'd like twelve white porcelain fingerplates and matching keyhole scutcheons, please.'

The counterman scowled at this upstart fluency in the Meakins idiolect and trudged off with resentful sluggishness, down the ranks of tiny mahogany drawers in search of a stepladder.

'What's a keyhole scutcheon?' asked a voice behind him, and Alec turned around to find Rachel, fetchingly dressed in white painter's overalls and with a dab of eau-de-nil emulsion on her nose. He had not seen her since the night of the washing-up disaster, the memory of which he had half succeeded in blurring, so that it now caused him to sweat with embarrassment only two or three times a day, as opposed to wanting to rend his clothes and smear his brow with ashes, which had been his first instinct on waking up the morning after Vivien's dinner party.

Had he really done that terrible thing? Could he, Alec, possibly have made a grab for a nineteen-year-old girl who had done no more than chat brightly over the washing-up bowl? The instant that surprisingly bony forehead of hers connected so painfully with the delicately arched bridge of Alec's nose he had known the truth. He had known that every sign he had read in Rachel's face, every invitation he had heard in her voice, were no more than reflections and echoes of his own lechery and loneliness.

Here was Rachel, having a polite chat with her tutor's famous publisher friend from London, and what does the famous publisher friend do? Within yards of her tutor and her boyfriend, with a tea towel tucked in his waist, suds up his forearms and with a Ratners wedding ring on his finger, he makes a pass at her with all the suavity and sexual poise of an overheated Labrador.

William, strangely enough, had been rather incurious about the whole business, even after Malcolm's shitty little story in the paper. He had accepted, without question, Alec's version of events. A casual little pat. Misinterpreted by this bloody neurotic woman. Obviously living in some sort of lather of feminist anxiety. Every man who passed the time of day with her was probably some sort of closet rapist.

And William had accepted it, which is not to say that he believed it, for there were few men Alec knew who entirely believed other men's accounts of their sex lives. They all had too much experience in doctoring accounts of their own. But in any case, Alec was grateful. He wouldn't have believed such a story for a minute coming from William himself – not that William would have bothered to concoct it.

His best friend adhered to the scattergun theory of seduction, which stated that if you asked practically every woman you met to go to bed with you, a fairly high proportion would say yes. Blast away at random, and you were more or less bound to hit something.

William had actually tested this theory once, outside David Greig's in Wykeham High Street, with Alec as witness. Very politely, but quite explicitly, he had asked strange women if they would like to go to bed with him. Three said no, but without calling a policeman and without any of the rage and indignation which Alec was certain would have been his own lot had he tried the same thing. The fourth woman said yes. She was the wife of a tobacconist from Wincheap, forty-three years old but not bad-looking. She caught the bus up to the university with William and they spent the afternoon in bed together. 'Three times,' said a drawn-looking William later, 'and a whole bottle of baby oil.'

The thing was, as he tried to explain to Alec when the tobacconist's wife had caught her bus back to Wincheap, women had fundamentally the same attitude towards sex as men. 'They all like fucking,' he told him, 'and they'd all like to fuck a bit more often than they do. The only difference is that they don't want their friends to find out they fuck, whereas, for the average bloke, having his friends find out he fucks is practically the whole fucking point. He wants to carve his notches on the headboard.'

Alec, in his first year at university and still without one, even metaphorical, notch on his headboard accepted this wisdom, but without believing it. Women for him were still alien creatures of unpredictable, arbitrary tastes. Sometimes, at a party, a pretty one would kiss you; sometimes an ugly one would not. There seemed no system or logic to it, no steady and predictable current of lust for the best-looking specimen of the opposite sex you could lay hands on, such as governed Alec's adolescence, and the adolescence of every male he knew. How could women want to fuck you as much as you wanted to fuck them? He didn't believe it, but in matters of sexual insight he deferred to William, as he deferred to him in practically nothing else.

'The trouble is, you still don't think that women actually enjoy fucking, or not as much as men do,' William would lecture him, when Alec complained of his lack of success. 'You think they fuck just to keep us quiet and to have babies. Of course, the brainwashing they get from their mums and schoolmistresses and *Jackie* magazine is so efficient that there are actually some women who believe it as well. But once they get away from their mums, and provided they don't vote Conservative, they usually learn that fucking is as much fun for them as it is for you.'

'What has voting Conservative got to do with it?' Alec asked him curiously.

'Ah well, as a politico like yourself should know by now, sexual relations echo power relations. Hierarchical and authoritarian societies always try to marshal, or suppress, the sexual instinct.'

Alec visualized the faces of what was then Her Majesty's Loyal Opposition. 'I'll grant you Edward Heath,' he said, 'but Margaret Thatcher doesn't look like somebody who's not getting any. And what about the Roman Empire? They were as hierarchical and authoritarian as you like, and they were at it all the time.'

'Only the ruling class,' said William. 'And only in private. The orthodox sexual ideal was the chaste Roman matron, and the strongest religious symbol the Vestal virgin.'

'Messalina was fucking centurions in the Forum,' said Alec.

'And Claudius *didn't know*,' said William triumphantly. 'The main way sexuality is controlled is through secrecy, suppression, marginalization. The fact that women enjoy sex is a prime example of the way society can manage to suppress a fundamental truth for the purposes of social control.'

'I don't see why society should give a toss,' said Alec. 'I mean, what does it matter to the balance of payments or the gross domestic product what people are doing to each other in bed?'

'Because sex is unruly,' said William promptly. 'It is a very straightforward, primitive drive which seeks satisfaction where it can. Sons with mothers, fathers with daughters, men with men, women with women, black with white. In a state of sexual excitement a duchess may screw a dustman, and in a well-ordered society that would never do.'

It hadn't made much difference to Alec. He still blushed and stammered at parties and discos, and, before Susan, there were still no notches on the headboard. At thirty-nine years of age, and accosted in a hardware shop by a chit of a girl in painter's overalls, with a dab of emulsion on her nose, he blushed and stammered now.

'A scutcheon plate? It's a little sort of cover for a keyhole.'

'To stop people peeping through?'

He blushed still more deeply.

'No, it slides to one side if, er, if you wanted to do that.'

'And why does one want to do that?'

Alec found himself getting irritated, which always restored his habitual fluency.

'I think the Victorians had a horror of apertures. Curtains and blinds on windows, screens on fireplaces, scutcheons on keyholes. They abhorred an unfilled hole almost as much as they abhorred an undecorated mantelpiece or an uncovered piano leg. Very *prudish* people.'

The intended note of adult superiority seemed to pass Rachel by completely.

'I'm painting my new room in Vivien's house,' she told him brightly, waving down at the overalls, whose rubber-buttoned side fastening, Alec had already noted, fleetingly revealed a very narrow strip of black knicker over honey-brown hipbone.

'With your nose?' he suggested coldly.

'You like the colour?'

'No.'

'Neither did Vivien. She wanted eighties colours, like pink and grey and yellow. But I've always wanted a proper boudoir, and Mummy would never let me do it to my room at home. How's *your* nose, by the way?'

'Slightly out of joint.'

'I'm very sorry if I hurt you. I was feeling rather angry with William, you see, and you sort of got caught in the crossfire. It was only partly intentional.'

Alec was somewhat mollified. He stole another glance at the scalloped section of naked hip, visible through the overall fastening.

'Well, I was only partly trying to get my hands down your trousers,' he said.

'You shouldn't really buy paint here at all,' he told her, as they waited. 'It's far too expensive.'

'I liked the name. Thos Meakin. One doesn't get Thos's and Chas's and Geo's any more. All the shops in London have stupid names, like Amazing Grates for fireplaces and Styx for furniture.'

'And hairdressers called Brian Waves and Head Jogs.'

'I used to go to one called 'Air 'Aid.'

'I know a greengrocer called Agent Orange.'

'You're making that one up,' said Rachel.

'No, really. And a butcher called Lights Fantastic.'

She had the most wonderful laugh. A real dirty honk, quite out of keeping with her 'Mummys' and 'ones'.

'Would you like some help back with those things?' asked Alec. 'I think we're going the same way.'

They walked with several feet between them, up the High

Street, Alec carrying a five-litre paint can in each hand and Rachel swinging his own, string- and paper-wrapped parcel. She stopped to buy a Marathon bar in Eastgate and chewed it as they walked. The pavements were crowded with parties of French schoolchildren and Americans with huge boots and rucksacks. Alec cast about for a neutral topic of conversation.

Most of the old shops had gone and been replaced by Next and Laura Ashley and Crabtree and Evelyn and Culpeper's and Liberty's. He pointed out the unfinished war memorial in the Cornmarket, which read 'To the men of Wykeham, who fell in.' He showed her the shop where Malcolm had once run his wholefood restaurant and which was now a Roman pizza parlour, with plastic Doric columns and waitresses in gilt vine leaf headdresses. He told her how, after university, he and Susan had planned to found a specialist publishers here, to reprint classic books on hand presses, with fine paper and original engravings.

'We'd had such a nice time here that we wanted it to just go on. But of course, people gradually left, and the students got younger and younger. And in a few years we both got restless. It had got to seem so bloody tiddly-pom, with its little teashops and the cathedral clock striking and the Bishop put-putting down the road in his Morris Minor; with Mr Beef the Butcher and Mr Green the grocer, all popping in and out of their little shops like Toytown. Everyone else was living the London life, and I'd begun to feel nostalgic for some proper urban grot: a few howling sirens and Coke cans in the gutter and something on at the cinema apart from *The Poseidon Adventure*.'

'They had *The Poseidon Adventure* on at the University Film Club last term,' said Rachel. 'And *Airport* and *The Towering Inferno*. One of the media studies lecturers put together a season of disaster movies. He said they were a sort of gentle introduction to Armageddon for the suburbs. "Packaging Apocalypse", it was called.'

Alec laughed. 'There's probably something in that. It's

funny how things you create for one reason can end up achieving something completely contrary. Horror movies that are meant to terrify people become a way to ignore real terrors. Mills and Boon is meant to glorify love, but actually helps people to get along without it. Barbara Taylor Bradford worships success, and her books become Bibles for failures. Dickens flays society for its callousness and greed and becomes court jester to the callous and greedy. The Cinderella myth probably still does more for social tranquillity than the Special Branch.'

Stop bloody lecturing, he told himself. She's nineteen, not nine.

'Was that what happened to *The Republican Reader*?' Rachel asked him.

'You've read it, then, have you?'

'I thought it was very funny.'

'Everyone thinks it's funny, apart from my wife. But it was a serious enterprise once upon a time. I was quite sure when we started on it that the monarchy was at the centre of everything that was wrong with this country, and it was meant to take the whole institution to pieces. Historical analysis, constitutional argument, satire, ridicule. And yet, by the time I'd finished, and it was into paperback and stacked up in display bins at Smith's, I found I'd created another institution and given the object of the attack a further lease of life. People have an astonishing ability to be entertained by what should enrage them. The Prince of Wales has an autographed copy.'

'You're kidding.'

'I wish I was. He came to our stand at the Frankfurt Book Fair and insisted I sign one for him. And he invited me to a Royal Garden Party. Apparently his dad thinks *The Republican Reader* is hilarious.'

'You could have told him to fuck off.'

'It occurred to me, and William said it would have sold us another 10,000 copies, but I actually rather like the Prince of Wales.'

They passed David Greig's, where William had picked up his lady tobacconist, and Alec told her the story.

'I'd love to see her now,' said Rachel.

'She must be sixty years old at least, with elastic stockings and false teeth.'

'William would still make a pass at her in a poor light.'

Alec felt encouraged by the coldness of the remark. William had still never mentioned Rachel by name, and he'd been too pissed to notice whatever had gone on between them at Vivien's party. But he had managed to work out by now that this was the girl William had been intending to see at Wykeham. On the other hand, they were supposed to be having a neutral conversation. Oh, what the hell.

'You do know William, then?'

Rachel said nothing for some minutes, until he began to wonder if she had heard the question, or decided to ignore it.

'I met him in Amsterdam at Easter,' she said eventually. 'Toby and I went there for a long weekend. A "Mini-Break", it was called. That was what Toby kept calling it. Have you got your passport ready for our Mini-Break? How much money shall we take for our Mini-Break? He comes from Chelmsford, you know. He does his hair like that, and wears these bow ties and so on, but he still uses Denim aftershave.'

'So you recoiled from his aftershave into the arms of William?'

'Toby got a cold, as it happens, only he decided it was 'flu and that he had to stay in bed at the hotel wearing winceyette pyjamas and a plaid dressing gown. He actually took these things with him to Amsterdam, you know? The Englishman Goes Abroad was the pose. When he got his cold I was supposed to be Nanny Bloggs, filling hot-water bottles, playing pontoon and reading to him from bloody Anthony Powell novels. Instead I went for walks along the canals. I'd never really been in a foreign country on my own before. Only with Mummy and Daddy, or on school trips. I was actually quite nervous: I couldn't read any of the shop signs, I didn't know how to order meals and I couldn't speak any Dutch at all. So I decided to be lonely and mysterious, like Greta Garbo. I drank chocolate on my own in the brown cafés and pretended to read *Die Welt* and *Le Monde*. I used to turn up the collar of my raincoat and stare over the edge of bridges, as if I might throw myself in. When I went to art galleries I would put my hands in my pockets and stare very hard at one painting for half an hour. I realized after a day or two that I was enjoying myself tremendously, and I didn't really want Toby to get better at all.'

They had stopped by the Stour bridge, where a Victorian reproduction ducking-stool hung over the sluggish, weed-choked river. He rested Rachel's paint cans on the parapet and they squatted companionably on the narrow ledge of a bridge pediment.

She had met William at the Van Gogh museum, where she was staring at that little picture he did in Arles of his pot of chives. You could actually stare at that a long time without having to pretend. It had this lovely salty bloom on the old earthenware pot and the blue background flickered through the green stems as if they were moving. Van Gogh was very good at those sort of oblique pictures of unregarded objects and fragments of scenes. As if it gave him a rest from looking at huge, overwhelming, frightening things.

'William came up behind me when I was looking at a picture,' she told Alec, 'and started peering over my shoulder and under my arm and through my legs. I wanted to be Garboish and stalk away with my nose in the air, but he's very good at being childish, William. So I started giggling instead and we went for coffee at the American Hotel. Then we went back to William's flat. And then we went to bed. A classic art gallery pick-up.'

'A classic William pick-up,' said Alec, trying hard to erase the envy and disappointment from his voice.

'So I gather now. So I gathered then, to be perfectly honest. William didn't spin me any stories. He told me he was living with this doctor and that we had two hours before she got back from the hospital. Two hours later he told me to sling my hook. I went back to Toby and his pyjamas wondering if I had daydreamed it all. A brown café fantasy over somebody who had walked past the window when I looked up from my newspaper. I simply didn't do things like that. I most certainly didn't do them with people like William.'

Alec avoided looking at Rachel's face. Below them on the river a string of ducklings was emerging from beneath the bridge, pedalling in solemn single file against the current. Further down river someone unseen, in the garden of The Ferryman, was flipping stones into the water.

She was the oddest creature: sparring one minute and blurting the next. Half an hour ago he was happy that she was willing to talk to him at all, and now he was rather afraid she was never going to stop. If he said anything she probably would stop, so why didn't he say something?

'The next day Toby said he felt better, but I became all Nanny Bloggs and bought him lots of Lemsips and told him he had to look after himself. And then I went to see William again. We just rode bicycles around the Vondelpark. Those heavy ones that you have to back pedal to stop and you ride like playing the organ. We kissed on the bandstand and we didn't go to bed even though I wanted to. He had got worried about me, I think. He cared enough to not want to hurt me, and that made it even worse of course. If he'd just been horrible, I might have been able to write it off as a casual fuck.'

She pronounced the last word uncertainly, without the proper relish that drunken men or angry women can give to it. Alec did look at her now, and found to his alarm that she was crying; big shapeless tears that wet her whole cheek like spilled water. He reached out to embrace her, then, remembering the headbutt, turned the gesture into an awkward pat on the shoulder.

'Have you talked to him at all? Does he know how you feel about him?'

Rachel's shoulders shook deeply and steadily under the

pressure of his hand. Her head was buried in her arms and there was wetness seeping through her knuckles. A few passing tourists glanced curiously at the odd pair crouched upon the pavement. The skin in the gap of her overalls had become greyish now and goosepimpled.

'Oh, Alec. It's not William any more. It's really nothing to do with William at all.'

CHAPTER EIGHT

From *The Republican Reader*:

The exclusion of 'ideas' from English literature parallels the exclusion of analysis from English political life. The aim of the Leavisite school of criticism is to rediscover and confirm eternal verities; to lay out for us an unshakable tradition. It is explicitly severed from ideas, just as political discourse is severed from ideology.

Malcolm was writing his Cherry Ripe column for *Sweet Sixteen* when the telephone rang, and he abandoned his keyboard without pain. Cherry Ripe was a seventeen-year-old secretary who lived in a flat in Chelsea and worked in a series of improbable jobs, as P A to film directors, pop singers and heart surgeons, with whom she never slept but who all fell in love with Cherry Ripe.

Cherry was gorgeous and witty and capable, and wrote breathlessly about the cocktail bars and chaste candlelit dinners she enjoyed with her employers. She flew on foreign assignments with them, rescued their children from drowning, repaired their film cameras, guitars and heart monitors with her nail file, and never did any typing.

She was entirely unlike any secretary Malcolm had ever met, but was by far the most popular feature in *Sweet Sixteen*. She had originally been created by an alcoholic newspaper astrologer, who had bequeathed her to a sports sub-editor in Manchester, who had in turn passed her on to

Malcolm in a pub in Fleet Street one rainy afternoon when he had grown weary of her.

The executives of *Sweet Sixteen* remained apparently unaware of Cherry's promiscuous career, or at least were indifferent to it, so long as she continued to sip cocktails and meet pop stars at regular intervals.

Malcolm had attempted for a while to inject more social realism into Cherry's life. He had given her a mild dose of non-specific urethritis. He had provided her with a drunken father, Sid Ripe, who had abused her as a child, and a thuggish boyfriend called Keith, who supported Arsenal and drank Hofmeister. But the innovations were not popular with *Sweet Sixteen* readers, and Malcolm had returned Cherry, sadly, to the life of the PA and the pina colada.

'Malcolm Rutherford?' said a fluty female voice that he did not recognize. 'This is Verbena Vallance, the features editor.'

'Ah yes,' said Malcolm, noncommittally. The name meant nothing to him. But then, newspaper features editors changed as frequently as newspaper editors' mistresses – which they often were.

'Malcolm, I just wanted to say how pleased everybody here is with all your pieces lately.'

'I'm very glad to hear it,' said Malcolm, searching his mind vainly for the articles she was referring to. The Famous Falsies thing on celebrity hairpieces perhaps? or the one on pop singers and gardening; what was it, Rock Gardens? it might have been the piece about religious mania in the police force, God's Squad, or something like that. It couldn't possibly be Cherry Ripe, could it?

'Everyone's very interested in the great education debate right now,' the Verbena person went on. 'Ronald Wilson is very *of the moment*.'

Ronald Wilson, his daughter Rachel and Malcolm's diary paragraphs about Alec slid successively into place in Malcolm's memory.

'Is he really?'

'Yes, and in fact, and this shouldn't go any further, but between you and me, there's just a little whisper that *She* is interested.'

'Is that right?' said Malcolm, impressed. For many years, in journalistic and political life, there had been only one person who could, without ambiguity, be referred to simply as *She*.

'Mmmnn. At the lobby briefing this week *her* press secretary put in a special mention of your piece. *She* feels very, very strongly about the crisis in the universities, you know?'

'No, I didn't,' said Malcolm honestly. 'I thought that was all made up by the newspapers.'

'Oh, *Malcolm*,' said Verbena with another fluty gurgle. 'She was having lunch with our editor just the other week. She's *most* concerned about falling standards and the anti-enterprise bias and all the Marxist ideology and the drugs and student protests and the contempt for basic morality and all that sort of thing. Well, aren't we all?'

Malcolm was forming a mental picture of Verbena by now. She had a pencil skirt and Nicole Farhi jacket and was well under thirty. She sent a lot of memos, signing them 'V'. She smoked, but only other people's cigarettes. She was very good at girlishly dangling jobs in front of people, and even better at sacking them. She had no opinions at all without clearing them first with the editor.

'Of course,' said Malcolm. 'Wasn't your editor at university in the sixties? The one who . . .?'

'Oh yes, the editor was at the LSE. He did that famous interview with Jagger. But he's very much on *her* side nowadays.'

'Right,' said Malcolm.

'Well, anyway, when this came up at conference, people were saying we should send one of our *top* feature writers down to Wykeham to take a proper look at this thing. Somebody like Linda or Anne or Geoffrey.'

Verbena paused significantly, and Malcolm deduced that he was expected to show proper amazement at this list of weighty names. He made a series of small moaning noises into the mouthpiece which he hoped were suggestive of awe and wonder.

'And of course, Linda would have been straining at the leash for this one,' said Verbena. '*Just* up her street. But I stood up and I just said "No." I said, "Look here, Malcolm has discovered this story. Malcolm has worked hard to develop this story, and I think we owe it to Malcolm to let him run with it. Let Malcolm run and see what he brings us."'

Malcolm made more moaning noises, this time suggestive of gratitude and appreciation. Although he was still not entirely sure what this Verbena person was talking about, he was clearly being favoured in some profound way.

'How much will you pay me?' he demanded finally, when his repertoire of appreciative moans was exhausted.

Another fluty gurgle. Clearly nobody had ever thought to ask Verbena before how much money they were to be paid for the privilege of not being replaced by Linda.

'You *are* funny, Malcolm,' she said at last. 'We really must have another drinky next time you're in London.' *Another drinky*? He was fairly certain he'd never spoken to this woman until this morning, and he'd definitely never met her. And yet here they were, apparently in the habit of having drinkies together.

And then Verbena crisply named a sum in pounds sterling so enormous that all trace of equivocation was instantly banished from Malcolm's mind.

'So, what we were wondering was whether you could use your contacts to provide some more stuff on modern university life,' she went on. 'This man Alec Smith, for instance. Wasn't he some sort of Trotskyite revolutionary when he was younger?'

'He was President of the Socialist Society when he was at the university,' said Malcolm, who had been the Secretary of the Socialist Society.

'That sounds promising,' said Verbena. 'Was it revolutionary?'

'Oh, quite definitely,' said Malcolm.

'And we could do with other things as well. More naughty goings on at parties and so forth. Left-wing bias in the teaching. Dubious books on the syllabus.'

'There's at least two copies of *The Communist Manifesto* in the library,' said Malcolm helpfully.

'That's wonderful,' said Verbena. 'What about sexy books?'

'Well, there's *Gravity's Rainbow* on the literature course.'

'I think D. H. Lawrence is probably a bit old-hat these days.'

'It's Thomas Pynchon,' said Malcolm, 'but there are lots of dirty bits in it, and it's full of criticisms of missile systems.'

'Sort of CND propaganda, you mean?'

'Oh, very much so.'

'That sounds just the sort of thing we need,' said Verbena.

The Sainsbury lecture theatre was packed to its polystyrene ceiling tiles, an almost unique event for the Literature department in the summer term. By the Easter of the academic year Vivien expected even her stupidest first-year English students to have grasped that lectures were a waste of time.

'You must not go to lectures,' Vivien always told her new students sternly, and they would titter and glance interrogatively at one another, with raised eyebrows. 'You will have noticed that the Literature department publishes an extensive schedule of lectures on important subjects. This is entirely for the benefit of your parents and other outside authorities. You must acquire the strength of mind to ignore this schedule completely.'

Was she serious? Vivien's students were never quite sure. She spoke with the same stern precision whether she was teasing or flaying, and had the habit of delivering her opinions in the form of solemn paradoxes which left them wondering uneasily which element of the inversion to obey.

'Seminars and tutorials you should try to attend, since

these are an aspect of social work. They prevent academics like myself from becoming lonely and depressed in our studies, and they provide you with an opportunity to make contact with members of the opposite sex and to arrange to meet them afterwards for coffee. Lectures, on the other hand, have no such function.'

But how were they to *learn*, a bolder student might ask anxiously, and Vivien would explain patiently that the lecture as a means for disseminating information ante-dated the invention of movable type, and if it had not died with Gutenberg, it should certainly have died with the advent of the Penguin paperback and the Xerox copier. The only purpose of a lecture these days, in Vivien's opinion, was as an initiation rite to test the mettle of a young academic, and also as a form of stylized sexual display in which the same young academics attempted to win the admiration of first-year women by tearing up Penguin copies of D. H. Lawrence.

'By not attending lectures,' Vivien said, 'you will learn, if you have not begun to learn already, that a university education is acquired in mysterious ways. It is acquired by getting up late and by going to bed late. It is acquired by having arguments with people in the bar, by vehemently espousing absurd political positions and then precipitately abandoning them. It is acquired by learning to acknowledge how little you have read, by reading what you can and by learning to lie fluently about what you can't.'

The clever students would laugh at this and the stupid students, who belonged to the Christian Union and the windsurfing club, would look stupid. What if they got found out? What would parents and other authorities make of it?

'Naturally,' said Vivien tolerantly, 'we cannot admit these facts to the likes of Alderman Foodbotham or Councillor Hackney, or whoever is the chairman of your Local Education Authority and is kind enough to pay your grant; nor can we admit them to your dear mama and dear papa, who are generous enough to pay my salary through their taxes. They would agitate to have us closed down. We don't need to tell the people who run the government or the University Grants Committee, because they have all been to university and know the truth already. They won't close us down because university is the cheapest way to keep you all off the unemployment register, and is the only recognized form of entry to the middle class that we have at the moment.'

If any of her students remained anxious, Vivien would advise them to go to the lectures of other departments than English, preferably those devoted to the practical arts. The most useful and stimulating, she told them, were some of the basic lectures on astronomy, jurisprudence, natural science and military history.

But the Sainsbury Theatre was packed, for however Vivien railed against the lecture system, everyone always came to her George Orwell lecture. It had once been part of the 'Aspects of Modernism' course, and then of the 'Signs and Meanings in Socialist Fiction' course, and now of the 'Lost Domain: The Literature of Longing' course. It had been running for ten years, and every year its fame grew.

Whispers of the Orwell lecture filtered down from generation to generation of students. This year all the literature people had come, and the history department, and a good sprinkling from Modern Languages. Bearded physicists with half-mast trousers and breast pockets full of biros had dropped in. Earnest, teetotal, Arab computer programmers with melting brown eyes and packets of Rothmans King Size up their sleeves had come along. Civil engineers on sandwich courses, who had never read a novel in their lives, waited eagerly. Stout and ageing academic colleagues wedged themselves into the plastic tip-up seats of the front row to see how the Orwell lecture had evolved since they last heard it five or ten years before. To sniff the vintage.

'Never,' began Vivien, 'did mediocrity expire more opportunely than when George Orwell, professional proletarian, and Eric Blair, old Etonian, coughed up his last Craven A in a private bed at University College Hospital in 1952.'

The audience sighed contentedly and settled itself into its seats. The Orwell lecture was going to be a cracker.

Though her eyesight was nearly perfect, Vivien wore small, steel-rimmed spectacles for lectures, so that she could peer menacingly over the top of them. To soften the effect today, she was also wearing her tightest green skirt and seamed stockings. Rachel, sitting in the back next to Toby, thought she looked very nice indeed.

'It is no part of literary criticism, of course,' said Vivien, 'but I have often been tempted to speculate on what would have been the career of this tweedy darling of the middle Left had he not been so intelligent as to treat his tuberculosis with sixty cigarettes a day.'

Toby, sitting in the back row, next to Rachel, leaned over to whisper in her small and downy ear. 'What part of the Left would you say Vivien belongs to?' he asked her.

Rachel told him to shush.

'Orwell would now have been eighty-five years old,' Vivien was saying. 'The same age as his friend, Malcolm Muggeridge, the sage of Croydon. A year younger than his mentor, Arthur Koestler, who committed suicide so recently and who so convincingly demonstrated his own faith in the hereafter by persuading his forty-five-year-old wife to top herself as well.'

A group of women near the front of the theatre with very short hair and very long earrings laughed loudly at this, and there were a few handclaps. Vivien frowned, but ducked her head in acknowledgement.

'What would Orwell have done with himself since 1952? An eighties version of *The Road to Wigan Pier* perhaps, entitled *The Motorway to Handsworth Marina*? Far more probable, surely, that, with Muggeridge and Koestler, we would now be finding our geriatric George peddling proto-Catholicism on breakfast television or prattling about the paranormal in the review pages of the *Sunday Times*, while trying to persuade the fourth or fifth Mrs Orwell to turn herself into a nun or a corpse for his greater glory.'

There was more laughter and clapping from the front. 'Can't see what all this has got to do with the Lost Domain,' whispered Toby, mainly for the pleasure of placing his lips again in close proximity to that perfect pinna. 'Toby,' said Rachel, loudly enough to make several people turn around. 'You are making my ear wet.'

'Apples do not fall far from the tree,' said Vivien, 'and the egalitarianism that afflicted Orwell in his thirties was of a particularly fleeting kind. That spasm of sentimental social-ism which so affected the Old Etonian, after his meeting with the beefy Italian militiaman in Spain, spluttered out within ten years in the last, tubercular pages of *1984*. It was a Church of England funeral and the feudal mulch of Sutton Courtenay which the one-time Imperial Police Officer chose for his last rest, but these are details which the Perrier set, in its determination to preserve its own Prince of Letters, pre-fers to forget.'

Toby leaned over to Rachel again. 'I seem to remember we had Ashbourne water on the table the other night,' he said, 'though I suppose, ideologically speaking, that is an entirely different . . . oouch.' Rachel had dug him hard in the ribs with a sharp elbow, and was now scribbling busily.

Malcolm phoned Alec.

'I can't talk long,' he said. 'I'm just waiting for some lights to change, but I was wondering when you're coming down to Wykeham again. I wanted to talk to you about something.'

'You've got a fucking nerve,' Alec told him. 'I had a good mind to put my lawyers on to that shitty little Tory paper of yours.'

'Ah, come on, mate,' said Malcolm uneasily. 'You know it's just a game, that sort of journalism. Show business. Nobody reads it and it's all forgotten by the next morning.'

'My son read it,' said Alec. 'And Rachel's father. And I haven't forgotten it.'

'Well, some of us have got to make a living,' said Malcolm.

'And you weren't so fussy about the wicked Tory media when you sold Prometheus Press to that Australian bastard.'

Alec said nothing.

'Look,' said Malcolm. 'I apologize, all right? I was scraping around for a story, and there's not a lot goes on down here.'

'What did you want to talk to me about?'

'I've got this commission,' said Malcolm. 'An in-depth feature on the modern university. Are we seeing a revival of sixties militancy? All that sort of crap. They'd like an interview with you as a major contemporary figure who was there at the time. It would be good publicity.'

'Don't need any publicity,' said Alec.

'Do it as a favour to me, then.'

'I'd want sight of copy before publication and a written undertaking from the newspaper giving me right of veto.'

'You know I can't do that,' said Malcolm.

'Then I can't do an interview.'

'I thought we were mates,' said Malcolm.

'So did I,' said Alec.

'Malcolm has got one of those new phones as well,' he told Susan.

It was a brilliant, dusty afternoon in Islington, but Alec had drawn the curtain in the living room. Susan was sitting at her drawing board, a complex structure of swivels and pulleys like a mechanical mantis, while Alec watched television with the sound turned down.

'I was thinking of getting one of them for myself,' said Susan. 'They're quite cheap now, and I can never seem to find a telephone box that works.'

'What on earth would you want a mobile phone for?' said Alec. 'I've certainly never felt the need.'

'And since I am merely an aspect of your personality, I suppose there is even less need for me to have one.'

'Prickly, aren't we?' he said. 'What's that you're working on?'

'It's a cover for the *Bystander*,' said Susan. 'Vivien put them on to me.'

'Nasty little fascist rag.'

'Vivien says the editor is more of a libertarian anarchist really.'

'People who work for Tory papers always pretend that their editors are closet lefties,' said Alec.

'Well, why don't you just regard it as a bit of harmless recreation for me, Alec? Think of it as a piece of needlepoint or crochetwork to keep the little woman busy while her husband wrestles with his destiny in front of *Neighbours*.'

The girl in *Neighbours* who looked like Rachel was back on the screen. She was washing up at the crap brown kitchen sink everyone seemed to have in Australia. She had the same strong, tapered back and pushed-back blonde hair. She was standing at just the same angle as when he had walked into the kitchen at Vivien's that time.

A chink of sunlight was bleaching out the colour from a corner of the Sony's screen and Alec stood up to adjust the curtain. When he sat down again the scene had changed to two men with Ian Botham haircuts mending a car. 'I think I'll be going down to Uplands again this weekend,' he told Susan, then added guiltily, 'Perhaps you'd like to come down and see how it's going?'

'Vivien's coming up on Friday. We're going to the *Bystander* party.'

'Really? I wouldn't have minded going to that,' said Alec.

'Nasty little fascist rag,' said Susan.

He wandered around the dim sitting room, silent but for the scratching of Susan's pen and the insect hum of the television tube.

'Would you like a drink?' he said eventually.

'It's only four o'clock.'

'I've got a fucking watch, thank you very much,' said Alec.

Vivien's George Orwell lecture was reaching its climax. The

Christian Union people had stalked out, as they always did as soon as Vivien said 'fuck'. A man who had started shouting something about ballbreakers had been ejected by the porter, to cheers from the women with the short hair and earrings. Toby was ostentatiously reading a copy of *The Face*, while Rachel scribbled busily.

'But it is to *Coming Up for Air*,' said Vivien, 'that we turn to see Orwell's Lost Domain most explicitly described. It takes the traditional form of a quest – for the Thames Valley village of Lower Binfield, where the protagonist and Orwell-proxy, George Bowling, spent his childhood. The atmosphere is the knickerbocker feverishness of Betjeman's 'Edwardian erstwhile'; a paradise on earth furnished with Raleigh bicycles, button boots and beanfeasts.

'As with *Le Grand Meaulnes*, we are in a picturesque, ante-diluvian countryside fitted out with meadowsweet and willowherb; copse and spinney; streams full of roach, dace and chub; and all the other sonorous Edenic trappings of the pre-1914, rural idyll.

'As with *The Magus*, *Great Expectations* and every other classic of this essentially juvenile genre, we find that the female characters of the Lost Domain are absent or, where not absent, then cursorily drawn pieces of crumpet, like Bowling's sweetheart, Elsie, or where not cursory then shrewish, like his wife, Hilda.

'You do not, as a rule, find love in the Lost Domain. It is the province of sentiment rather than sensuality; of titillation rather than fulfilment. Nicholas D'Urfe is alone at the end of *The Magus*; Alain-Fournier leaves Meaulnes still wandering; Pip finds Estella, but it is a publisher's afterthought neither we nor Dickens believe.'

She closed her notes with a snap at this point and marched to the edge of the platform. The women with earrings gazed raptly up at her fierce and handsome face, and the Arab programmers with the liquid eyes down at her slender, stock-inged legs. The theatre was silent. Even Toby looked up from his magazine.

'But George Orwell's defection from adulthood is far more explicit. George buys a rod and line. He goes searching for the great fish which eluded him in childhood. Orwell's yearning for an eternal pubescent stasis is expressed not by passion for his sweetheart, who has aged into a hag, nor by a reconciliation with his wife and children, who are caricatured and dismissed, but in one of the most solitary, the most pointless, the most onanistic of all male activities. Not fucking, my friends, but *fishing*!'

'Perhaps I should take up fishing,' said Toby later, in the squash court, as Rachel removed his thumbs from the elasticated waist of her knickers.

'You could take up playing squash,' said Rachel, and served a wall-hugging lob which Toby failed pitifully to excavate from the back corner of the court. When they had first played squash together, months ago, he had been wildly excited to discover, after two games, that Rachel was wearing no knickers beneath her tennis dress. It improved her game, she had told him, and after she had generously permitted him to finger fuck her to a climax against the back wall of the court, she had proved it by taking the next two sets five–love, five–love.

They had agreed, very seriously after Easter, to a period of celibacy in their relationship. But there was an implied eroticism in the isolation of a squash court, and a very present eroticism in Rachel's brown legs in a short, white, pleated dress, which never failed to arouse Toby, and to shoot his game to pieces.

'Six–two,' said Rachel.

He returned the next serve, but too hard and too high. She volleyed softly on to the right-hand wall and the ball drifted diagonally across court, kissed the front wall an inch above the tin, and lay stone dead in the corner.

'Seven–two,' said Rachel.

'That's a good shot.'

'It's one my father taught me.'

'Is he very good, then?' Toby asked her.

'I've never taken a game off him yet, and he's fifty next birthday.'

'I'm looking forward to meeting him when he comes down.'

'Oh, I don't think there'll be time for that,' said Rachel quickly. 'He's only meeting me for tea, you know. He's really here to talk about this dreary reorganization project with the VC and the bursar's committee and people like that.'

Toby's next return of serve smacked hard into the tin skirt below the base line with a dull 'Brabapapapap'.

'Eight–two.'

'You seemed very keen on me meeting your family, before Amsterdam.'

'I'm sorry, Toby, but I don't want Daddy to get the wrong idea about you. He's very old-fashioned and Scottish, and he'd be bound to think I was introducing you as my intended and take you off for brandy and cigars and ask you about your prospects. You know that's not what it's like with us.'

Toby leaned a damp hand on the chalky, scuffed wall of the court, and spun his racket hard in the other, feeding air to the sweat-soaked towelling of the grip.

'What is it like, then, with us?'

'It's . . . nice. We're friends.'

'We've been sleeping in the same bed for six months, Rachel.'

'Not any more.'

She served again, breaking the sequence of lob serves, with a hard, low drive to Toby's left, catching him on the wrong foot. He caught the ball on its rebound from the back wall and smashed an ambitiously low forehand into the corner.

'Brapapapap.'

'My game. And set,' said Rachel.

Toby collected racket covers and sweaters from the base

of the tin and trudged slowly back down the court to where Rachel was bent over, shaking her damp hair over her face.

'Shower with me?' he asked.

'I'm going down to Vivien's for lunch. I can shower there.'

'With Vivien, I suppose?'

'Don't be pathetic, Toby.'

Malcolm bought Toby another drink. It was one of the strong foreign lagers, with an old-fashioned ceramic cap like ginger beer, which all the students seemed to drink, straight from the bottle. It was Toby's sixth, while Malcolm still nursed his second gin and tonic.

'So Vivien tells people not to go to other people's lectures, does she?'

'Says a same thing ev'ry year 'parently,' said Toby thickly. He rarely drank at all, and never in the afternoon, after fierce exercise.

'And did she really say all that stuff about wanking?' asked Malcolm.

'Talked about wanking all a th'time,' said Toby. 'Dickens is a wanker; Fowles sa wanker; Fournier sa wanker. Orwell sa biggest wanker of the lot. Whole of the male lit'ry world devoted to self-abuse, 'cording to Vivien. Prob'ly Conrad 'n' James 'n' Joyce too. Great Tradition's a sort of giant jerk-off circle fulla chaps who're frightened of fucking Vivien, and really want to go to bed with their mums.'

Toby stood up and lurched off in the direction of the lavatories, leaving Malcolm alone at the corner table. The student union bar was deserted so early in the evening and smelled unpleasantly of the beer-sugars in the carpet, the disinfectant in the slop pails and scorched zinc ashtrays. Malcolm took out a small notebook and scribbled hastily: 'Foul language – Dickens a wanker – feminist interpretation . . .'

'You're not going to use any of this, are you?' said Toby, sitting down heavily.

'Oh, no. It's just background for this general feature they want on life at the modern university. Something light, pegged to Wilson's visit, you know.'

'It's not a formal visit he's making, is it?'

'It will be by the time the newspaper has finished with it.'

'Rachel won't let me meet him, you know that? Prob'ly going to introduce him to Vivien, though. Hello, Daddy. This is my English tutor. She teaches me Leavis and lends me her dildo.'

'You think they actually do that?' said Malcolm.

'I looked out the window the other week after she came to dinner and they were kissing on the porch.'

'There's nothing peculiar about women kissing each other.'

'Oh, no? This was real tongue wrestling stuff. Tonsil tickling. Would have taken the East Kent fire brigade to get them apart with a high-pressure hose. They're probably down there now, sharing a bar of soap in the shower.'

Malcolm bought Toby another lager and a fresh bottle of slimline tonic for himself, making the barman grumble with a £20 note. Journalism really was paying remarkably well these days. Verbena had given him his own expense account number and an advance and a credit account with the local Hertz agency. Malcolm had rented a Cellnet telephone with the advance and a Mercedes estate car from the Hertz agent.

'Did she talk about politics at all?' he asked Toby.

'She was quite rude about private health care at the start,' said Toby vaguely. 'And she went on about religion and Malcolm Muggeridge and imperialism.'

'No attacks on the government, though? Anything rude about the Prime Minister, for instance, or the Department of Education?'

'She did say something about England being a "grey dystopia run by power-worshippers".'

'That's marvellous,' said Malcolm. 'Do you mind if I write it down? It's just the kind of image I'm looking for to illustrate the campus malaise. A grey dystopia.'

'She might have been talking about *1984* at the time,' said Toby.

'Doesn't matter,' said Malcolm. 'It's the phrase I like.'

'Well, so long as you don't actually use any of this stuff,' said Toby.

CHAPTER NINE

From *The Republican Reader*:

The length of time taken over a hat, and hence
its price, varies according to the Queen's move-
ments . . . From June to October is not an uncom-
mon length of time for the making of a hat.

– Colin McDowell, *100 Years of Royal Style*

On Saturday morning at the Smiths' house in Islington
Susan was getting dressed in Vivien's bedroom. The two
Smith children were still away at school and the women had
slept late, after sitting up over two bottles of Chablis. Now
they were going shopping.

The bedroom belonged to Susan's daughter, Dora, during
the school holidays and was still decorated in nursery colours
of pillar-box red and banana yellow. Posters of the Pet Shop
Boys and Bros argued with Susan's stencilled murals of
Pooh and Piglet and Mr Toad. A junior disco dress of
shimmering turquoise hanging on the back of a wardrobe
door disagreed violently with a pink polythene Wendy
House. Vivien, who was still in bed, a duvet up to her nose,
squinted through the glare at her friend, now clipping together the two halves of a black-lace brassiere between her
breasts.

'Do you always wear tarty underwear like that?'

'Well, you never know your luck, do you. I might get run
over by Melvyn Bragg.' She stepped into a pair of black
French knickers and pulled them up over her suspender

belt. 'They're actually very nice to wear, you know. All silk, and plenty of air around *yer parts*.' Susan had switched into her funny cockney voice. 'Though I 'ave to say I fink I'd prefer 'em in summink more *femnin*. Summink pastel like yer coral or yer oyster.' She changed back again to her normal crystalline county. A voice to straighten the back of a shop assistant. 'Alec buys them for me in fact, just like those funny little husbands in the *New Yorker* cartoons. I think he's trying to tell me something.'

She wandered back through the connecting door to her own bedroom to collect more clothes, while Vivien burrowed deeper into the quilt. Real down, firmly packed, and for the nursery!

Vivien was putting off getting out of bed, partly because it was nice in bed, with the sun coming through the blinds, and partly because she wasn't as good as Susan at waltzing around in front of other people with no clothes on. Susan had gone to boarding school in the breezy Malvern Hills, where she had been made to shower with ten other girls after hockey and compared the development of her teenage breasts with twenty more, before all going to bed in the same room. Susan now regarded her body with the same brisk detachment with which she had once regarded her childhood ponies: scrubbing it down with her loofah to keep it hygienic, having it seen to by her doctor when it went wrong, grooming it for special occasions, commenting frankly on its inadequacies. 'And French knickers are kinder to an arse the size of mine,' she called, through the open bedroom door.

Vivien had grown up in a Wolverhampton council house of locked bathroom doors and forbidden bedrooms, where her arse was known as her botty well up to the time she went away to university. Breasts were your 'bust' or, more daringly, your 'bosom'. She actually used to blush at the Methodist Sunday School in Wergs when they talked about 'the bosom of Abraham' and the 'sons of his loins'. What was a loin anyway? She had never been sure, except that it was something muscular, masculine and vaguely indecent.

Shopping with her mother, in the Bull Ring, she glanced surreptitiously at the pink meaty torpedoes of pork loin in butcher's windows and wondered. It couldn't be *that*, could it?

Genitals in Wolverhampton were referred to only as 'yourself', as in her mother's injunction to the infant Vivien, 'Stop scratching yourself. You'll make yourself sore.' Straightforward Susan had inspected her *self*, squatting on a dormitory mirror, at the age of nine and had surrendered her self to a paraffin wax candle at the age of thirteen. 'My first love was a red Prices barley-sugar twist,' she had once told Vivien in the first year at Wykeham, 'reduced after Christmas. And better value than most of the ones since.' But Vivien's *self* had been a forbidden zone, less familiar to her at fifteen than the surface of the moon, of which there was at least a geographical globe in the school library.

Your *self* was this terrible complicated crack where it seemed that shit and piss and blood and babies all happened at the same time, and from an indeterminate number of different holes. Not that Vivien's mother would have had such words spoken in her house. Piss and shit were number ones and number twos. Babies, until they were born, were – incredible to think now – 'little strangers', and menstruation was 'Women's Problems' – a euphemism like the Curse being far too chic and metropolitan for the suburbs of Wolverhampton.

What Vivien did glimpse between her teenage legs was alarming. Viscid cavities and glistening fronds of offal red and nacreous pink, as if your insides were right there, hovering on the very edge of the real, tidy, pale-skinned you. It summoned up that terrible phrase her mother would whisper sometimes over tea with friends: *a prolapsed womb*. So-and-so had been taken into the General with *a prolapsed womb*. So-and-so would be *on the table* tomorrow.

What was a prolapsed womb and what happened to it *on the table*? Vivien had imagined it vaguely as the result of doing the things to *yourself* her mother had warned against.

You scratched yourself, sat on cold steps, did the splits or let yourself be interfered with. And then, the prolapsed womb. The terrible crack would open too wide and everything would just *prolapse* with a glutinous suck and wheeze and glop, like a Christmas turkey.

Much safer to leave it alone. Far better to just wash it gingerly and pat it dry with lily-of-the-valley talc and to wear the enormous sanitary towel like a wound compress which her mother gave her and which all the other girls wore. Hammocks for mice, they called them in school, and though they bunched up like damp rope after a day in class, at least the hammocks were better than the tampon things, which *took your virginity* if you weren't careful with them.

It was all that sort of nonsense the sixties did away with. Guilt and ignorance, sin and shame. In 1968, when Vivien left the world of busts and locked bathrooms for university, there was a golden bubble of an idea in the air, never explicit but understood, that it was possible by a simple act of will to make a caesura with the past. No more war. All you need is love. Let it all hang out. The slogans had been breathtaking in their unlettered simplicity, infuriating to the grown-up world in their adolescent arrogance. But while the nascent scholar in the eighteen-year-old Vivien had scoffed at them, her heart had leapt.

No more hammocks for mice for Vivien, then. And no tampons either. A feminist biology student explained to her that pill periods were phony periods, imposed by male doctors to keep women in chains. So Vivien took the pill twenty-eight days a month and abolished menstruation as well as guilt. Her blood pressure rose slightly; her blood platelets coagulated more readily, raising the risk of thrombosis; her tissues retained water; and potentially cancerous cells increased slightly in her breasts. But the biologist feminist had not mentioned these things to her, and Vivien was too young and healthy to notice. Five men in one week. Two in one day. Marie, Marie, hold on tight. And down they went.

Susan straightened the sleeves of her black cashmere sweater and then picked off the floor a calf-length kilt in Black Watch tartan. Vivien noted that it was the proper kind of kilt, with two leather straps which buckled at the side, rather than the sort which had a zip and sewn-in pleats. Susan always had *proper* things without even knowing they were proper. Huge cotton towels in solid colours; Sony Trinitron TV sets; mild steel cook's knives that you could sharpen properly; hardback novels from Hatchard; Manx kippers; Clinique scent; German car. Vivien surreptitiously gorged on snob guides in the Sunday magazines, but Susan just knew.

'It doesn't work, by the way,' Susan said now, gingerly prodding a jet stud through her earlobe.

'Sorry?' said Vivien, telling herself off automatically, for forgetting once again to say 'What?' Sorry was even worse than pardon.

'The tart's underwear doesn't work. Alec can't get it up any more. Goes on about it all the time. He's half convinced he's got something wrong with him, like cancer of the balls. But personally I think he just drinks too much and wanks too much. He keeps these awful magazines upstairs, hidden behind the books in his study.'

'Nothing wrong with that,' said Vivien loyally, though the image of Alec frotting himself over *Fiesta* did not much appeal. 'Perhaps he should keep them on the bedside table,' she said, 'so you can read them in bed together.'

'Well, sank you for zat advice, Doctor Root,' said Susan. 'Ze only trouble iss, ve neffer in bed togezzer any more are finding ourselves. Alec sleeps in here. When he's here.'

Vivien looked again around the nursery with its fading primary colours, dusty paper lampshade in the shape of a hot-air balloon and the bald patches left by Blu-Tack on the paintwork – and her heart went out to Alec. They were both her friends, Susan and Alec, Alec and Susan. And she was loyal to the Alec–Susan institution in the same way that William was, and even Malcolm. They were the couple who had always been together, while others fell apart. Clever

Alec and beautiful Susan. So well matched and so comple-
mentary. Plebeian and posh. Voluble and clipped. But agreed
on all the big things: on politics, on books and on people.

Through the 1970s Alec and Susan had been an institution
with open doors and spare beds to those who needed them.
It was an illustration to those of their friends who feared
such things that marriage and children need not bring bore-
dom. Alec and Susan proved that success need not be altogether a sell-out and that not all comfortable lives were
compromised ones. They provided the reassurance of a path
not taken but always, in theory, available.

'Have you thought of marriage guidance counselling?' said
Vivien. 'Sex therapy, that sort of thing?'

Susan snorted. She was brushing mascara on to her long
eyelashes now, peering down her nose into a plastic-framed
mirror shaped like an owl.

'Instrumental Vivien. You're as bad as Alec. Fix this,
rebuild that, patch the other and our marriage would be
good as new. I think if Alec could find the right sort of
spanners in his little toolkit he would take our libidos out
there in the shed, jack them up and give them a good over-
haul.'

'There are things you can do . . .'

'Like go to bed with a bottle of baby oil, and a *Joy of Sex*,
I suppose? Listen, dearest, the problem with Alec and me
doesn't start in bed, though of course, being a man, that's
exactly what he believes. It starts with someone who thinks
you can run a marriage like a fucking board meeting.'

Susan adjusted her voice again to a fair parody of Alec's
mockney accent. 'Fed up with all the 'ousework, Sue? Tell
yer what. We'll draw up a new contract of employment. Feel
like you're takin' secon' place to my career, Sue? Tell yer
what. We'll table a motion against it and take a vote. Emotionally bulldozed by your 'usband? I'll put it on next week's
agenda. Nah, then, any uvver business?'

'He's not like that.'

'Try living with him.'

'Anyway,' said Vivien, 'you knew all those things about Alec when you married him. Everyone assumed that was *why* you married him.'

'Perhaps people split up for the same reasons they got married in the first place,' said Susan.

'So what *are* you going to do?' Vivien asked her.

'I don't know,' said Susan. 'Fuck the plumber perhaps. But for today, and if you ever get out of bed, I'd like to go shopping.'

They took the bus to Oxford Circus, a mildly left-wing act now that patronizing public transport had come to be seen as something vaguely subversive, a relic of the *ancien régime*.

'I wish I knew,' said Vivien, gazing out of the smeary window at broken, littered pavements and the garish, haphazard shop fascias, 'if London has always been as horrible as this, or if I just notice it more, now I live in the country.'

'It's hardening of the arteries,' said Susan promptly, always loyal to her adopted city. 'Noticing litter is one of the symptoms of middle age, like complaining about pubs and thinking that there are no good tunes in pop records any more. Alec goes on about them all the time.'

'I don't think there *are* any good tunes in pop records any more.'

'There never were,' said Susan. 'All those wonderful tunes you thought you could hear when you were sixteen were actually just the sound of your mother gnashing her teeth.'

'Do you do any gnashing of teeth over the Pet Shop Boys?'

'Not with Dora and Jonathan away at school most of the year.'

'You miss them, then?' Vivien asked her.

'Quite a lot.'

'I never understood why people like you and Alec would want them to go to public school in the first place.'

'Well, it's hardly Eton, dearest. Jonathan addresses his housemaster as "Baz" – he's this hairy individual with launderette-coloured clothes and a strong whiff of dope about his person. He's not even a housemaster, he's a "house-parent". And speaking of parents, Dora tells me there were two girls who got pregnant in the fifth form last year.'

'I suppose they had to leave?' asked Vivien, who had gone to a girls' grammar, where smoking cigarettes behind the bikeshed had been an expulsion offence.

'Oh, no. I think they're rather proud of their pregnancy rate at Beddington. They'd probably like to commemorate their gymslip mums on a fumed oak tablet in the hall, next to the sporting honours – not that they've got any sporting honours, or gymslips for that matter. Alec always says Beddington is one of the few socialist institutions left in the country, and for once I rather agree with him.'

'I'd have thought the state schools would be quite good in an area like yours,' said Vivien.

'Oh, God. No. The local comp has become frantically aspirational since all the ambitious middle-class parents took over running it. The children spend their entire time programming computers and sitting examinations and marching about in horrible grey uniforms like the Freikorps.'

'But if you *miss* them . . .'

'Well, I do,' said Susan, 'but I don't think they miss us all that much. And at least at Beddington they wear normal clothes and do some music and art and messing about in workshops.

'Anyway,' she went on, 'when Daddy died he left some money which could only be used for their education, so it seemed a bit bloody-minded not to spend it. Of course, he rather hoped he would be saving them from their awful socialist parents. Get Jonathan doing something manly at Mill Hill and Dora learning to look after hamsters and make mayonnaise at Heathfield. I don't suppose he thought his grandchildren would be going to a place where they smoked marijuana in the lavs and did aerobics instead of lacrosse.'

Vivien fell silent, thinking about children. She never wanted any that badly, which was just as well, because she had never managed it. Not even when she and Malcolm had tried, that year they spent together living in the basement flat at Uplands.

Such madness it seemed now. She had been researching her doctoral thesis on William Faulkner at that time, toiling away among the humming, air-conditioned carrels of the university library, while Malcolm worked at the wholefood restaurant, in between trips to Brixton to stock up the magic briefcase.

He was passing through his whole-earth phase at the time, reading Alvin Toffler and Rachel Carson, filling sweetshop jars with muesli and bran and boasting to Vivien about the buoyancy of his turds. He had already dug up part of Alec's back lawn and planted vegetables; he had banned salt from their food and had stopped dropping acid in favour of the more organic mescalin when he started on the baby business.

People made too much fuss about babies, he told her earnestly. Look at Alec and Susan, with their cots and prams and nappies and bottles and expensive Beechnut babyfoods. All that fuss. All that *hardware*. Babies were *natural*. All you needed for a baby was a sling to carry it in, some mother's milk, a handful of muesli as it got older. He told her that in Mongolia babies didn't even wear nappies. They just sat in a little earth box with their heads poking out of the top and were perfectly happy.

Malcolm had seen himself working down at the wholefood restaurant with a gurgling baby on his back in a leathern sling and a multicoloured Mongolian hat knitted by Vivien. He was going to take it on demos with him; bring it up to the university library for Vivien to breastfeed; fix a seat to the back of his bicycle for it.

The baby – it was going to be called either Patchouli or Nipper – would complete the reconstruction of their lifestyles which Malcolm was determined to bring out. It would be an engagement with the natural processes of the earth; a re-proach to the bourgeois *artificiality* of academic life; a departure from the Peter Pan self-indulgence of the receding 1960s. And for his parents in Weybridge, who still thought

Malcolm should have been a lawyer and that Vivien was a little *common*, it would be a decisive poke in the eye.

And Vivien, her mind absorbed in the influence of the French symbolists on the early novels of William Faulkner, her ankles puffed with five years of twenty-eight pills a month, had absent-mindedly agreed. Even with the five men in one week, Vivien had never had an orgasm without the aid of tongue or fingers. Making a baby at least seemed to add a certain zest to sex with Malcolm, who, despite the restlessness of his interests, was an unimaginative lover, believing an application of K-Y jelly to be an adequate substitute for foreplay.

Six weeks after giving up the pill Vivien had become pregnant. Two weeks after that Malcolm had left the basement flat at Uplands for a magic briefcase trip to Brixton and had never come back. The back garden had returned to weeds, and Vivien had returned gratefully to her undergraduate diet of Mars Bars and fish and chips. Susan heard from William that Malcolm had become a New Romantic, 'whatever that might be', and Vivien had received a card with a Chelsea postmark and a picture of Marlon Brando as Fletcher Christian. ''Tis a far, far better thing that I do now,' it said. 'S W A L K, Malcolm.'

'Ignorant sod couldn't even get the book right,' said Vivien savagely, 'and whoever sealed a fucking postcard?' She shredded the card into the bin. A week later she miscarried, copiously but painlessly, in the library lavatory, and thanked her stars. After another month, and a week of stomach ache, she awoke with a knife in her belly and a soaking bed, and found she was lying in a pool of her own blood. *The prolapsed womb. Taken into the General.*

Susan got her washed and dressed and Alec phoned 999 for an ambulance, which didn't come. So they wrapped her up in a nappy of sheets, like Gandhi, and drove her to the hospital in the middle of the night. There a bad-tempered Indian woman doctor rummaged around inside Vivien's abdomen with a pair of stainless steel barbecue tongs.

'You've got an infected womb from a partial miscarriage,' she told her crossly. 'Why didn't you report the abortion to the ante-natal clinic?'

'Never went to the ante-natal clinic,' said Vivien, through gritted teeth, and gripping the sides of the couch as the barbecue tongs seized her liver, or perhaps her kidney, in their icy, serrated jaws. 'We were going to have a whole-earth baby.'

'You'll be lucky if you ever have any sort of baby now,' said the doctor. And then she pumped a blessed syringe of pethidine into her spinal cord, scraped out her uterus with a curette and shot a massive dose of penicillin into her buttock, while Vivien stared at the ceiling and tried to cheer herself up by thinking of Cash in *As I Lay Dying*, with his broken leg going rotten in a concrete cast.

They shopped quite differently, Susan and Vivien, with Susan favouring the comfortable, cigar-box interiors of Jaeger and Laura Ashley, and Vivien the poky little shops along South Molton Street and St Christopher's Passage, with their expensive, designer dilapidation. Vivien had wanted a suit for work, but instead she bought a tight black dress which she didn't need and which cost £300, from Joseph Tricot. She told Susan that it was £250, and she would tell her mother, who shopped at the Wolverhampton C&A, that it was only £30. 'I can wear it to the *Bystander* party tonight, anyway,' she told herself.

Why did she worry? Susan actually spent more money: £50 on a sweater from Jaeger; £150 on a linen suit from Laura Ashley; £80 each on two shirts from Margaret Howell. But Susan spent money as only the moneyed do – steadily, largely and deliberately; Vivien knew she shopped like a shoplifter – rapid, furtive and flushed. It wasn't that she couldn't afford it. Salary, book royalties and freelance articles all begin to add up when you are thirty-eight and single, but Vivien would never be able to spend it as if it were hers.

Susan too shopped to an orderly scheme, filling in gaps of

a seasonal wardrobe that had hardly varied except for slight concessions to fashion since she was twenty-one. Wool suits for winter and linen for summer. Six skirts, a dozen good sweaters and a dozen good shirts. Three best frocks, and three for everyday. The whole lot fitted, pressed and lavender-scented, in a single wardrobe and a small chest of drawers, while Vivien's clothes bulged from a half-a-dozen closets around her house, filled with guilty, expensive, unworn secrets.

She wore the Joseph Tricot, though, to the *Bystander* party, and Susan her linen suit. It was in the ground floor and garden of the house in Amwell Street: three Georgian rooms with office desks pushed against the wall and paper cloths spread with calculatedly unfashionable foodstuffs. Bridge rolls, crisps, sausages on sticks poked into halves of grapefruit. There was even, Susan noted, jelly and blancmange.

She had expected to find young men in their father's suits and flowered Hackett waistcoats, but most of the people looked fairly normal. The professor of history at Birkbeck, wearing jeans and a 'Remember '68' t-shirt, was standing in the corner, talking to the *Bystander*'s editor. He was saying something about new agendas for the Left, and gave her a wink over the editor's shoulder.

Vivien disappeared into the garden with the books editor of the *New Statesman*, and an immensely tall young man with wet lips, wearing baggy harem pants, filled her glass from a two-litre bottle of Safeway's claret. 'My name is Gideon Gibbs,' he told her gravely. 'Institute for the Study of Subversion.'

'My husband's a subversive,' said Susan. 'And I've been studying him for years. Do you think I could get a grant?'

'We take our work very seriously,' said the young man, and disappeared with his claret.

The professor of history took his place at her elbow. 'Susan. You're looking very beautiful. How is Alec?'

'I was just trying to betray him to the CIA agent in the pyjamas.'

'Oh, Gideon. He's the young man who was arrested in Warsaw for handing out Liberty League pamphlets. One of my ex-students, in fact.'

'Was he telling the Poles to become capitalists?' Susan asked.

'Oh, no. It wasn't that. They can't become capitalists fast enough in Eastern Europe these days. They didn't like all the bits about legalizing heroin and sexual freedom and abolishing the Royal Family. They're very conservative, the Poles, even about other people's royalty.'

Susan pondered. 'How come it's the Liberty League lot who can say all those things now? It was our side that used to have the monopoly on being barmy.'

The professor tapped the slogan on his t-shirt.

'Failure of nerve at the crucial moment, my love. 21 May 1968. The French students handed over the revolution to the workers, just like Marx said they should. But the workers weren't interested in freedom or revolution. Just bigger colour tellies.'

'Nothing wrong with colour televisions,' said Gideon Gibbs, who had reappeared with his bottle. 'Trouble with socialists is they're all fucking elitists who think the working man should be reading Shelley and watching Shaw.'

'Whereas you think they should be reading *Sunday Sport* and watching *Blind Date*, while you pick their pockets,' said the history professor.

'I didn't realize you were Alec Smith's wife,' said Gibbs, turning to Susan. 'I thought *The Republican Reader* was brilliant. In fact, we all did at the Institute.'

'I'll certainly let him know,' said Susan. 'It should make his week.'

An hour later she found Vivien out in the garden, still talking to the *New Statesman* books editor, a boyish-looking fifty-year-old with a wasted leg and a grey fringe flopping over one eye that gave him a permanently quizzical expression.

'Susan, do you know Tony? Tony, this is . . .'

'If you say I'm Alec Smith's wife, Vivien, you shall have to find your own bed for the night. I'm beginning to feel like the Duke of Edinburgh. Anyway, I know Tony.'

'Susan designed the jacket for my book on Soho in the fifties,' explained the books editor. 'And very nice it was too. A collage of John Deakin photographs. The publishers decided to use a Francis Bacon for the paperback. One of those horrible things like a flayed pig wearing a bishop's mitre or something. Do you still design, Susan?'

'Not really. I teach a few days a week at Camberwell.'

'That's a shame. The covers you used to do for Prometheus were wonderful. Even for that bloody *Reader* thing.'

'God,' said Susan, 'the man who didn't like *The Republican Reader*. Say that in there' – she waved in the direction of the party – 'and they'll probably start throwing bridge rolls at you, and flicking jelly. You're in a minority of one, Tony. Or two, anyway. The rest of eighties England thinks it was the best thing since oven chips.'

'It would have been fine if only Alec had resisted the temptation to be funny as well,' said the books editor seriously. 'True words may occasionally be spoken in jest, but it's the joke you remember afterwards.'

'I think after ten years of scraping a living my husband decided he would rather make people laugh than make them listen,' said Susan.

They drove home through the London twilight to Islington in Vivien's Volkswagen Golf. The great plane trees on Highbury Fields were silently unwrapping their fistfuls of sticky foliage for the summer and horse chestnuts in full bloom glowed like candelabra in the dusk.

Susan's teaching term would be over soon. She thought about Alec, down in Wykeham, and the children, down in Beddington, and the empty, unplanned summer that lay ahead. They'd been good at organizing summers once, just as they'd been good at parties. Two weeks bucket and spading in Cornwall with the children. Three weeks in Italy or

Greece while Dora and Jonathan stayed at grandparents. When things began to fall apart, it seemed, it was planning that went first.

'Saturday nights always make me miserable,' she told Vivien.

'Parties are never so exciting now that you know you aren't going to get off with someone by the end.'

'There was nothing to stop you, if you'd wanted,' said Susan.

'Not much to stop you, from what you were saying about Alec this morning.'

'No, I've definitely decided on a nice simple plumber with a canvas bag full of glottal stops. I've had enough of literary gents. Mind you, I could quite fancy Tony.'

'Well, then?'

'Well, nothing,' said Susan. 'I know his second wife. And besides, they send their children to Beddington.'

CHAPTER TEN

Alec was making mayonnaise in the Uplands kitchen, trickling a thread of thick green olive oil into a white china pudding basin while his other hand worked the egg yolks into golden ointment. The gentle piddle of oil into the bowl, the suck and click of the wooden spoon in the thickening goo, was soporific in the hot, sunlit kitchen where William sat, dozing over the Sunday papers on a table white with plaster dust.

'It's an argument for the existence of God, you know.'

'What?'

'Mayonnaise,' said Alec. 'It's one of those things that couldn't have been discovered by accident. Nobody could ever have guessed that simple eggs and oil would do this when you mixed them together. Even when you know how to make it, you can often get it wrong if you rush, or if you're feeling bad-tempered. My mother used to say a menstruating woman should never try to make mayonnaise.'

'If you feel your period coming on,' said William, 'there's some salad cream in the fridge.'

'Toothpaste,' said Alec dismissively. 'Dried eggs, chip-shop vinegar, anti-oxidants and E numbers.'

William took a jar of Safeway's mayonnaise from the refrigerator, set it down next to the pudding basin and scooped up a dollop of each on to his grimy forefingers. 'Right,' he said, 'close your eyes.' Alec did as he was told, and took two ginger licks.

'Okay,' he said. 'Number one was Polyfilla and number two was sand and cement.'

'This is a serious exercise,' said William. 'If you can't do this, you can never bullshit me again about wine smelling of pencil shavings and blackberries.'

'All right, seriously. Number one is Safeway's toothpaste and number two is my own mayonnaise.'

'Lucky,' said William.

'Luck has nothing to do with it,' said Alec smugly. 'The Safeway's is a good 10 degrees colder.'

'Funny thing is,' said William, just to keep his end up, 'they were both Safeway's.'

The house renovation was proceeding slowly. Mr Truss had produced a retarded nephew called Lewis, with shoulders the size of a phone box. 'He comes from Glamorgan,' said Mr Truss gnomically, 'but he's a good worker.' Lewis had knocked down many walls, some of them the right ones, with a twelve-pound sledgehammer, and then departed, claiming a prior commitment in Herne Bay and leaving the hallway stacked with plastic fertilizer bags of rubble.

'Prior commitment,' said William bitterly, as they humped fertilizer sacks down the driveway to the skip, which was too big to come through the gates. 'Mick Jagger and Princess Di have prior commitments. The only commitment Lewis ever had was a Section Three to Colney Hatch. Why don't you get a proper builder? Someone who can read the headlines in the *Sun* without moving his lips and can make his own roll-ups and who moves the dishes before he pees in the sink.'

But Alec was being weird at the moment. He would

mumble vaguely about wanting to manage the job himself and then go off on one of his little shopping expeditions. Buying expensive new door knobs for all the doors they didn't have, or some Osborne and Little wallpaper for all the walls that didn't exist any more. Or he just disappeared for hours, swimming over at the gravel pits or reading novels upstairs in the bedroom that was just a lot of carrier bags full of dirty clothes.

William had cleared the basement of fifteen years of student debris: mildewed cardboard suitcases; motorcycle crank cases; boxes of Penguin paperbacks, the pages fused and corrugated with damp; broken guitars; a pair of homemade, concrete loudspeakers; the rotted scenery of a 1970 *Beggar's Opera*, painted by Susan; a rack of Boots homebrew, dated 1982, unopened but all turned to vinegar; clinking hillocks of empty wine bottles; and slithering dunes of ancient magazines.

The basement had been a self-contained flat once, where Marcie, the American girl, and her boyfriend had lived. The bloke who played the saxophone and had driven his car over a cliff in Mauritius. And then Malcolm and Vivien, before Malcolm went to London. And then one-legged Geoff Bright, who had owned all the motorcyles. And then . . . William could not remember then. There had been a kitchen and bathroom before, but the basins were cracked and the lavatory was full of sump oil like black molasses. So William had pulled them out, cemented over the holes and dumped the broken china, inarticulate pelvic shards, on to the skip at the end of the drive.

He didn't need them. The cellar would make a decent furniture warehouse for a while so long as it was kept dry. He hired a cowboy damp-course company, which sent a man to inject the soft red bricks with silicone for the third or fourth time in their lives. He had lost the guarantee with its impressive crests and seals and solemnities, and did not trouble to find it again. Abbreviated empires, damp-proof companies were always fated to expire just before their works did.

He dry-lined the walls with wooden battens and plaster board and hired another cowboy to skim the broken stone floor with smooth rubber paste. None of it would last. The oozing Wealden clay on which Uplands was built, and the wet orchard mists, would have their way with porous brick and spongy sandstone. But it would do for a while.

Alec came downstairs to inspect the work now and then. 'I was thinking we should have got a proper lead damp course this time,' he would say. 'You could cut right through the outside walls with one of those tungsten chainsaws and cement it in.' Or he would prod the rubber floor with his toe and say dubiously that he had thought of having the flags taken right up and relaid on a new base. But he didn't seem very interested. He handed over his Amex card for the cowboys, rummaged dreamily through the piles of old magazines and salvaged odd curiosities from the skip.

William was relieved by this new ineffectuality. In university holidays they had run their own housepainting business in London. Working for the sharp-toothed minnows of the speculative building boom, William had met the businesslike, omnicompetent Alec and been depressed by him. Alec with the cleanest overalls and the grit-free glosswork. Alec who chased around with pursed lips and a critical squint, straightening the edges of William's painting, picking up his stray bristles and paint dribbles.

It wasn't the university Alec of the six-joint sessions over the latest Dylan album, and he liked him not nearly so much. 'They're only speculators' hutches, squire,' he told him touchily. 'Woodchip paper and magnolia emulsion is what they want, not fucking David Hicks.'

But Alec seemed incapable of the genial slovenliness which William felt was all their gold-braceleted employers deserved, and which, in any case, came naturally to him. They were only making a few quid in the holidays, after all. Taking a ride on the property spiral. But as they tarted up plasterboard bedsits in Finchley, Alec was dreaming of Highgate restaurants and Hampstead mansion blocks. He talked of fleets of white Mini vans, power spray guns, industrial wallpaper strippers, illustrated catalogues and a special line in decorative finishes. He took to saying 'Islington Interiors' when he answered the telephone to their clients, while William enraged him with a cheerful 'Quickslosh Decorators'.

William knew that like most friendships – like most of the marriages he knew – theirs was based on the past. It had been founded on common undergraduate appetites for dope and Dylan records and mildly subversive behaviour. It had been cemented by shared houses and minor ordeals: rebuilding the old M G, hitching across Turkey, hustling a living together in the building trade. Over the last fifteen years, and through long separations, it had been kept adequately topped up with pints in pubs and do-you-remember conversations.

But he had often thought, in the years since university, that if they had met now, for the first time, their worlds, their boundaries, would have barely intersected. They would have tapped and diverged like billiard balls. Alec with his houses and children and board meetings. William with his string of unsuitable girls and addresses scribbled on cigar packs. He was not displeased with his life, and he was not especially jealous of the solid accumulation of property and achievement which was Alec's. But as he watched this sudden wobble develop in his best friend's steady trajectory, it was not without a trace of satisfaction.

'What's all this stuff for anyway?' he asked Alec, waving at the soft-boiled eggs in their shells, and pâtés and pots of crudités and French sticks with which Alec had covered the only clean surface in the kitchen.

'A picnic.'

'Great. I'm fed up with all this mess. Where shall we go? What about giving Malcolm a ring?'

'I thought I'd go with someone else actually,' said Alec, his face bent low over the open refrigerator.

'Vivien? Isn't she still up in London with Susan?'

'Well, it's Rachel, as a matter of fact.'

'Oh,' said William. 'I see.'

Alec pulled a bottle of white Rioja from the freezer compartment of the fridge, where he had placed it for rapid cooling, and detached a frosty fish finger from its gold-mesh corset. '1978. Nose of fresh hay and plums. Slightly acid. Long finish.'

'It makes no difference to me, mate,' said William. 'But she's a bit weird, you know?'

'We're only going swimming,' said Alec, 'and anyway, weird might be just what I need.'

William phoned Malcolm.

'Fancy going down The Ferryman for lunch? I'm melting here.'

'Bloody hot, isn't it?' said Malcolm. 'Can you pick me up? I'm in the hammock at the end of the garden if I don't answer the bell.'

'You've got one of these flash phones as well, then, have you?'

'They're great, aren't they? I keep having baths so I can ring people up from it. I even called my mum yesterday. She thought I must be ill. What about Alec?'

William contemplated the wisdom of entrusting Malcolm with any information about Alec. But why should he, William, be manoeuvred into dishonesty by Alec's philanderings? And then there was Susan, an equally old friend to consider. In a mild glow of righteousness he said: 'He's meeting Rachel.'

Malcolm took over a second to compose an adequately casual response.

'For a return bout, I suppose?'

'They seem to have kissed and made up actually,' said William, 'or made up at any rate. They're going swimming. At the gravel pits. And we were definitely excluded.'

'She does get around, doesn't she?' said Malcolm. 'Her friend Toby was under the impression that she'd clubbed together with Vivien on a vibrator.'

'There's no telling with young people nowadays,' said William. 'I'll see you at one.'

Alec drove Rachel south through Bedgebury Forest in his Audi Quattro and worried about his stomach. He had been fat once, nearly sixteen stone, and had made himself thin again by swimming and starvation and by drinking gin instead of beer. But the paunch had remained. It was a compact little apron of suet, which had never spread to his hips or breasts but had also proved immune to sit-ups or to Susan's Trim-wheel. He had got up to 200 sit-ups a day at one time, but the paunch had just changed from being flabby and prominent to rubbery and prominent.

Fashionably baggy trousers in the 1980s had made it less of a problem and on Greek beaches it could be camouflaged with a sun tan. But after nine months in London the paunch was codfish white and swimming trunks, however generously cut, were unforgiving. With Susan it didn't matter so much. In the democracy of decline, his gut and her bum cancelled each other out. But without ever having seen Rachel in anything more revealing than a decorator's overall he already knew she was going to make him feel about sixty.

She was wearing her swimming costume when he collected her from Vivien's. A sheeny black one-piece, which, so far as he could see, had no back at all, just an endlessness of honey-coloured skin. Around her waist she wore a billowy white skirt of some heavy, coarse-textured stuff and on her feet a pair of red plastic beach sandals, like children wore when they were shrimping. It was the same red as the plastic clothes peg that held her hair bunched from her neck.

'You look terrific, Miss Wilson,' he said honestly. 'If this old man offers you a sweetie, will you come for a ride in his car?'

'Well, I dunno. This is a very flashy motor you're driving, Mr Smith,' she said, peering around the cream leather interior of the Audi. 'One of those Four-spring Dutch Knick-knacks, as my mother calls them. She'll still only drive Austins.'

'And my father will only drive Rovers. He calls this "Alec's Nazi car". But the four-wheel drive is a must for getting up the ramp from the Safeway's car park.'

'I don't know any more than I've already told you,' said William wearily. 'Alec is a bit miserable. He's rowing with Susan over coming back down here. He's been seeing a bit of Rachel. That's it.'

He was sitting, with Malcolm, on a rotted Rexine sofa in the back garden of The Ferryman, while geese pecked at the sandwich crusts William had thrown down for them on the lawn. The Ferryman was the most squalid, inefficient and empty pub in Wykeham. It had no music, no gaming machines, no food but cheese sandwiches and only two beers, drawn from barrels behind the bar into greasy pewter jugs. It had been favoured by William since he was eighteen, for all those reasons, and for the fact that he was permitted to smoke marijuana in the back garden.

It was run by Mrs Bishop, the widow of the last landlord: an immensely fat woman with permanently bandaged feet and soiled kaftans which smelt strongly of damp carpet. The bar mirrors were the colour of dull brass from fifty years of nicotine, and it was furnished in broken-down living-room furniture, apparently salvaged from skips, which, as it became older and more broken-down, was gradually tossed out into the beer garden. This was a strip of dandelions, creeping buttercup and goose shit, fringed by the river. If there had ever been a ferry at The Ferryman, it would have been a short trip, for at this point it was possible to cross the sluggish Stour, bank to bank, with a light leap, though a drunken William had once tried it and fallen in.

'Just doesn't sound very likely to me,' said Malcolm. 'It's not as if Alec was ever much of a stud, is it? He was always the sort that women like, but not go to bed with.'

'He went to bed with Vivien.'

'Who hasn't? And in any case, from what Vivien used to tell me, there was not a lot went on when they did.'

William had begun to regret mentioning Alec's assigna-
tion, if that was what it was. He considered sharing with his
friend Vivien's opinion of Malcolm's own sexual prowess
during the year in the Uplands basement, but decided against
it. The afternoon was pleasant. Mrs Bishop was filling up
the second beer jug. And at thirty-nine you don't make
many new friends.

'I hope you can swim properly,' said Alec. 'The water here is
very deep and quite cold, and there's only one or two places
on the banks where you can climb out.' His swimming was
his only real sporting accomplishment and he was rather
proud of it. Too short-sighted for rugby and cricket at
school, he had found, rather to his surprise, that he could
swim miles with his choppy, head-up breaststroke. At home
in Watford, Alec's lifesaving certificates had been the only
sporting trophies on the mantelpiece of the unathletic
Smiths.

'I never knew this place existed,' she told him, as they laid
out hamper and rug beneath the beech trees.

'We used to come here quite a lot when we all lived at the
house,' said Alec. 'William's old M G is down at the bottom
somewhere. We had to dump it after he got done for tax,
insurance and M O T, and he told the policeman that his
name was Kim O'Sabe.'

Two windsurfers a quarter of a mile away were the only
occupants of the gravel pit. The whole south-east of England
was brown as sisal after six weeks without rain, but the lake
brimmed from its underground springs and the grass of its
banks squeaked underfoot, swollen with sap. The beeches
and alders were bigger and covered most of the northern
shore now. The only other sign of change in twenty years
was a mossy-looking ski ramp, moored a hundred yards out
from the shore.

'Fortunately, it's a bit small for watersports,' said Alec, as
he tried not to watch Rachel unhooking her skirt. 'They all
go over to Bewl Water. And families with children don't

— 123 —

come here because it's too dangerous.' He fiddled with the hem of his t-shirt and decided to leave it on for a while. It wasn't all that hot in the shade of the trees. Rachel's armpits were shaved and he had wondered, in the car, if the rest of her was. The cut of her swimsuit, which curved an inch above her hipbone, left him in no doubt. It wasn't.

'Well, I'm very sorry,' said Malcolm, 'but it doesn't seem right to me.'

'You've never been exactly noted for your stern moral sense before, you know,' said William.

'Well, some of us grow up,' said Malcolm. 'And that's just the trouble with Alec. He's thirty-nine and she's, what, nineteen. He's got a daughter of sixteen.'

'Dora,' said William, 'the one you said that you fancied.'

Mrs Bishop appeared, unbidden, with a third jug of beer and graciously accepted a pull from William's joint. 'Beautiful day,' she remarked. 'A right shame you having to work to them exams in weather like this.'

'A great shame,' agreed William who had taken his third-class honours degree in 1972, and without doing any work at all.

'You'll be off to London soon, I expect, practising law and medicine and all of that.'

'Oh, I expect so,' said William, as he had said to Mrs Bishop, off and on, for the last fifteen years.

'Can't take to these new students at all,' said Mrs Bishop. 'All pina coladas and Perrier water. Give me that sex and drugs and rock and roll every time.'

'An example to us all,' said William, as Mrs Bishop teetered back towards her kitchen, still bearing his joint and trailing a loose end of foot bandage through the goose shit.

'Someone else who can't come to terms with change,' said Malcolm crossly. 'All this living in the past. That's what this Alec business is about, you know. He does very well out of the new enterprise economy, thank you very much. Churns out all these negative, knocking books of his, makes a fortune, and then retires to the country on the proceeds, where he picks up the daughter of a Conservative minister – probably as some kind of puerile political gesture.'

'Whereas you, of course, are very good at change,' said William, with his broadest smile. 'You who have changed from being a hippy, to a socialist revolutionary, to a narcotics wholesaler, to a wholefood freak, to a New Romantic, to the oldest punk in Neal Street, and now to some kind of lick-spittle apologist for the new totalitarianism – of market freedom wedded to social repression. You who've been a superficial poseur for so fucking long that you can't tell a vacuous pose from a vicious political dogma.'

He watched Malcolm's face shift gradually during this speech from a grin to wary amusement to the beginnings of anger.

'Are you serious, William?'

'Of course I'm not serious,' said William, smiling even harder. 'You stupid wanker.'

'I think I'm going to keep this dry for the way home,' said Rachel, and peeled down the shoulders of her swimsuit. Alec tried the usual techniques for looking casual: staring up at the leaves above his head; tracing patterns on the ground with his finger; whistling noiseless tunes between his teeth. Then he gave up and looked instead at Rachel, who was naked now and picked her way gingerly through the litter of broken twigs and beech mast to the water's edge.

The perfect hemispheres of her rump, with their brief triangle of white skin, were painful to Alec. The buried pipeline of her spine sliding smoothly beneath her skin was agony. The hint of spun sugar pubic hair that flickered in the blue V of sky between her thighs was quite intolerable. He pulled off his t-shirt and bathing trunks, and marched resolutely to the water's edge.

'Stop sucking your stomach in,' called Rachel, bobbing and shuddering in the cold water. 'You look lovely.'

They swam side by side out to the ski ramp. The

windsurfers had disappeared from the far shore, and the sheet of water was dark and flat as engine oil in the still afternoon. The only sounds were the tiny splashes of their arms breaking the water now and then, and the susurration of their own breathing.

He enjoyed the strange sensation of the cold water coursing between his buttocks as they clenched and unclenched with the steady stroke. Even in a hundred yards you could begin to feel the heat starting to retreat from the skin, inwards to the body core as the coldness pressed in. Half an hour, he knew, and muscles would begin to knot with cramp. An hour in this sort of water and you would be unconscious.

Alec imagined himself down on the dark floor of the gravel pit, 200 feet below, looking up at the insect scurrying of their own bodies on the calm surface of the water. Way down there among the rusted cars and supermarket trolleys and the jumbled bones of birds and badgers and the odd, unlucky swimmer.

He could see from there that he and Rachel, splashing happily across the surface of a sunny pond, were feeble little heat engines, leaking energy into the millions of tons of freezing water beneath them, seeping inexorably towards equilibrium with the chill indifference around. Down there at the bottom of the gravel pit Alec Smith stopped worrying about his wife, Susan, and his children, Dora and Jonathan, and about the indignities of age and paunch. His testicles were shrunk to the size of lentils and his penis was a bluish acorn, but he knew with great certainty that he wanted to fuck Rachel.

They rested either side of one float of the ramp and Alec noted mournfully that Rachel's breathing slowed long before his own. In the clear water he could see the whole length of her body glimmering against the blackness of the gulf beneath them and feel against his skin the small eddies she made as her legs pedalled lazily to keep afloat.

There seemed to be nothing to say that was worth upsetting the calm. They gazed at each other across the wooden float for a minute and then Rachel lifted herself and kissed him hard on the mouth. The heat and salt of her lips and tongue shocked him in the cold neutrality of the water. Her belly grazed briefly across his own as she turned and then she was gone, swimming a brisk crawl, much faster than he could have managed, towards the shore.

Mrs Bishop set down a fourth jug on the table and accepted another toke from William. 'He should go a long way, this lad of yours,' she told Malcolm, resting a benevolent hand on his brown and polished pate. William smiled beatifically through a wreath of marijuana smoke.

'It's what you miss at our age, isn't it dear?'

'Now look,' said Malcolm, 'I'm not his . . .'

'Everything to look forward to,' said Mrs Bishop. 'The Age of Aquarius.' She shuffled back towards the pub, trailing more bandage and humming tunelessly, 'When the mooo-on is in the Seventh House . . .'

William poured more beer.

'So you're going to stitch him up, then, are you?' he said.

'What do you mean, "stitch him up"?' Malcolm tossed a pebble at a row of half-grown ducklings that were solemnly pedalling past the foot of The Ferryman garden. 'I haven't written anything about Alec that wasn't true.'

'What about the "all-night rave-up"?' said William. 'Where "drink flowed freely and drugs were taken"? What about the "drunken groper" left on the floor with "a bloody nose"?'

'Well, so what? She did hit him for feeling her up,' said Malcolm. 'Toby told me so.'

William fingered the lapel of his flying jacket. 'What about the "leather-jacketed Hell's Angels"?'

'Oh, come on. You've got to put some colour in these things,' said Malcolm, 'or nobody is going to read them.'

'Make it up, you mean?'

Malcolm threw some more pebbles into the river. 'It's different when people are in the public eye,' he said. 'Ordinary people are interested in them and the papers have a duty to inform. If you've sought fame and publicity, then you don't have the same rights of privacy.'

'And just for the sake of argument,' said William, 'what if I decided to tell someone like the *Daily Mail* about Malcolm's magic briefcase?'

Malcolm shifted uneasily on the Rexine sofa. 'I'm hardly a person in the public eye, am I?'

'Oh, I don't know,' said William, 'we could work on it.'

'I want you to rub this stuff into me,' Rachel told him when they were dry, 'or my skin goes like a crocodile.'

So he sat naked astride her buttocks, rubbing oil, with long, sweeping strokes, into the strong, tapered back and marvelling at the good fortune of it all.

'Why don't you get fat with all the sweets you eat?'

'Because I don't eat anything else,' said Rachel.

'When I was about six,' he said, for something to say, 'I remember my Uncle Jack giving me a ten-shilling note to spend on sweets.'

His hands swept lower to the incurve of her waist, spreading the oil on to her hips, then buttering down the inner thighs. She stirred beneath him, opening her legs to make it easier.

'It was a huge amount of money to give a child,' he went on. 'Dozens and dozens of packets of sweets. I kept it for days. I was almost too frightened to go into the sweet-shop.'

'Oh, come here, Smith,' she said impatiently, and reached behind her blindly for his groin.

But it was no good. Something flew away. He carried on stroking her back with oil, and then her front, until they were both sweating in the afternoon heat beneath the beech trees. They had oil all over them and pieces of grass, and she was twisting hard underneath him, with her eyes wide open, arching her back to push her breasts into his slippery hands.

She moved on top of him after a while and took his penis into her mouth and raked it gently with her nails, but it was no good.

'It doesn't always work for me,' he told her some time later. 'I don't know why. It's always been a bit erratic, but it seems to have packed up altogether these days.'

'It's all right,' she said earnestly. 'It happens to lots of men. Performance anxiety. They're always having these articles in *Cosmopolitan*.'

She took him in her hand again, rolling his scrotum gently in her palm. 'Actually, I like it small. I think it's sweet.'

'I don't want to be sweet,' he said sadly. 'I want to be like a fucking crowbar. I want to split you in two with it. I want you so much my balls are aching, but the stupid fucker just won't stand up.'

'All that stuff,' said Rachel, 'about men being goal-oriented and women not minding so much. It really is true you know. I would like to do it, but I like just being here with you as well. I like feeling your hands all over me. You use your hands beautifully, you know. And in any case, there'll be plenty of other times.'

'Really?' said Alec.

'Promise,' said Rachel.

He rolled a joint for them then and they smoked it, lying side by side and staring at the sky through the tracery of beech leaves. 'I brought some of Malcolm's coke in case you'd like some,' said Rachel.

'Shouldn't waste your money,' said Alec. 'Malcolm sells more talcum powder than Boots the Chemist. Anyway, it would wake me up and I think I'm going to go to sleep.'

They lay there together a long time in the heat, their skin sticking gently with the oil and perspiration, until her breathing slowed and grew regular and she was asleep. When his arm beneath her shoulders grew numb and the ground began to dig into his hip, he gently pulled himself away, folded his half of the rug across her sleeping body and walked quietly to the water's edge.

The cool water soothed the dull ache of his bachelor's balls. He dribbled it over his forearms and ran his wet hands over his hot forehead. 'Useless bloody item, aren't you?' he told his penis. 'You get presented with what is probably the best body in the whole of the south-east of England and you're as much fucking use as a wet piece of string.' It bobbed flaccidly in the water, nodding its acorn head in apologetic agreement.

When he turned back to the shore the rug had slipped from Rachel's body and she lay sprawled, face upwards, in an attitude that would have been ungainly in anybody less than perfect, but in her was merely heartbreaking. Her high, round breasts hardly sagged at all on her arched ribcage. A breeze ruffled her pubic hair. Alec sat down beside her again and rummaged around inside the picnic hamper, looking for the plastic container.

Lubricated, his fingers coursed softly through her folds, finding smoothness, and heat and new lubrication. Her body stirred beneath him as his fingers worked gently, and he felt a hand run softly down his own back as he leaned forwards between her legs.

Salt and oil. Rainwater and lemon. Then just the taste of her. His mouth worked delicately, hardly touching, and her stomach began to flex strongly upwards towards him, her legs involuntarily to spread and the hands to claw at his back. He dug his own fingers in then, hard into her buttocks, as the flexing became rhythmical, then demanding, then overwhelming.

'I thought women weren't supposed to be goal-oriented,' he told her afterwards.

'God, that was good,' said Rachel. 'Though I'm sorry you didn't have more fun yourself.'

'It's all right. I haven't enjoyed myself so much in years,' he said truthfully.

    'What was it?' she asked, touching herself. 'That stuff you put on me?'

    'Mayonnaise,' said Alec. 'It's an argument for the existence of God.'

—— CHAPTER ELEVEN ——

From *The Republican Reader*:

> Flashed from his bed, the electric tidings came,
> He is not better; he is much the same.

–Alfred Austin, Poet Laureate, on the illness of
the Prince of Wales

'Definitely not Chippendale,' said William. 'A good Edwardian repro, I'd say.'

'Daddy always said it was Chippendale,' said Susan, who still found it hard to believe that William could really know anything about something serious, like furniture. 'It's got the fluted legs and the bow front and all that sort of thing.'

The Smiths' living room in Islington was scattered with Susan's good pieces of furniture, assembled from odd parts of the houses. Some were upside down, some partly dismantled, with drawers and leaves stacked against the walls. It had been a difficult day for William. Driving all the way to London to price all these wonderful things Susan wanted to sell. And then finding the only thing she actually seemed to want to get rid of was a rotten card table that might have come from John Lewis last week, and would fetch no more than £500 if he was lucky.

'Chippendale was the Terence Conran of the eighteenth century,' he explained to her patiently. 'And you don't find many Habitat tables with Tel's personal chisel marks, do you? He sold through catalogues, pattern books, workshop franchises. And he was copied. There are Chippendale tables like this from Vladivostok to Fort Worth.'

'How do you know?'

'Because I sold half of them,' said William, 'and, in any case, the colour's all wrong.'

'What do you mean, the colour's all wrong? It's fucking brown, isn't it?'

'Yes, it is fucking brown, and that's what's wrong with it.' William picked up an eighteenth-century wheel-back carver from the corner and held it overhead to display a blackened underside, decorated with fossilized gobs of Dora's infant chewing gum. Susan found herself admiring the way he hefted the cumbersome thing by one leg; the flare of his dorsal muscles under the grubby Jean-Paul Gaultier t-shirt. 'Now this is the real thing,' he told her. 'Look how dark the stretchers are underneath, where the beeswax has accumulated. Look at the way the wood shades from dark to pale along the legs. Look at the colours in the seat.'

Susan stared obediently at the seat, buffed by a thousand Georgian and Victorian backsides. She stared hard, in the way she was used to staring at paintings or photographs. And gradually the flat brown plane of the wood, punished by 200 years of sweat and gravy, wax and water, began to resolve into its elements. Burgundy, russet, tawny, silver – even blues and greens. Colour.

'All right,' she said finally, grudgingly. 'But I'm not selling that. I'm selling the Chippendale.'

William sighed. 'Come on. I've got an auction to go to this afternoon. You can put your Conran card table in, if you like, and see what it will fetch.'

Susan used to enjoy sleeping with William very much, but she had promised herself never to do it again. She made this promise the night all three of them had gone to bed together, and Alec had crashed Malcolm's motorcycle, and then told the doctor at the General that he was a famous violinist.

She slept with William, off and on, for the first six months at university, but they didn't *go out* together. William hated the couples who went out together. Waddling round the campus, locked together like a three-legged race. Writing each other's names on their ring-binders. Sharing psyche-delic Morris Minors with names like Car and Maurice. Playing the mums and dads game.

William just used to turn up in Susan's room at Uplands two or three times a week, and they fucked. And that was it. He used to arrive at around nine in his flying jacket and cowboy boots; roll joints, play his *John Wesley Harding* album on her stereo and then they would go to bed; or floor; or chair; or table. He was very good at it too. Gentle, unfussed and funny. Not like Malcolm, who finished before you got started; or bloody Alec, who was all anxiety and attainment scores and a post-mortem on every orgasm.

Susan got to know her body and William's better than she had known anything before. Better than times tables; better than *Great Expectations*; better than the Otto Pann pastel on the wall of her room at home in Gloucestershire, which she had stared at every night before going to sleep since the age of two. She got to know that she liked sex as much as William did, and she got to know too that there was nothing in sex that you shouldn't do, as long as you liked it.

The only thing she didn't know was that at twelve o'clock, when William shrugged on his flying jacket and collected his dope tin and skins, and ambled off downstairs, he was climb-ing into bed with Alison or Vivien or Marcie, and doing the whole thing again. It was Malcolm who had thoughtfully pointed this out to her and Malcolm she had then gone to bed with as an act of ineffectual revenge.

'But we weren't *going out* together,' said William, baffled by her rage, 'and in any case, I thought you knew.' And perhaps she really had known, for nobody who had de-mystified sex as much as William could ever have mystified monogamy.

'Why aren't you bidding?' she whispered to him. They were sitting in the Foulkes auction room in Kensington Church

Street – a sort of shabby corridor with a pine pulpit at the end, like a Baptist chapel.

'My bids are already in the book.' He pointed out the green-coated porter with his ledger. 'You look at the furniture beforehand and register your bids. Saves a lot of hassle. You don't spend more than you can afford, and you don't even have to turn up if you don't want to.'

She thought for a moment. 'How do you know there aren't higher bids in the book already?'

'Because you bung the porter £20 to have a look at it.' Susan, who instinctively disliked conceding any kind of expertise to William, was impressed by this display of insouciance. William's role in her life, since he had stopped being her lover and become Alec's best friend, was that of the amiable slob. He was the friend every marriage needs who is discovered crashed out on the downstairs sofa in a greasy sleeping bag every six months or so. Someone who played nicely with the children; drank all the Remy Martin; melted his nylon socks in her tumble drier; and then disappeared back to Amsterdam or Paris or wherever it was that he was practising his amiable slobbery that particular year.

It was an effort to remember that William had also managed to make some sort of a living in the last fifteen years. Not a comfortable, predictable living like her own, of course. But it was at least a living that had included flats in foreign cities and cars and telephones and Jean-Paul Gaultier t-shirts. William, she was forced to admit, knew something that she didn't.

She had never been to an auction before and it was a good deal shabbier than she had expected. The auctioneer looked about right, in his oversized pinstripe suit and Trumper's haircut. A Dominic or a Simon, pretending to have a proper job while he waited to inherit. But most of the buyers were men like William, in bomber jackets and jeans, sprawled listlessly on plywood and gaspipe chairs. She had seen more tension and theatre at a Wykeham jumble sale.

The Simon or Dominic person chanted rhythmically but

unenthusiastically, and Susan craned her neck to find the source of the bids.

'I can't see anyone bidding at all.'

'They probably aren't. The auctioneer just makes them up until he reaches the reserve. It's called "taking them off the wall". Then he sells it to the highest bid in the book, unless a real punter jumps in. This is your table next.'

They had agreed to put a £400 reserve price on the Chippendale. The auctioneer whisked it swiftly from £200 up to £423 and then knocked it down.

'Told you it wasn't worth more than £500,' said William complacently.

'Do you know who bought it?' asked Susan, looking around.

'I did,' said William.

'*You* bought my table?'

'Could fetch £1,000 in Paris if I'm lucky,' said William. 'The French wouldn't know a Conran from a Chippendale if it had a Design Centre label on it.'

She had been going out with Alec for about a year. Really going out this time, with the three-legged race around the campus and the Valentine cards and meals together at the Anglo-Asian, when they all went to bed together.

They were playing the tennis-elbow-foot game in the big Uplands living room, with everyone tripping on blotter acid from Malcolm's magic briefcase and a bottle of Jim Beam. There was always just that little hint of orgy in the air with the tennis-elbow-foot game, but it never quite got there somehow, until that night.

The only straight person was Daisy Dee, who was with William, and Daisy wanted to try some acid too, because she kept asking William what tripping was like, in that silly squeaky voice she had.

'It's like coming,' William told her, 'but continuously. A twelve-hour orgasm.'

'What, *really* coming?' said Daisy, 'or just feeling like you're coming?'

'No, no *really* coming,' said William solemnly. 'That's why I have to tuck my jeans into my boots.'

Daisy stared at William's boots then, and Susan started choking and Daisy went red. But in the end she dropped some acid too and played the game.

Daisy was naked first because she was deaf in one ear, and because she was one of those people who just like taking their clothes off all the time. She climbed on William's lap and started squirming about, but people pretended not to notice because it wasn't cool to notice. William was fully dressed anyway, as he always was in tennis-elbow-foot, and not paying much attention to Daisy either, but staring across at Susan, sitting there in her jeans and nothing else.

Vivien didn't have anything on either by the end, or Alec, but he had a cushion on his lap, because he was embarrassed about his gut. It all broke up when Malcolm got paranoid because people were picking on him and he went downstairs with Vivien. Daisy started crying for no particular reason and saying she felt sick, and Alec took her into the kitchen. And she and William looked at each other.

Everything got much vaguer then. They'd been asleep about an hour, too stoned for sex, when the wedge of light from the landing fell across the bed and Alec climbed in. It was all right at first, sort of warm and comical, with William and Alec talking across her and everyone giggling and half asleep. They played the mental Monopoly game for a while, with Susan being the dice.

And William had started doing it to her, which had been sort of weird but very exciting. And she remembered that Alec just lay there watching them, getting more still and further away on the edge of the bed and not saying anything, until after a while she stopped noticing. And then when she could notice things again, Alec was gone, and there was the metal grunt of the motorbike in the driveway.

'Any stiffness in the mornings?' asked Dr Dougal, stubbing out a Craven A into his crowded ashtray.

'Oh, no,' said Alec. 'We've got this orthopaedic mattress at home now that . . .'

'Stiffness in the member, man,' said Dougal impatiently. 'Morning glory.'

'Oh, right. Well, yes, I suppose I do, most mornings. But isn't that just from lying on your back, or wanting a pee or something?'

Dougal was the last doctor Alec knew who smoked, and probably the last in the world who smoked during consultations. It was the main reason he still came to see him. He could have afforded some Harley Street suit by now. With the BUPA policy he had acquired on the takeover of Prometheus Press, he wouldn't even have had to pay. But he liked his doctors flawed.

'Didn't I hear you on *Stop the Week* a while ago?' said Dougal.

'*Start the Week*,' said Alec. 'Yes, that's right.'

Alec had not smoked since he was thirty, but he still got cancer all the time. A strange twinge under his jaw when he yawned; a stabbing pain in the left lung; a spot on the knee that refused to go away. But he never went to the doctor. Susan would go sailing serenely up to the Highbury medical centre almost every month to have her rigging checked, or her bilges scoured, or her barnacles scraped, or whatever it was they did to women at all these clinics they were always going to. It was why women lived to be eighty while men nursed their *timor mortis* until the day they dropped dead at their retirement dos. Alec stayed at home, fearfully studying his latest wart for melanoma in the lavatory and brooding over his ancient copy of the *Complete Home Doctor*, inherited from Harry.

Alec had his first wank with that *Home Doctor*, over the picture of the naked woman on page 42. She had been drawn to be as unstimulating as she possibly could be, with marcelled hair and the vacuously healthy outdoor face of the 1930s fresh-air faddist. Her genitals were as sketchy as a Barbie doll, but she had breasts and that was good enough for a hard-on when you were twelve.

Mind you, practically anything was good for a hard-on when you were twelve. The smell of swimming pools; the feel of glazed cotton sheets on bare skin; the bakelite pudenda of shop-window dummies; the simple word 'naked', in print, in a Famous Five book would have the pubescent Alec reaching for his groin. The stout corsets in the Kay's mail-order catalogue could give him an all-night stonker, a burning spear, welded to his lower belly, that raged cluelessly under knotted bedclothes.

What a fucking waste it was. All those hard-ons. The things he could do with them now. But then he hadn't known, had he? Nobody had told him. What were you supposed to do with this thing? What was it for? His mother had given him maddeningly unspecific pamphlets from the Methodist Counselling Service, and talked to the ceiling about self-control. But it was *The Complete Home Doctor* that had given him his first clues, and he was still grateful.

'I don't know why you read that stupid book,' Susan would say irritably as he mooned over its ragged, sellotaped pages. 'People don't get things like Plagues of Boyles and Surfeits of Lampreys any more. See the doctor if you're really worried. He won't kill you.'

But Alec knew that was exactly what a doctor would do one day, unless he was lucky enough to be flattened first by one of those runaway juggernaut heart attacks when he was walking down the street. It would be a doctor who one day would gently tell Alec the name of the disease that was going to kill him. It would be a doctor who would kindly, tactfully, write out the last, meaningless prescriptions. And it would be a doctor who would, with a tiny shrug, mercifully flip the final switch which separated Alec from not-Alec.

They were all complicit, these doctors, united in the know-ledge of what he liked to view only from the corner of his eye. Like Rabelais, wasn't it, who used to taste his patients' turds to form his diagnoses. They were too engaged to be repelled. They jousted with death in the languages of clinical detachment, or comic brutalism. They were more complete than Alec and they scared Alec to death.

And so he liked Dougal, with his Craven As and his bottle of Famous Grouse in the cupboard, the cigarette burn in his tie and the pee stains in his tweedy crotch. Dougal should have been dispensing pessimism and horse pills in a rural Scottish slum somewhere and instead found himself in a north London health centre, with a Well-Woman clinic and a Fight the Cuts banner and an alternative medicine group every other Friday.

'Bladder bonk,' said Dougal now, lighting another cigarette from the untidy flare of his petrol Zippo. 'Full bladder in the morning exerts pressure on the prostate gland, producing involuntary erection. But it shows the essential parts are in working order, d'ye see? It tells me you have no physical problem, like nerve damage or diabetes or blocked arteries. But we'll have a look at you anyway. Pants down and on the couch, if you please.'

Alec was disappointed. He had been rather hoping it was something physical, though nothing too nasty of course. Just a bunged-up pipe in the plumbing or a blown fuse in the electrics. Or perhaps some undiscovered erogenous zone, lurking like a forgotten switch beneath the skin. Just remember to press this before you go to bed, Alec, and you'll have six inches of rampant sinew, ready for action.

'The unruly member,' said Dougal reflectively, and squinting through the smoke, as he kneaded Alec's suet apron with horn yellow digits. 'The one part of us we twentieth-century men cannot order or command. Popping fly buttons at the vicarage tea party and shrivelling to little acorns when you need them most: "Thou treacherous base deserter of my flame/False to my passion, fatal to my name."'

'Shakespeare?' said Alec.

'Right century,' said Dougal. 'John Wilmot, Earl of Rochester.'

A fragment of ash from his cigarette dropped into Alec's pubic hair, where it flared briefly and expired in a nest of ghost-grey filaments. Dougal flicked it aside and calmly continued his prodding.

'Some spasm here in the lower bowel. Any wind?'

'Well, yes, sometimes.'

'Top or bottom?'

'Er, both . . . only sometimes.'

'Offensive?'

'Not to me,' said Alec.

'That's W. H. Auden, isn't it?' said Dougal approvingly. '"Every man likes the smell of his own farts." It's probably only stress in any case.'

The idea of psychiatric treatment depressed Alec profoundly. He could picture it already. Some old mitteleuropean hag in Belsize Park, with a basin haircut and a kaftan, telling him that he really fancied his mum. Or, more likely these days, a bashful circle of pussy-whipped men in baseball boots, manipulated by a monster called Bill in a lumberjack shirt, who would tell him his impotence was really the expression of his repressed violence against women.

'You're saying I need therapy. See a psychiatrist?'

'It's the modern age needs a psychiatrist, dear boy. You and I must survive as best we can with the crutches of alcohol, tobacco and drugs. Sit up and breathe deeply so I can listen to the bellows.'

Alec did as he was told and tried not to squirm as the icy kiss of the stethoscope patrolled his back.

'I see three or four young men like you every week. Spend their lives in traffic jams, eating mucky food like pizzas, shouting down the telephone. Think their unruly members should perform like their motor cars. Want to knock their superegos into shape like their squash backhands. And then there's the ladies, of course, with their magazine nonsense of G-spots and the clitoris and bridge techniques. When I began to practise medicine, all that a nice young woman wanted from marriage was bairns and then twin beds. These days I get plumbers' wives of sixty-five coming to me demanding multiple orgasms or their money back. New washing machine, fitted kitchen and a blissful bunk-up twice a week. No wonder the poor wee member becomes nervous.'

'Are you saying there is nothing I can do about it?'

'You could become simple, Alec. Simple like the beasts of

the field. I've never met a dog yet with a potency problem or a goat that grappled with its superego. You could live on an island, far from the telegrams and anger, the horns and motors. Find yourself a cabin of clay and wattles made.' He raised his stethoscope theatrically and recited to the humming fluorescent striplight.

Nine bean rows will I have there, a hive for the honey bee,
And live alone in the bee-loud glade.

'Gerard Manley Hopkins?' said Alec.

'William Butler Yeats,' said Dougal reproachfully, 'and I thought you were the literary man.'

'Exile wasn't quite what I had in mind,' said Alec, 'and anyway, it's sort of what I've done already.'

'Then it's the quick fix for you, my boy,' said Dougal, taking a writing pad from his desk. 'There's a consultant at St Barnabas's Hospital who does erections on demand apparently. Urino-genital department. A bit of a weird bugger by all accounts, but I've sent a few there and they've never come back.'

He sealed the note in a manila envelope and scribbled an address on it. 'You'll have to go private, of course, unless you want to wait until Doomsday, or the next proper socialist government, which amounts to the same thing. But you can afford it these days. You might let me know how you get on.'

William barked his shin hard on a protruding drawer and swore viciously and unfairly at the Smiths' cat, Nelson, which was observing him blandly from the top of the refrigerator. The drawer was overflowing with plastic carrier bags and grated unpleasantly when he tried to kick it shut with his bare toes. He was dressed only in an old dressing gown of Alec's, which fell six inches short of his knees, and the floor was unpleasantly tacky beneath his bare feet, as if someone had spilt orange juice a few days before and failed to wipe it up thoroughly.

The double sink was stacked with dirty dishes, which

spread out across the melamine worktops and tottered insecurely on the rings of the gas hob. The cat-tray on the floor looked as if it hadn't been emptied in a month and was scattered with miniature cigars of cat shit, powdered grey with fuller's earth. There were two empty bottles of Chablis on the kitchen table, more carrier bags and an opened bottle of milk, turned solid. A half-pound of butter, partly wrapped, bore on its exposed surface a sprinkling of black toast crumbs and what looked like one of Nelson's pawmarks.

William was not a fastidious man, but in the Smiths' house, as in a good hotel, he expected order, and what he saw disturbed him. There was no bread in the Edwardian enamelled bin and the Ryvita packet he found there yielded only crumbs. In the refrigerator were an opened packet of McCain's oven chips, two Birds Eye frozen pizzas, a Findus Arctic Roll and three flattened milk bottle tops sticking to the brownish goo that had gathered in the bottom of the door compartment.

The Smiths were not supposed to live like this. They were supposed to have crusty loaves of wholemeal bread from Rumbolds and tasty cheeses from Camisa Fratelli. Their fridge should be full of Marks and Spencer salads and Waitrose salamis and the delicious leftovers of ratatouille and roast chicken. It was a kitchen where you could roll up stoned or jet-lagged at two in the morning and positively count on a beef and horseradish sandwich, or at the very least a bottle of Becks and a handful of cold potatoes, sprinkled with rock salt. Rubbing his sore toe in the chaotic kitchen, whole new vistas of loss opened up for William.

He contemplated heating up the frozen chips, but as he did so Nelson, who was still on the top of the refrigerator, reached out in deferred revenge and sank his claws deep into William's scalp. He yelped with the unexpected pain and grabbed a fridge shelf for support, which promptly slid from its housing. He staggered across the sticky floor, caught his ankles on the protruding drawer and fell backwards into Nelson's cat-litter, amid a shower of frozen chips.

*

'What on earth were you doing downstairs?' said Susan, when he climbed back into bed. 'And what is *that*?'

He carefully balanced the slice of cherry cake, smeared with peanut butter, on the edge of one of the wine glasses which crowded the bedside table and took off his dressing gown. 'Just about all there was to eat. What happened to your kitchen?'

'My little Mrs Mop decided to go and live in Wykeham with you, didn't he?'

'I don't think you've got any intention of going down there, have you, you old slut?' he asked her. 'All this crap about valuing the furniture.'

'It was his idea in the first place,' said Susan. 'A new life. Back to the basics. Susan at the easel and Alec at the type-writer. But I don't know if he wants me to come down there any more. I've only seen him once in the last week. Popping in for clean clothes and his mail. He hasn't phoned at all.'

'You haven't phoned him either,' said William.

'No, I haven't. I was rather afraid I might get this girl he's been seeing.'

'How do you know he's been seeing a girl?' he asked curiously.

'I didn't,' said Susan. 'But I do now.'

William took a bite of cake and peanut butter. 'You know I think I got some cat shit on his dressing gown,' he said, through a mouthful of crumbs. He picked up a glass that still contained a dribble of Chablis to rinse the salty goo from his palate. Susan kissed his shoulder, then slid her tongue lazily across a nipple and down the groove of his hard stomach towards his groin. The tongue dipped into his navel, teased a nest of hairs and then continued, very slowly, downwards. William waved his arms in the air, searching vainly for somewhere to deposit cake and wine glass.

'Have you heard the one about what's smooth and salty and sticks to the roof of your mouth?' he asked her. But Susan's answer beneath the grey-striped, real-down duvet was completely lost.

*

It was the first time in what, nearly twenty years, since that night in Uplands when Susan had started the tennis-elbow-foot game and been such a bitch to that girl he'd been with. Daisy Dee, her name was, who'd been deaf in one ear and had amazing nipples like wine corks. Someone had told him she was married to a judge now.

She'd been pretty thick actually, old Daisy, but it was her first time in the house and Susan had absolutely carved her up. She'd sat next to her in the tennis-elbow-foot game and fed her abstract nouns until the poor little cow was starkers while everyone else was sitting around in their overcoats. And then she ran off to the kitchen, where he had found her crying and trying to get both feet down one leg of her jeans.

So he'd helped her get dressed and they'd put her to bed in Vivien's flat. And when he got back upstairs there was Alec crashed out with all the acid and whisky, and Susan sitting in his bed for the first time in a year.

As far as he could remember they hadn't done very much. Too smashed probably, but somewhere along the way the door of the bedroom had opened and electric light had flooded the room and Susan had said something sharply, before he had woken up properly, and then the next thing was the sound of the motorbike in the drive.

Alec had only gone about a hundred yards when they found him, lying at the side of the road with the bike on top of him and blood all over the place. The only injury actually was a couple of shredded fingertips on his left hand, which had whacked into the gatepost at the end of the drive and tipped him off. William drove him to the hospital in the old MG and Alec kept going on about his fingers and how they mustn't cut them off because he was the next Jascha Heifetz. And he'd never played a fiddle in his life.

That had been the last time.

William was wakened by the doorbell and the sound of somebody rattling the letter box. He felt for his watch on the bedside table and knocked over a wine glass. It was only 11 o'clock.

He heard more rattling at the front door, then the chink of something falling on the path and then, unmistakably, the sound of a key in the front door.

'There's someone coming in,' he hissed to Susan.

She sat up in bed and turned on a light. The sight of her breasts, free from the duvet and swinging rosily in the dim glow of the reading-lamp, did nothing at all for his libido. William was not in the mood to encounter burglars.

'That will be Alec,' said Susan calmly. 'He's much later than I expected.'

'You said you'd only seen him once in the last week.'

'That's right,' said Susan. 'He popped in this morning on his way to the doctor's.'

CHAPTER TWELVE

From *The Republican Reader*:

In 1969, when the Duke of Edinburgh complained that the Royal Family was about to go into the red, a group of patriotic London dockers started a fund to buy him a new polo pony.

On the university campus the summer term continued, miraculously hot and dry. The cerulean wash of bluebells in the birch woods around the colleges was crushed to sappy salad by furtive couplings, then overwhelmed by unsprung reels of sharp green briar and the waist-high drifts of creamy flowering weed, which Alec called cow parsley and Rachel, Queen Anne's Lace.

Grizzled professors of politics and economics, nostalgic for the Summer of Love, took seminars out into clearings in the woods, where they sprawled at ease, while their students picked twigs from their trouser turn-ups and stirred uncomfortably on the Next carrier bags they had brought to protect good skirts from spiky grasses and juicy slugs.

In the valley below the university, the spires of the cathedral were clear only for an hour after dawn each day, and then surrounded in grey banks of mist from the Stour and traffic fume from the ring road; a greasy pelt like Hoover fluff, which lay still all day in the bowl of the city until evening breezes drove it away across the Weald.

On the hilltop campus the sun burned down unimpeded, on white concrete and smoked glass. Ring pulls became embedded in sticky asphalt paths and the college newts retreated to the bottom of their shrinking pond beside the biology labs. The Master of Marcuse fussed over the *Clematis jackmanii* he was striving to train up the concrete cliff of his college, watering its roots twice daily and fretting over the tender leaves that crisped and shrivelled away from the scorching cement. The Master of Saussure paid twice-daily visits to his breezeblock cellar of '82 clarets, to cluck over their temperature and to order the floors hosed down once again.

In Senate the issue of the college names had been debated once more and Humanities had surrendered to Business Studies. Admissions continued to decline and a working party was appointed to consider new, more acceptable titles for the 1990s. Galbraith College could be rechristened Friedman without its American star shape causing problems. Saussure could be renamed Stoppard, who if modern was at least anti-communist and more-or-less British. Marcuse, built as it was in the shape of an M, was more of a problem. There was a shortage of respectable Ms. Marx was obviously unthinkable and Milton had republican connotations. In a satirical spirit the student union rep suggested Mengele, but the working party settled eventually for Malthus, which had overtones of both piety and chastity.

There had been a brief rent strike at the start of term and a minor occupation of the registry in protest at the indexation of college charges. But in the heat of June, militancy had melted like the Stour mists and a mood of weary resignation fallen upon the campus.

In the humming grey carrels of the library, final-year students, with exams a fortnight away, were stricken with library lassitude and slumped unconscious over Collingwood and Carr, Russell and Rousseau. The library was the biggest and most expensive building in the university, the gift of a chocolate manufacturer, magnificently built and scantily stocked. Sitting in the centre of the campus, humming away behind massive buttresses of brown-burnt brick and molten cascades of mirrored glass, it seemed the source of the sleeping sickness. The whole building hummed, sending soporific vibrations across the campus to strike down lecturers and professors, students and technicians where they walked or stood chatting, until the hard yellow lawns of the university were strewn with sleeping bodies.

In her study in Marcuse, Vivien dozed over her unfinished biography of Mrs Oscar Wilde, a book that had been due at her publisher's two months before. In the Sainsbury lecture theatre Toby slumbered through the Film Society's matinée of *Un Chien andalou*, his favourite movie in the world. In his stifling room under the eaves of Uplands, with an empty bottle of St Joseph at his side, Alec slept, with the salty ghosts of dried tears on his cheeks.

Rachel was still in bed in her new, eau-de-nil room that smelled curiously of banana milk. She had slept ten hours straight. She had heard the postman call at eight-thirty. She had heard Vivien leave at nine. She heard the cathedral clock strike eleven. Still in bed, still half asleep, it was possible to imagine you were in the last wisps of a bad dream. Still possible to suppose there was not that terrible reality outside, arranging its filing cards, booking its appointments, striking the days from its calendar. She slept again.

No birds flew across the Wykeham campus in the morning heat. The dogs at their bones, the fire in the hearth, the flies on the wall: a princess somewhere had pricked her finger on a spindle, a great hedge of sharp briars had sprung up around the domain, and everything was asleep.

Only Malcolm was busy, weaving phosphorescent words into spiky patterns on the matt-black screen of his word processor. The grey metal leaves of his louvred blinds were clasped tight against the sunshine. In the morning bright fragments of light crept shyly into the dimness of his room, falling upon the stone-grey carpet and the charcoal grey of his new stereo, the chromium complication of his coffee table, only to retreat again as the sun rose higher in the sky.

The only colour in the room was the tiny red monitor light of the word processor; the only sounds the whirring of its cooling fan and the patter of its plastic keys. On its screen the glowing blob of the cursor shuttled steadily to and fro, to and fro.

'In the increasingly turbulent atmosphere of Wykeham University,' said the screen, 'radical activists now see a potential for unrest unrivalled since the 1960s.'

Malcolm contemplated the sentence for a moment, then substituted 'militant' for 'radical'. He pondered again, and changed 'increasingly' to 'politically' and inserted an 'increasing' before the 'potential'.

'In the politically turbulent atmosphere of Wykeham University militant activists now see an increasing potential for unrest unrivalled since the 1960s.'

That was much better. But should he have said 'militantly turbulent' or 'turbulently militant'? It was very flexible, this vocabulary. Malcolm took a swig from the cold bottle of Grolsch beside his keyboard. His fingers pattered and the glowing blob of the cursor shuttled, to and fro, to and fro.

Rachel felt fine when she got up. She ate three digestive biscuits quickly and a slice of bread and honey, and she still felt fine. So perhaps it was all right after all. She awarded herself a small salt spoon of Malcolm's coke in celebration and put the kettle on for tea. Alec and Vivien were both surprisingly stuffy about coke, for supposedly liberated sixties people. But talc or no talc, it certainly set you up for the morning.

There were three letters set out for her by Vivien on the kitchen table. One from her mother, one from her father and one from Michaela.

Dearest R,

Daddy says I can come to the RGP this year. Isn't it exciting? Hats! Do you suppose I can net myself an HRH?!! There's still a few that aren't married, aren't there?

M and P positively flipped over H's resits but she says she doesn't care and she can do the Montessori course anyway without silly maths! The aged P keeps going on about you living in a den of vice. All those stories in Dempster. M says it was *his* idea for you to go there in the first place. Sounds more fun to me than bleedin' Berks anyway!

Labby preggers again. Positively *last time* according to M. Rolly lost a shoe on the first draw last Sat, and H got back before we'd even finished breks, swearing like the Princess Royal.

Must dash now. Ghastly Gordon for tea. Told P that I quite fancy Linley and he said no daughter of his would marry a chippy!

Much love, M.

Why did her sisters always write as if they were working for MI5, Rachel wondered. She opened the letter from her father, which was in one of the stiff little yellow envelopes, with the House of Commons waffle iron stamped on it.

Dear Rachel,

I am most surprised to learn that you find yourself short of funds. As I make up your income to the level of the full State grant, you must be better off than many of your colleagues. I discussed the matter thoroughly with your mother and we both agreed it would be better for you to make do for the remainder of this term, and perhaps to look for some employment during the Long Vacation, as I myself was obliged to do in university days.

Of course we do not wish you to go short of necessities. However, you managed to get into your present predicament and I have agreed with your mother that she should send you some wholesome provisions if that would be of any assistance. No Mars Bars!

I shall be visiting Wykeham on the 12th, and look forward to seeing you then. I shall be spending most of the day in meetings with the Vice-Chancellor and Senate, but perhaps you could arrange for us to have tea somewhere pleasant? Until then,

Love, Daddy.

It would have made a fine departmental memo, she

thought, lacking only the list of 'copies circulated' at the bottom. The letter from her mother contained a £50 note and a Royal Academy postcard written in swooping violet ink.

Darling,

 Don't breathe a word to Daddy but I managed to embezzle a few pounds from the HKP. Fill him up with buttery crumpets and sticky eclairs when he comes to Wykeham and he might become more mellow.

Your ever loving, Mummy.

It was very sweet of her, of course, because Daddy was very careful over the housekeeping, and bound to find out sooner or later. But she wished that she had not mentioned the crumpets and eclairs. With a hand over her mouth, Rachel fled to the bathroom.

Malcolm's fingers pattered.

'Trotskyist lecturers who have lain dormant – "scholastic sleepers" – within the academic community for twenty years are now "seizing the time", as militant Black Panther leader Bobby Seale urged that they should.'

Malcolm knew that nobody who read the paper would know who the fuck Bobby Seale was. Verbena Vallance had warned him against that sort of thing. But he liked the bit about 'seize the time'. The headline writers would be bound to pick that up. Nothing they liked better than a resounding cliché, unless it was a plonking alliteration: 'Scholastic Sleepers Seize the Time,' they would probably go for. He decided to leave Bobby Seale alone. Everybody, more or less, knew that the Black Panthers were baddies.

Malcolm was enjoying his new career. He had his own picture now and his own eighteen-point byline: 'Special Education Correspondent Malcolm MacIntyre: In the Crazy World of the Campus, a Still Small Voice of Reason'. He had asked for twenty-point, but Verbena said it would come with time.

It was so easy too. They never wanted any facts; they never asked him to attribute any quotes. They hadn't even sent a photographer down yet. They were just using old library pics from Warwick and East Anglia. Malcolm's fingers pattered.

The unrest at Wykeham is centred around radical government proposals to rationalize runaway spending on wasteful sixties universities, and to form new alliances between academe and industry, which, the militants say, will interfere with academic freedoms.

The subversive elements have produced plans to rename colleges of the university after Marxist revolutionaries and to vet purchasing of library books that contain what they describe as capitalist dogma and heterosexist ideology.

Self-confessed radical feminist lecturer Vivien Dawes has been at the centre of another major row over her use of English literature lectures as a vehicle for political propaganda.

Moderate students have protested to the authorities over her exploitation of her privileged position for attacks on subjects as diverse as the Christian faith, the British Empire and private health care.

According to students 'Ms' Dawes has regularly dismissed the entire Great Tradition of English letters – of universally revered writers like Dickens, Conrad, James and Joyce – as 'a male sexist conspiracy'. She has forbidden students to attend the lectures of 'reactionary' colleagues and she has not hesitated to use her own lectures as a platform to attack the present government for imposing what she describes as 'a grey dystopia, run by power worshippers'.

Malcolm wondered for a moment what Vivien would think of this, then as swiftly dismissed the compunction. She certainly owed him one anyway. He thought of the time when they were living together at Uplands and she was playing around with her eternal bloody thesis and he was bringing home the bacon. Growing vegetables to help stretch out the grant, cooking them decent meals, trying to lay the foundations of a proper family life. She'd probably never have *got* her doctorate if it hadn't been for him. Or her bloody tenure for life.

Malcolm's mother wasn't right about many things, but she had been right about Vivien. Why was he throwing himself away on this girl, she used to ask. Why was he helping with *her* career? Why wasn't he fulfilling his own potential, in law school, or publishing, or the BBC? Vivien owed him. And she would never read it in any case.

Dawes is also known as a close associate of another 'scholastic sleeper' – sixties student leader Alec Smith, publisher of the notorious *Republican Reader*. Smith has recently returned to the area, together with other former student agitators from as far afield as Paris and Amsterdam. He is now a familiar figure on campus – frequently as the companion of Rachel Wilson, daughter of the Education Secretary, Ronald Wilson, and a student of Dawes's.

The Department of Education and Science has failed to confirm or deny reports that Wykeham is now a candidate for closure or merger. But sources close to the Education Secretary say he is now 'extremely concerned', both by his daughter's new comrades and by the swelling tide of militancy and disruption. The same sources confirm that he is observing the situation closely, and is expected to pay an emergency visit to the campus in the next few weeks.

Malcolm took another swig of Grolsch and read through the article again. Some of the details would need filling in later. But the general tone was all right and, so far as libel was concerned, it looked pretty fireproof to him. He decided to throw in a few more conditional verbs and 'allegeds' in any case, just to be on the safe side.

The monitor light glowed, the cooling fans whirred, the keys pattered and the glowing blob of the cursor shuttled, weaving together the spiky patterns of words. To and fro. To and fro. To and fro.

'I need to borrow £300,' said Rachel. 'To buy a motor bike.'

Vivien set down the Ellmann biography of Oscar Wilde, parallel to the edge of her desk, and put on her spectacles.

Rachel was standing, unsurely, on the threshold of her study. The door behind her, into the corridor, was still ajar, as if she had taken a while to decide whether to come in and was already half sorry that she had.

She looked awful. Her blonde hair was greasy and stuck to her neck; there was a ripe spot on her chin, smudged over with brown foundation. She'd put on weight lately and her face looked waterlogged around the eyes and jaw. All those sweets.

'Tutors don't normally act as bankers for their students,' Vivien told her, 'and neither do landladies for their tenants.'

'I've already got an overdraft,' said Rachel, 'and I've paid your rent to the end of term. That's partly why I'm so broke.'

'You could ask your parents. You could ask Alec for that matter. Alec has got money coming out of his ears. Why me?'

'Because I thought we were friends.'

'I thought at one time we were rather more than friends.' Just a minute, cancel that remark, she thought. But a flicker of superiority had already passed over Rachel's face.

When Rachel had moved in with her Vivien had made several resolutions to the effect that if anything *happened*, that was going to be up to Rachel. She was not about to start making passes at her students. She wasn't even sure that she liked that sort of thing in the first place. But she still found herself irritated with her own irritation when nothing had happened at all.

There had been that first kiss in the street, of course, and one or two others that had more than a hint of tongue about them. Rachel had wandered into the bathroom now and then, and even soaped her back for her. A week after her arrival, when Vivien was almost asleep, the bedroom door had opened and there had been a whisper of bare feet on the carpet and a sudden weight in the bed beside her. Rachel, in a cotton nightgown, and cold as a trout.

They had said nothing at all to each other. Their breathing, unsynchronized, had seemed absurdly loud; the bed had creaked and Vivien had felt her backbone tight as wire. Did she reach out and pat the thigh which she could sense, an inch from the back of her own? Did she pull one of those chilly hands that brushed her shoulder blade over to her breast? She felt no desire at all, only a need to do something. She did nothing.

Vivien had lain there in silence, for half an hour or so, gradually feeling the cold weight in the bed behind her grow warmer and softer, and the breathing grow deeper and pucker into little adenoidal rattles and gruntings. Eventually she realized she was alone in the room. Rachel was snoring.

She put up with it for another hour; her own pulse running quickly and mind too busy for sleep. And then she had got out of bed and made herself some tea and toast in the kitchen, and spent the night in Rachel's bed, in the spare room, with the rather squashy mattress, breathing in the smell of drying emulsion paint and Camay soap.

'My father doesn't really approve of grants and parental contributions at all,' said Rachel now, finally closing the study door behind her. 'He thinks that students should have to take out loans. He's always telling me and my sisters how when he was at St Andrews he spent the summers working on the shipyards.'

'When there were still shipyards,' said Vivien. 'The miserable bastard. He must be on £60,000 a year. Does he tell your sisters they should have to pay for their horses with loans as well?'

'No.'

'I bet he doesn't. Mind you, it will be jolly nice for the government when everybody is on loans. Then all the students will have to do Business Admin degrees, and go and get jobs with Price Waterhouse when they graduate, and spend their careers sequestrating union funds and surcharging local councillors.

'The really rich ones will still be able to do Arts degrees, of course. You'll need a few of those to run the Courtauld and the Summer Exhibition and the Royal Opera and Glyndebourne. And you'll have to replace the Catholic novelists, and the snob travel writers, as they pop off. Just enough to supply a drip-feed of middle-brow conservative culture, and to reassure people like your father that he isn't a total fucking barbarian.'

The speech made Vivien feel better, restored a little of her slipping ascendancy. She unzipped her sleek black leather shoulderbag, and removed the Coutts chequebook. 'There are only three conditions. One, you pay it back on the first day of the Autumn term. Two, you do not tell anyone else where you got the money. Three, you buy the most expensive helmet there is.'

'It will only be a moped,' said Rachel. 'Just a way of getting to and from the university now I'm living out.'

'And to and from Uplands, no doubt,' said Vivien grimly, as she handed over the cheque. 'Get the helmet anyway.'

'My father's not that bad, you know,' said Rachel. 'I think it's just that making your own way in the world seems to affect people in different ways. You either feel sorry for everyone else who hasn't made it too or you despise them for not having the gumption. He's actually quite a sweet man when he's not being a Cabinet Minister. Quite funny.'

'Was he ever "funny" with you?' said Vivien.

'I don't understand.'

'You understand me perfectly well.'

'That's none of your business.'

'So he was, then.'

There were red blotches on Rachel's neck and her head was down. Her fingers were rolling the cheque into a tight tube, thinner than a cigarette.

'That's ridiculous. You've got absolutely no . . . You can't . . .'

Vivien stood up from her desk and freed her damp blouse from the small of her back. 'Look, I've been personal tutor to a hundred-odd young women in the last twelve years, and

I've taught God knows how many thousands. One in ten belongs to a certain type. They're clever. They have a washed-out, downtrodden mummy they never mention. They have a pumped-up, powerful daddy they mention all the time. They often came here somewhat against his wishes. They form haphazard, promiscuous relationships with unsuitable people.'

She was standing at her study window, looking down at the sunbathers on the hard yellow lawns. Immediately below, among a scatter of Faber poetry books, a brown boy in cut-off Levis was rubbing oil into the back of a girl wearing nothing at all but a white bikini bottom. Eden on the rates.

'As I say, they're about one in ten, and I reckon on a ten-to-one chance that if daddy hasn't actually had his hand up their skirts, it wasn't for want of trying.'

Rachel was looking furious by now, her spot even redder and her eyes full of tears. 'I'm sure my father would be interested to hear these fantastic speculations of yours.'

'I'd be delighted to meet him,' said Vivien levelly. 'I gather he's going to be visiting us soon.'

There was a long silence. Adam and Eve downstairs had pulled on t-shirts and were collecting their books together. The library clock was striking eleven, which meant one. There was a hostile edge to Rachel's voice when she finally replied:

'These "haphazard, promiscuous relationships with unsuitable people,"' she said. 'Does that include you?'

'Yes,' said Vivien sadly, 'I'm afraid that it does.'

She found him asleep in the stifling attic bedroom at Uplands. His knees were drawn up to his chest and there was a dribble of wine on the single sheet that covered his body. Moist black curls were plastered to his forehead. His breath smelled of rusty iron and he hadn't shaved for days. She noticed, tenderly, that the patches of stubble on either side of his mouth were silver grey.

She undressed quickly and climbed into the bed behind him, moulding herself to the shape of his back. After ten minutes or so the texture of his skin began to change, from damp and slack to warm and elastic, and she knew that he was awake.

'There's a hole in your roof,' she told him.

'Hello,' said Alec. 'I'm hiding from the world.'

'It's an enormous hole.'

'I know. The world's trying to break in and get me.'

Lewis had made the hole on Wednesday, to take out the rusty steel water tank from the loft. He had stripped off half the old Welsh slates, thick as tortoise shells and burnished gold with lichen, and thrown them down in the driveway, where they had shattered. He had sawn through four of the roof timbers, and then slid the heavy tank down the slates, tearing off the rain gutter on its way, bouncing in the bed of dwarf azaleas and then rolling into the drive, where it still rested. Alec had found it there when he drove back from London on Wednesday night and smashed into it with the front offside wing of the Audi Quattro.

'What should Lewis have done with it?' asked Rachel.

'What anyone with half a brain would have done. Cut it up and carried it out down the stairs.'

'What did you do to Lewis?'

'I haven't seen him yet. Mr Truss says he has another commitment in Herne Bay.'

'And what about William?'

Alec told her about his day in London. About seeing Dr Dougal, about getting drunk, about arriving home and finding William and Susan. He only left out the bit about St Barnabas's Hospital.

'I suppose there was a terrible scene.'

'Not really. William trod on a wine glass when he jumped out of bed, so we spent most of the time bandaging his foot and trying to get the blood out of the stair carpet. It was the most awful mess. Susan and I started giggling. It was William who was angry in the end. He'd managed to get cat shit on my dressing gown as well, so that was all over the sofa. Perhaps they'd been doing it in the cat tray.'

'You weren't angry?'

'I don't know. I pretended to be a bit. I was actually quite relieved. I'd been going to tell Susan about you, and how I didn't really want her to move down here any more. So at least there wasn't any need for that.'

'But you won't be friends with William now,' said Rachel.

'Oh yes, that's all right. He's coming down next week with some furniture. All of this has happened before, you see. William used to sleep with Susan long before I knew her, and a bit afterwards as a matter of fact. I think that's why Susan is generally so nasty about William. She's always fancied him more than me.'

'Can't think why,' said Rachel, running a hand luxuriously through the damp mat of his chest hair.

'I haven't had a bath in three days,' said Alec.

'I know. You smell like an old tomcat.'

She pushed back the sheet that covered them and straddled him, brushing her breasts softly over his face and chest and groin. He groaned happily, and began to run his hands, paper light, down the arrowhead of her back, teasing into the cleft of her buttocks, smoothing down the insides of her thighs. Back and fore in light, long, body-long strokes as she swayed above him, licking the saltiness of his collar bone; the triangle of her tongue and nipples drifting and grazing, hardly touching, then pressing and burning, then drifting.

It had become ritual by now, this clasping and stroking and swaying. He didn't understand how he could be so aroused, and so unaroused, but he knew that he was learning something new. His genitals mysteriously uncoupled from his lust, he had become half woman.

He was full of her smell and feel. Sitting in a pub or car his skin would goosepimple to the touch of her hand and at once he would want her naked. Greedily he swallowed her body with his mouth and eyes and hands. He never became tired of it. Making love with Susan, they copulated, cuddled, lay still and slept. But this was addiction. Always wanting more skin, more contour, more taste, more smell. Sometimes she demanded her orgasm, and his tongue and fingers had become clever. But more often it was this slow, luxurious clasping and unclasping, stroking and smoothing, drifting, grazing, burning.

'I don't know how you can be so *flat* about it all,' she said later, still lying on top of him. 'Your best friend in bed with your wife. I mean, Susan must have arranged things so you would find them like that.'

'It was all those sixties orgies we were always having,' said Alec, his voice muffled between her breasts. 'Got rid of our sexual hang-ups, you see. That's how come I'm such a great stud these days.'

'Oh, shut up. I keep telling you. I've gone right off sex. I don't want to be *screwed* at the moment.'

Skrud. He loved the way she wrapped her tongue so awkwardly around those words. Like an American saying 'bastard', it never sounded quite right. Lazily, his mouth abandoned one swollen, glistening nipple to search for its partner, which was showing sad signs of detumescence, but she pulled herself away.

'Did you really have orgies?' *Awjiz.*

'No. Well, yes, I suppose we did, once. Though it was hardly *Satyricon*.'

'Tell me.'

'You're a dirty little swine, Wilson. Underneath the alabaster skin and Bambi eyes, a seething cauldron of unnatural lusts and warped . . . Ouch. That hurt.'

'Tell me.'

Reluctantly, he peeled his perspiring body away from hers and lay back, his arms behind his head.

It was twenty years ago today. Or very nearly.

Susan was sitting opposite him in jeans and nothing else, smoking a cigarette probably. Everybody smoked then. Alec used to drive to get the cigarettes in his car. It was the old Rover that Harry had given him, with the dope seedlings growing in a tray in the back window, so you always had to try and park it in the sunshine.

The cigarettes used to come 1,000 at a time from the newsagent in Wincheap who did discounts. And he used to get the Tampax there as well, in those enormous boxes like cornflakes; 200 a box, because every women in Uplands seemed to menstruate simultaneously, like nuns. Apart from Vivien, who had abolished menstruation.

The sitting-room was full of smoke, anyway, and dirty plates, and six or seven tripping people, sitting on sag bags and on the carpet. Susan, Alec, William, Malcolm, Daisy, Alison. William was doing his lotus position. He was learning yoga, he told Daisy, so that he could suck himself off. Alec had been too stoned to play really and was down to his t-shirt, and Daisy was down to nothing.

Alec: 'Window.'
William: 'Pane.'
Susan: 'Malcolm.'
Daisy: 'Um . . .'
Malcolm: 'Oh, fuck off, Susan. She hasn't got anything else to take off.'

'What about your diaphragm, Daisy?' said Susan. 'Daisy's always got her diaphragm in, just in case, haven't you, dear?'

'Susan,' said Alec, 'why don't you . . .'

'I was talking to Daisy,' said Susan. 'You could take off your hearing aid, couldn't you, Daisy? Yes, that's right dear, HEARING AID.'

She had started miming sign language then, which had made William snigger, which was pretty shitty, because he was supposed to be with Daisy. And then Daisy had started crying and gone off to the kitchen to be sick, and Alec had taken her downstairs to the flat and put her to bed.

She'd been nice, Daisy. Plump and warm and pink, like a sugar mouse, even if she did smell a bit sicky. Someone had told him she was married to a judge now. She had asked him to stay with her and he had lain down, awkwardly for a while, on the counterpane, and then she had told him he could get in with her if he wanted. And he had, only it hadn't been any good, not that Daisy had noticed.

It hadn't been any good for a while. Because even then, when he was twenty, there were times when it all went wrong. It would be all right for a while, and then not, and Susan would be patient, or not. She was impatient that night, and very faraway on Malcolm's acid, with her face very pale and her eyes very bright. She was looking at William all through the tennis-elbow-foot game, and though William wasn't looking at her, you could see he knew.

So he had sat and smoked cigarettes in the kitchen for an hour or so after Daisy had fallen asleep, then gone upstairs. Susan and William had been quiet when he had climbed into bed with them and he had thought they were asleep, but they weren't. They had started moving again after a bit, and Susan had giggled in the darkness and said, 'Perhaps this will turn him on.'

Alec and Rachel lay, staring at the ceiling, with its tatters of wallpaper and tracery of ancient cracks.

'Was that it?' she asked.

'That was it,' he said. 'It was this room actually.' Then, after a long silence, 'Probably this bed.'

'Why do you think you did it?'

'It may have been voyeurism, I suppose. A cheap thrill, watching your best mate having it off with your girlfriend. Perhaps I was punishing myself for not being very good in bed with Susan. Perhaps I secretly fancy William. Fuck knows. I stayed with them for a while, anyway, but they weren't very interested in me. It all got a bit embarrassing. So I just went off for a ride on Malcolm's motorbike, off up the A2 on my own, with the sun coming up and feeling really rather happy. That was my orgy.'

Rachel filled a bath for them, emptying half a bottle of bubbles into it, and they sat together in the gritty iron tub, up to their necks in warm suds, with her between his knees, his hands roving gently over the front of her slippery body as she lay back against his chest.

'You know, I really like you, Alec Smith. I like you more than anyone I can think of at this moment.'

'And I thought it was just my rampant member.'

'I'd like you to meet my father when he comes down this weekend. I'm going to take him to tea at the Eastgate. But you must shave,' she told him, nuzzling her wet cheek against his softening bristles. 'You're not to turn up looking like the richest tramp in Wykeham.'

'He'll hate me, you know. Left-wing spiv having his goatish way with his precious teenage daughter.'

'No, he won't. He likes people who have done things. Made their own way in the world.'

'Meaning people who have got lots of money,' said Alec.

They got dressed then, taking turns to dry each other, and Rachel made tea and found some Ryvitas and marmalade, and they picnicked, in towels, on the unmade bed.

'We look like Romans,' said Rachel.

'That wasn't all true, you know,' he told her then. 'I didn't really ride off up the A2 on the motorbike. I smashed it into the gatepost at the bottom of the drive. Broke two fingers.'

He showed her the two scarred fingertips on his left hand with their misshapen nails.

'You don't have to tell me everything if you don't want to,' said Rachel. And he knew that he didn't. It was a masculine thing, this urge to confess. The feeling that everything could be wiped out and made clean by acts of self-revelation. Women knew better than that, sensing perhaps that confessional was not just the end of one passage of life, but the beginning of others. There were no breaks, no absolutions and no purgations; just one muddied stream merging with another. But he went ahead and told her anyway.

'Me and Susan and William, lying here in this bed after the tennis-elbow-foot game. I didn't just lie there watching them that time. I wasn't just the voyeur. I let William do it to me as well. I let William fuck me.'

'Oh, Alec,' said Rachel, pressing the two scarred fingertips to her lips. 'Dear, sweet Alec.'

'You're quite right,' he said later. 'I am angry about Susan and William. I used to believe once that we were different from our parents. More tolerant. Less hung-up. All that. But I don't think so any more. We weren't all wonderfully liberated and guilt-free and wise then. There was always plenty of bitching and squabbling in this place when we all lived together. Always people storming out in tears and having it away on the quiet.'

'You've got marmalade on your chin.'

'You can't exorcize the past just by wanting to. You can't remake yourself just by an effort of will.'

'You don't believe that.'

'How do you know?' said Alec.

'Because all of that is exactly what I like about you.'

'Well, there is part of me wants to shove a wine glass down William's throat and stamp on Susan's face,' he said. 'I suppose the only reason I never have is that I'm thirty-nine years old and you don't make many new friends once you're over thirty.'

'There's me,' said Rachel.

'Yes,' said Alec. 'By some extraordinary, ridiculous, un-thinkable, miraculous, unbelievable and incredible fucking absurdity . . . there is you.'

CHAPTER THIRTEEN

From *The Republican Reader*:

We are members of the British Royal Family.
We are *never* tired and we all *love* hospitals.

> – Queen Mary to her son, Edward VIII

Alec took a taxi from Waterloo to St Barnabas's Hospital, his bowels watery with dread. He had left the British Rail breakfast untouched and spent the journey thinking about hospitals. All the hospitals he would visit in the years to come.

What would it be first, he wondered? Blood pressure perhaps, then something like gallstones, prostate, a touch of angina, the first heart attack. The week-long stay, then the month in hospital. Then the kind, bored faces of his own, middle-aged children through the cellophane of the oxygen tent. And then finally the shuffling, slippered, paper-skinned exit.

He felt old and frail already, braced in the back of the bucketing cab. London potholes multiplied in proportion to the city's wealth, it seemed. The landscape of council blocks and chain hotels along the Westway, which still seemed new to Alec, was already being demolished and replaced by childish buildings with brightly coloured rigging, like the tents of an occupying force. The Post Office Tower in Charlotte Street displayed its third new name; the Television Centre at White City its fourth. He flinched as a sports car knifed across the taxi's bows and horns howled.

The city which had once excited, now frightened him with its blares and squeals and shouts and shoulderings. Cars missing by inches and people by millimetres. All those London words for life: dodging and weaving; ducking and diving. The city was a massed orchestration of skids, swerves, near-misses and sometimes collisions.

He had left the Audi yesterday in a railway arch on the Ashford Road, in the charge of a pessimistic mechanic recommended by Mr Truss who circled warily around it, sucking his teeth and cracking pewter-coloured knuckles.

'Not so easy to come by, body spares for these foreign motors. Could be a few days.'

'It's an Audi,' said Alec, 'made by Volkswagen. Well-known German company. Largest volume car manufacturer in Europe.'

'It's still foreign.'

'*All* the cars in this country are foreign. What do you expect people to drive? Humber Snipes? Jowetts? Lanchesters?'

'*That* was a car,' said the mechanic wistfully. 'The Humber Snipe. Built like a tank. Not baco-foil, like these foreign things.' He booted the crumpled wing savagely and the chrome trim of the headlamp tinkled on to the ground. 'And you can't get the parts for them.'

'There's an Audi main dealer in Maidstone,' said Alec. 'Twenty miles away. Perhaps I'd better go there.'

'Dealers,' said the mechanic bitterly. 'Fitted carpets. Pot plants. Computers. They'll put three blokes with white coats on this and charge you a thousand quid. You don't want to mess about with dealers.'

'I want a proper job,' said Alec.

'Well, you've come to the right place.'

'And I need it by tomorrow evening.'

'I'll do my best, but I ain't promising nothing.' Reflectively, he booted the wing again and the unbroken indicator light fell out and shattered on the greasy cobbles of the forecourt.

*

The hospital was old, built of cinder-coloured brick, with high ladders of tiny window panes and loose parquet floors that rattled underfoot. Alec wandered through long, echoing corridors. Dirty cream walls scarred at waist height with the passage of trolleys. Sickening school smells, of Jeyes Fluid and steamed food.

There were metallic crashes in the distance, and shouts, and once or twice the sight of a nurse's uniform whisking through a faraway door. He studied clusters of bland signs: radiology, cytology, gynaecology, haematology, urology. Why didn't they use capital letters? Why didn't they use serifs? Too much like tombstones probably, or *Times* obituaries. This chummy, Postman Pat lettering was meant to reassure you, whereas in fact it terrified, by suggesting you were in the hands of sub-literate infants.

A yellow-faced woman patient in a candlewick dressing gown, smoking a cigarette, directed Alec to urology, and he followed the Postman Pat signs up stairs, along corridors, under buzzing strip lights on furry chains, past locked and empty wards. In urology he stopped a fat young doctor jogging along the corridor in Reebok trainers.

'Dr Ellis-Lloyd?' he panted.

'You want the Pahlavi clinic. First door on the left after the gents. Good luck, mate.' And he jogged off, with, Alec thought, a rather speculative backward glance at his groin.

It was a heavy, new-looking door in blond oak, with deeply moulded panels. No Postman Pat letters either but a chunky brass plate, etched in a cursive, mock Arabic script: 'Dr Evan Ellis-Lloyd, FRCS, CPT, Pahlavi Clinic, 1978.' The handle was brass as well. Massive, smooth and silent.

When he had opened the door and looked in, he took a step backwards for a moment, to stare up and down the corridor. The hospital was still there. The grimy cream walls. The buzzing lights. The crashing metal trolleys. A patient shuffling along in a tartan dressing gown and slippers. The receding figure of the jogging doctor.

He looked back inside the Pahlavi Clinic. The ceiling

must have been knocked through at some time into the ward above, because the roof soared up a full fifty feet, climaxing in a sunlit dome of richly coloured glass, depicting the vanquishing of Rustem by Sohrab.

The lofty walls were of polished, veal-coloured marble, patterned with geometric designs of a darker stone. Bokhara rugs shimmered on walls and floor; plangent chords of an unknown music filtered from concealed speakers; fountains played; carp swam in an onyx basin; the air was heavy with scent of sandalwood and crushed rose petals. A dusky nymph in a pure-white sari, clasped at one shoulder and with nothing underneath, drifted towards him from the direction of a small grove of flowering camellias.

'I am Staff Nurse Patel,' said the nymph. 'You have an appointment with Dr Ellis-Lloyd?'

He sat in the waiting room among the plashing fountains and tinkling chords, reading a copy of *Forbes* magazine and avoiding the eyes of three or four dark-skinned men, all similarly employed. They had all, he noticed, crossed their left leg over their right. He uncrossed his legs and began studying a consumer report on the Gulfstream executive jet. When he looked up again, five minutes later, the other men had uncrossed their legs.

'The doctor will see you now.'

He followed the triangle of smooth brown shoulder into a small chamber of marble and gilt, furnished with a silk upholstered divan, a kidney-shaped marble desk and a tapestry screen of scenes from the *Rubaiyat*. From behind the screen there emerged the sounds of running water and eventually a small, red-haired man in his thirties, with damp and freckled forearms. He was wearing a white linen tunic over black pyjama trousers, with black canvas espadrilles on his bare feet. The effect was half medical, half clerical; an impression he immediately dispelled by patting Staff Nurse Patel on her shapely rump.

'Five minutes, please, love, and then bring in the tray.'

She left with a rustle of silk and a lingering smile over her shoulder. 'Smashing girl,' said Ellis-Lloyd. 'Rescued her from the bed pan and the enema pump.' He turned his attention to his desk, which was empty apart from an onyx and gold telephone and a thin sheaf of medical notes in a burgundy leather folder, stamped with the same gilt, cursive script as the brass plate on the door.

'I wondered when I saw your name,' said Ellis-Lloyd. 'Are you the Alec Smith who . . .?'

'Yes,' said Alec.

'Smashing book. Great. Laugh! You were on *Question Time* a while back as well.'

'*Any Questions*,' said Alec. 'That's right.'

'Absolute discretion, of course,' said Ellis-Lloyd. 'The newspapers would pay millions for the names of some of the people who have lain on that couch.'

'I'm not ashamed that I . . .'

'Of course you're not, man. And no reason to be. But not everyone has your sensible attitude. Politicians. Film stars. Royalty. Pop singers. That one with the leather trousers. Always on *The Tube*. What was his name . . .?'

'I wondered when I saw your name,' said Alec, gesturing to the burgundy folder, 'what the CPT stood for.'

'Companion to the Peacock Throne,' said Ellis-Lloyd proudly. 'One of our many satisfied customers. Though of course we had to wait for him to . . . ah . . . *go* before we could use the name. We do a lot of foreign trade. Keeps us afloat, see, through all these cutbacks. In fact you must be the first Anglo-Saxon I've seen since Easter, or should I say Ramadan. Ha, ha.'

'You get Muslim patients?'

'Nothing against it in the Koran,' said Ellis-Lloyd, glancing nervously towards his waiting-room, 'but why don't we just keep off theology altogether, and you tell me about this little problem of yours.'

Alec began the familiar recital. The long adolescence; the timidity; the early, unsuccessful encounters; meeting Susan and things being all right, then not all right. He noticed after a minute or two that Ellis-Lloyd was drawing a line of fat red rabbits on his prescription pad and swinging an espadrille to and fro beneath his desk.

'I don't know if this is what you wanted to . . .'

'No, no, you're doing great, man. Smashing. Getting the picture perfectly. A classic history. Standard pattern of minor dysfunction amplified through compulsion-introversion. Nothing at all we can't deal with. Do you mind if we talk about money?'

The clinic had considerable overheads, Ellis-Lloyd explained. Pioneering medical techniques; making its own contribution to the hospital budget. Purchasing of new and expensive drugs and equipment. Specialized training of staff. 'My charges are therefore £200 a consultation, and we require patients to contract for a minimum course of five consultations, payable in advance.'

There was an expectant pause.

'You want me to give you £1,000?' said Alec.

'Yes.'

'What, now?'

'Yes.'

He had never actually put money in a doctor's hand before. It seemed vaguely indecent, like publicly bribing a policeman, but there didn't seem much point in going back now. He reached for his chequebook.

'Shall I make it out to the hospital or the clinic?'

'Organic Developments Ltd, please,' said Ellis-Lloyd. 'Just our little joke.'

'There are psychological approaches, of course,' said Ellis-Lloyd, when he had tucked the cheque into the burgundy folder. 'Counselling, sex therapy, group therapy, deep analysis even, if you want. Unpredictable results, though, and a lengthy business. And we are all busy men, are we not?' He smiled conspiratorially. 'Personally, I'm an intervention man. Don't mess about. Get straight to the root of the problem. And what is the root of the problem? Piece of tissue won't perform its proper biological function. So we make sure that it will.

'There are various techniques. Device which fits over the penis with a vacuum pump attachment. Quite effective, but not very suitable for the casual romantic encounter, right? More permanent solution: a surgically implanted prosthesis connected to a fluid reservoir operated by a small pump in the scrotum. But that's really for the old boys. Clapped-out vascular system and the neurones shot to pieces with booze and fags. In your case I think we are looking at something less dramatic. Injection with a mild muscle relaxant, paparavine derivative, providing a reliable erection for three or four hours. You can even learn to do it yourself. Take a pack of syringes and bottle home. Keep it in the fridge. We find in most cases that it becomes unnecessary after three or four injections. The psychological log jam is broken, see? Confidence restored. And the injection is always there as a kind of psychological crutch if you think you need it. Right?'

'Er, right,' said Alec.

'Smashing,' said Ellis-Lloyd. 'Nurse!'

Deft brown fingers unzipped his flies and swabbed his penis with an antiseptic gauze pad, while Ellis-Lloyd loaded a large syringe from an unlabelled bottle.

'This . . . stuff,' said Alec. 'It's all properly tested – and so on?'

'Fully licensed in France and Switzerland,' said Ellis-Lloyd, 'and widely used for anti-spasmodic treatments in this country.'

'Have you ever tried it yourself?' asked Alec.

'Only once,' said Ellis-Lloyd, with a wink, and Nurse Patel giggled.

'I didn't think you were going to do anything to me straight away,' said Alec anxiously. 'I mean, I've got a train to catch this afternoon. A four o'clock appointment.'

'Can't you cancel it?'

'I'm having tea with the Secretary of State for Education.'

Ellis-Lloyd looked unimpressed. For one accustomed to leather-trousered pop singers and detumescent royalty, a secretary of state evidently counted for little.

'Then wear a tight pair of pants,' he advised, 'and you'll be all right.'

Alec flinched as the gleaming steel needle sank into the side of his shrivelled organ. The fluid reservoir fell in the syringe and a cool numbness spread through his tissue. 'There seems to be an awful lot of it,' he said faintly.

'Might get away with less,' said Ellis-Lloyd, 'varies with body weight. But as it's the first time we like to be sure. It'll start to work in about fifteen minutes, and it should wear off completely in five hours or so.' He looked at his watch. 'That's around six this evening. Any problems, you can give me a ring. I'll see you the same time next week. Try and make the most of it.' And he winked again.

In the gents lavatory next door Alec examined his penis. There was a faint red dot where the needle had entered. It was still flaccid, but distinctly larger. And the cool numbness had become warmer; a tingling sensation that suffused his testicles and groin. He poked it experimentally with a forefinger and the head nodded upwards a fraction of an inch. Perhaps it really did work.

Unconsciously, he had taken a step back from the urinal, and he suddenly became aware that a male nurse in a white Nehru tunic was regarding him with interest from another stall. Peculiar bloke waving his willy about in the middle of the bogs. Alec wiped the wondering expression from his face and replaced it with the traditionally businesslike and eyes-front demeanour of man-peeing. He stuffed the organ, which was becoming increasingly springy, back inside his boxer shorts.

'Haven't seen you around here before,' said the nurse, lingeringly.

'No you haven't,' said Alec, and made for the door.

By the time he was standing in the taxi queue outside the hospital car park it was a quite definite erection, nosing its way below the hem of his boxer shorts. With his hand in his trouser pocket, he surreptitiously eased it to a transverse position, and buttoned his suit jacket. As he did so a white Porsche Carrera pulled up and a smoked glass window whirred down. 'Any signs of life down below yet?' shouted Dr Ellis-Lloyd.

The other members of the taxi queue examined Alec's lower half curiously for clues to this gnomic question.

'Er, yes. Looks quite promising.'

'Smashing. Now don't waste it, man. It's a long time to next week.'

And with a scrunch of fat radials the Carrera was gone. There had scarcely been time to catch a glimpse of Staff Nurse Patel's naked brown shoulder in the passenger seat, but there had been long enough.

It was strange, he thought in the taxi, that a horny brain could not produce a hard-on but that it worked the other way around. He had not had so much as a wisp of a sexual thought since going to bed with Rachel the day before yesterday, and yet suddenly, here was his brain, teeming with images of concupiscence.

The injection, as Ellis-Lloyd had explained, was not an aphrodisiac. It produced only a physical reflex: relaxing the vascular muscles and flooding the spongy tissues of the penis with blood. So why were the streets of West London suddenly filled with girls in filmy summer dresses; tender navels in brown midriffs; straining nipples in cotton t-shirts; gauzy skirts, breeze-blown around brown thighs and moulded into pelvic vees? Why was every poster filled with skin and lip and curve? Every image and building and scent headily redolent of sex?

He sat back in the friendly diesel throb of the cab, cradling his erection proudly across his lap like a sabre. The great council blocks of the Westway looked less bleak and ominous to Alec now. The vivid blue and green exo-skeletons of new building looked playful and cheery. A fertile, youthful new city, springing into being. The red sports cars knifing past in the fast lane were boys' toys to Alec Smith. The Post Office Tower seemed to nod respectfully to him from the skyline.

He felt powerful, restored. And he thought bitterly of all the months, all the years of anxiety and misery and shame. And all fixed. One little prick! For a moment he even contemplated an act of treachery in Greek Street with the miserable Melanie, or better still, the cheerful Woolwich. He could, perhaps, with a certain amount of tact, even donate his hard-on to Susan. But at once he scolded himself for the idea. A hard-on has no principles, but this hard-on was for Rachel. She deserved this hard on.

And he deserved Rachel. All those hours of stroking and rubbing. Teasing, tickling, drifting, burning. All those loyally administered orgasms, slogging away down below with thumb and tongue. It was nice, of course. Even wonderful at times, yes. A new experience. An erotic concerto of unfulfilment which had revealed to him new nerve endings, new sensitivities, a new languorousness and luxury in the flesh. Voluptuous horizons of tender deferment. All that stuff. But it wasn't the *business*, was it? It wasn't, quite, ever, the *real thing*. And let's be honest. Was it not sometimes, just sometimes, a little dutiful, a little bit *boring*?

If he could just get his hard-on to Rachel in time. Anxiously he planned the race across the country with his perishable cargo. Half an hour before he could get it to Waterloo and load it on to the train. Another hour and a half to transport it to Wykeham station. Get the car for it. Drive it to this bloody tea with Rachel's father. That couldn't last more than an hour, could it? That would take it to five o'clock. Just enough time. He prayed the mysterious chemical arithmetic of Ellis-Lloyd's magic injection was reliable.

In the Sock Shop at Waterloo he bought the tightest underpants he could find: a red nylon bikini brief for £1.50, and hobbled back across the station concourse to the gents lavatory. Locked securely in a cubicle he took off his trousers and examined himself with mingled awe and glee. The stuff was amazing. A good 45 degrees up from the horizontal and, he could swear, an inch longer than he'd ever seen it before. It twanged triumphantly erect when he tried to force it down between his legs. It struggled like a jolly puppy when he tried to restrain it in the nylon sausage skin of the underpants: popping boisterously out of the leg-hole, peeping cheekily over the waistband.

He took off his tie and tried strapping it to his leg, but found it was now impossible to stand upright. Eventually he managed to entangle it in his shirt tails and to wedge it sideways through one leg of the pants. That would have to do.

He was running with sweat by the time he boarded the train. He bought two cans of warm lager from the buffet bar and drank one straight off. Clutching his jacket shut in front of him, he shuffled to an empty section in first class where no one was likely to join him. And it was only as the train actually pulled out from Waterloo that the two teenage girls, demanded by the spirit of tragic irony, came and sat down in the seats opposite him.

On any ordinary train journey, of course, the girls would have been fat and plain, with straining stone-washed denims and outsized t-shirts stencilled with tediously jocular slogans. They would have eaten crisps and read horoscopes and possibly listened to fizzing personal stereos. But as it was this particular journey the spirit of tragic irony had provided them with tenderly lovely faces and shining bobbed hair and sweetly lissom bodies squeezed into the impossibly brief, second-time-around mini-skirts, to which, in the fifteen years since the first time around, Alec had entirely lost his acquired immunity.

It was very hot in the carriage. There was something wrong with the heater beneath the seat and it was blowing a furnace breath over his lower legs. The hard-on seemed to have got bigger since Waterloo. It was hot as a poker, trying to burn its way through the material of his pocket in a bid for freedom. Moisture trickled down the backs of his legs in their itchy woollen trousering. His crotch was a scalding tangle of elasticated nylon, shirt tail and tumescent tissue, smouldering beneath two layers of tweed suiting like an atomic pile, threatening to go critical. He laid a copy of the *Independent* across his lap, and one of the girls whispered something to the other, who giggled.

By the outskirts of London Alec had ravaged them both twice, across the seat, on the floor, against the window and in the luggage rack above his head. They had declared themselves his sex slaves for life and he had agreed to let them live in the basement of Uplands, now fitted-out with water beds, bondage apparatus and a docile eunuch, who rather resembled William. He drank his second can of lager.

By Orpington he needed to go to the lavatory badly, and by Sevenoaks there was no choice in the matter. An urgent, undeniable cry. Stiffly, he hauled himself upright, and sidled down the gangway, Quasimodo-like, clutching the newspaper to his groin. A ripple of girlish giggles followed him down the train.

With the lavatory door shut behind him he stripped off his jacket and wringing shirt. The hard-on bounced gleefully from his trousers, bigger than ever, and very red. Its veins were swollen like hawsers and there seemed to be a swelling near the end behind the head, giving it a ferocious, knotty appearance like a cartoon caveman's club.

The problem was how to pee. The organ had fixed its beady monocular gaze upon the ceiling. He tried a high trajectory at first, standing well back from the lavatory bowl. But the train was rocking too much and he had sprinkled the roller towel, the mirror and the complimentary tablet of Network South East soap before, with a massive effort of will, he could clench his sphincter muscle and stem the arcing stream.

Pouring with sweat in the tiny space, he mopped the

grimy floor with a handful of tissues, then tried again, crouching low over the bowl, but it was fixed too close to the wall to allow him to bend properly. The situation was becoming desperate. With his trousers around his ankles and his fist clawing at the now leaking organ, he shuffled to and fro, like a caged panda, casting about desperately for possibilities.

He contemplated pissing out of the window, he pondered the washbasin, he considered the ashtray. Furiously, he plotted angles, calculated trajectories, but everywhere he looked, damnable geometry confounded him. Somebody outside was rapping at the door and there were voices in the corridor. 'Is everything all right in there, sir?' The ticket collector.

'Just be a minute.' He pinched his organ hard but it was not to be quelled now. It was going to piss into the light bulb or burst. At last, with a flash of enlightenment, he saw that by standing astride the toilet bowl, and leaning forward against the door opposite, he could perhaps manage to aim the thing downwards.

His organ dribbling greedily in anticipation now, he scrambled out of his trousers and underpants, straddled the pan, and with a sob of relief lunged forwards into the arms of the ticket collector. There was a piercing scream from one of his two sex slaves, who were waiting in the corridor outside. There was a gentle, cosmic titter from the spirit of tragic irony. Alec Smith had forgotten to lock the lavatory door.

When he peed at last, it was a powerful amber parabola, his face lifted to the sun in gratitude, among the dock leaves and nettles, behind a Skol hoarding at Wykeham station.

The ticket collector had been quite decent really, in spite of those stupid girls screaming. Just a 'bit more careful in future ... sir'. Why did girls always go to the lavatory together anyway? And hadn't they ever seen a naked man before? Well, perhaps not a naked man with his shoes and socks on, sprawling across the floor of a train and sporting an eight-inch erection.

Wincing but spent, he levered himself back inside his damp tweeds, and limped to the taxi rank. Four-fifteen. He was going to be half an hour late for tea with Rachel and her father, and there were only ninety minutes left before detumescence.

At the railway arch garage he found the scarlet Audi in the forecourt, its wing repaired with fibreglass which had flopped slightly over the headlamp, giving the car a lewd, drunken appearance. The repair had been hazily resprayed the colour of tomato soup and a fine dusting of the same colour decorated the bumper and headlamp glass. Several greenfly were embedded in the fresh paintwork, through which the crosshatching of the rubbing down was still visible.

Inside the car black fingerprints covered the cream head lining of the roof, sun visors and the stitched-leather wheel cover. On the floor was a paper mat printed with two stylized footprints and the words, 'For Your Hygiene and Convenience'. According to the mileometer, Alec noted, his car had managed to cover 247 miles between the forecourt and the inspection pit of the garage. The bill came to £370.

'Everything all right, sir?' said the mechanic.

'Give me the fucking keys,' said Alec.

He hardly noticed the tea at the Eastgate, or Rachel's father. A sallow man with a Foreign Office slashback and a pilled polyester collar. The mother must be quite something to have diluted Ronald Wilson enough to produce Rachel. Two heavy men in light-brown suits and cowpat haircuts watched them carefully from a corner table.

Wilson had gone on a bit about declining standards in education. Alec had tried to reassure him by pointing out how the myth of decline from a golden age – in education, morality or society in general – had always been central to conservative political programmes and seldom had any empirical basis. Wilson seemed to understand this line of reasoning. It had gone quite well, really, if he hadn't had to keep worrying about the time and nudging Rachel's leg under the table as the clock crept around to five-thirty.

He was exhausted when they got back to Vivien's house. Hot, sticky and with the beginnings of a lager hangover needling at his right temple. He hadn't eaten all day. He wanted a bath, a sleep, a decent meal. But the kitchen clock was standing at a quarter to six. What if it just disappeared on the stroke of six, like the ballgown and coach and horses?

'I'd love to go to bed with you,' he announced, as warmly as he could manage.

'What, now?' said Rachel.

'Yes.'

'Vivien might be back soon. And there's something I've got to talk to you about.'

'We could talk later, couldn't we?'

'It's quite important,' said Rachel.

'It's just that I've been thinking about you all day. And I've got this feeling that it's going to work this time, you know?'

'Oh, all right, then,' said Rachel kindly.

They undressed in the little spare bedroom with its eau-de-nil walls, Blu-Tacked posters of Klimt paintings and a pink teddy bear with matted fur.

'Christ, what's that?' said Rachel when he turned around.

'Only me,' lied Alec.

Fantasy time.

They did it with him on top, and then they did it again with her on top. They did it with him sitting on a chair, and they did it standing up against the wall. They did it from in front and from behind and leaning over the desk and they did it again on the floor. He did not know how many times they did it.

'Doesn't it go down at all?' she asked him at eight o'clock.

'Well, it's been a long time for me,' said Alec modestly.

'I think I'm going to be bloody sore,' said Rachel.

*

He turned on the light in Vivien's bachelor bathroom and had to choke off a shout at what he saw.

Erect, yes, and two hours after Ellis-Lloyd's deadline, but he had put that down to the variable effects of the drug. Red and sore, certainly, and hardly surprising after two hours of the most savage friction he had ever experienced. But black?

Half-way along his organ was a hideous midnight stain about the area of a matchbox. Its edges were greenish blue and it was slightly puffy, standing proud of the surrounding flesh. He hardly dared to touch it in case it gave beneath his finger, like a rotten orange. Gangrene? A dirty needle? Some hostile reaction? That bastard Ellis-Lloyd hadn't even given him a blood test. Too much of a hurry to get his money. He felt tears of self-pity start suddenly to his eyes and shudders swept his frame.

Hot with panic he wrapped a towel tightly around his waist and almost ran back to the bedroom. He snapped on the main light and began grabbing clothes.

'Look, I'm afraid I've got to go. Someone's calling at the house to see me in half an hour.'

'Okay. I'll come with you.'

'No, really, it's just a business thing. You'd be bored.'

'I'll read a book upstairs until he's gone.'

'I'd rather you didn't come, really.'

She was sprawled naked on the bed. He noticed a long smear down the inside of one thigh, and how heavy her breasts looked in the harsh electric light. As if conscious of his scrutiny, she pulled herself upright, making a fence of her knees. There was a fold of fat at her middle. She had got distinctly thicker around the waist lately. All those sweets. She was going to have to watch out as she got older.

'There was this thing I wanted to talk to you about,' she said.

'Well, sure, but I think we'd better leave it until tomorrow.'

'I'm going to London tomorrow. I'll be gone for a few days. It was quite important.'

His penis throbbed dully under the towel. He felt irritation mingling with the panic. Important! What was important? Her last essay mark? Her sister's pony had lost a shoe? Mummy had come last in the flower-arranging rota? Important! His dick was falling off. That was important.

'Look, I'm very sorry, but I've really got to go.' He was scrambling into his trousers, his back turned to the bed.

'Alec, you've screwed me for the last two hours without saying a word apart from "turn over". I can't believe this mysterious "appointment" is so important we can't have a ten-minute conversation.'

'What do you mean I've *skrud* you?' He was talking shrilly, imitating her accent. 'I thought we *skrud* each other? I seem to remember you saying how you were as keen about getting *skrud* as I was. Or are we reverting to the innocent maid and evil seducer scenario?'

'I . . . just . . . want . . . to talk . . . to you.'

'Well, I'm very sorry. I wish I could. But I really can't. I'll phone you later. I promise. I'm sorry.'

And he was gone.

At Uplands there was a removal van blocking the driveway but no lights on in the house. He dialled the phone number on Ellis-Lloyd's card, but there was no reply. Nine o'clock at night. He imagined the horrible onyx tart's phone trilling, a hundred miles away in the darkened clinic among the tinkling fountains.

Upstairs he pulled off his clothes again. How many times had he undressed today? The hard-on seemed more swollen than ever, throbbing painfully, and it was now almost completely black. Whimpering he rushed to the shower and turned the cold water on full. After half a minute it trickled to a dead stop. Lewis and that fucking water tank.

Still wet and naked, he stumbled back downstairs to the kitchen, pulled ice trays from the refrigerator and pounded them furiously in the sink. He found a Safeway's carrier bag, filled it with the ice slush and wrapped it gently around his organ. The red eye of the erection glared up at him from its blackened sheath. Clutching the compress tightly around the black terror he hobbled to the hall again and dialled the St Barnabas switchboard. After forty-eight rings a laid-back West Indian voice answered.

'I need to get in touch with Dr Ellis-Lloyd. Urology department.'

There was a long pause. 'Cain't contact no consultant doctuh this time o ni', man. This Sa'day ni'.'

'It's very urgent. A . . . treatment he's been giving me has gone terribly wrong.'

A contemplative silence filled the crackling line from London. Alec was shuffling from foot to foot in agitation, the plastic bag of melting ice dripping on to the hall floor.

'You wan' ring 999 if'n you got an emergency there.'

'It's not that kind of emergency.'

Another long pause. 'Then I cain't help you.'

The phone went dead, the front door opened and Susan and William walked in. He was carrying an armful of tinfoil takeaway food cartons and a bottle of Riesling. She had just been laughing at something. There was a long silence while they took in the nude, dripping figure in the hallway, one hand on the telephone, the other clutching its groin.

'Hello, Alec,' said Susan, eventually. 'I told you that carrier bags always came in useful in the end.'

At the General a bad-tempered Indian woman doctor prodded Alec's groin with harsh, unsympathetic fingers, while William waited outside with the bag of melting ice.

'What was this stuff called that he gave you?' she asked him.

'I don't know, ouch. A mild dose of muscle relaxant, he said. Paparavine derivative or something.'

'How big was the dose? This big?' She waved a syringe at him from the enamel kidney bowl of instruments at her side.

'No, bigger than that.'

'And you've been playing with yourself all day.'

'No, I have not,' said Alec indignantly.

'Then you've been playing with somebody else. You didn't get these contusions from watching television.'

'Look, I . . .'

'Don't worry, Mr Smith. Your little willy is not going to drop off. But I'm going to have to take some blood from you, to reduce the swelling. About 20 cc should do it.'

She plunged a horse needle into Alec's penis, swore softly as she missed the blood vessel, withdrew it, plunged it in again. He hardly stirred on the couch. Feeling seemed to have almost vanished by now, along with shame. Inspected and injected. Battered, abused and exposed. The thing was practically public property now. A comic rubber prop in somebody else's idea of a farce.

From the corner of his eye Alec watched the horse syringe slowly fill with bright blood and the black terror slowly, gratefully subsiding into the damp foliage of his crotch.

'You did this book on the Royal Family,' said the doctor, as she swabbed the perforation.

'Yes.'

'You are going to have to stop playing with yourself for a fortnight until the bruising has gone down,' she said, grinning widely at him now. 'Start work on another book. Only nastier this time.'

It was after midnight when they left the hospital, and raining hard. Great cold gouts of water slapped across the windscreen of William's removal van, sending wet earth smells through the cab.

'Do you realize this is the first time it's rained since May?' said William.

'A bee sting, the doctor thought it was,' said Alec. 'Sunbathing this afternoon. Probably set off some kind of allergic reaction.'

'I was wondering,' said William, 'how you'd feel if I moved in with Susan.'

'Oh, Jesus,' said Alec, 'I forgot to phone Rachel.'

── CHAPTER FOURTEEN ──

From *The Republican Reader*:

> But now the globe's light hardens. The dreams
> go
> And what is so, is so.
>
> — Ted Hughes, Poet Laureate, on the 85th
> birthday of the Queen Mother

The man had been completely mad, of course. He could see that now. He had thought for a while it might be some kind of elaborate joke, to *épater* the bourgeois father. But Rachel had been too embarrassed for that. The man simply had to be a dangerous lunatic.

It was Sunday morning and the Right Honourable Ronald Wilson, MP, was sitting at home, working through his weekend boxes. Vivaldi drifted upstairs from the drawing room, where his wife was working through her *Mail on Sunday*. Unseeingly he signed minutes, underlined paragraphs and scribbled question marks in margins at what seemed like appropriate intervals, while his mind replayed the events of the previous afternoon in growing disbelief.

He had to be mad, didn't he? He had lurched into the restaurant three-quarters of an hour late with his wet suit and a damp, shredded newspaper clutched to his groin. Drunk obviously. Peed himself in all likelihood and absolutely stinking of beer.

'Daddy, I'd like you to meet Alec Smith. Alec, this is my father . . .'

He was a podgy little man of around forty, with a hot and sticky handshake. Greasy, greying curls, far too long for his age, and razor cuts all over his neck. His eyes darted frantically. His mouth gabbled words about trains and motor cars. He paid no attention at all to Wilson's own courteous conversational openers about the publishing business, but launched instead into some kind of half-baked leftist attack on the government's education policy. *His* education policy.

He had one of those insistent north London voices like a local radio disc jockey. Scattering false emphases to give weight to pseudo profundities. Swallowing his glottals like a barrow boy.

'What you gotta *realize* . . . wivaht any empirical *basis* . . . traditional reactionary *programme* . . .'

After a while Wilson had noticed, to his horror, that the man appeared to be feeling him up under the table. Pressing his damp, tweedy knee against Wilson's own and rubbing his foot against his ankle. He even placed a hand on his thigh and squeezed confidentially. Still more appalling, he began to realize, there was something wrong with the man's crotch. He was shifting uncomfortably in his chair, adjusting the filthy newspaper in his lap, scrabbling furtively in his trouser pockets.

It hardly seemed credible, in a Wykeham teashop, on a Saturday afternoon, and with two Special Branch constables on the adjoining table. It simply defied belief, but could this disgusting little man – a friend, perhaps more, of his own daughter – could he actually be *playing* with himself?

Wilson made up his mind by the time he had finished his boxes and the wholesome smells of roasting meat were drifting upstairs from the kitchen. He hadn't paid much attention to all the newspaper gossip, but even after a single visit he could see that Wykeham was clearly a third-rate institution. College structure hopelessly uneconomic. Falling rolls. Staff mostly dispirited remittance men. Something might be done with Business Studies and Electronics.

He just couldn't imagine how he had ever allowed his

daughter to go there in the first place. Heroin or no, socialism or no, pregnancies or no, she could not possibly have been worse off at Oxford.

The address was in Richmond, somewhere near the Thames. She didn't know that part of London very well, but she could sense the river close by and feel cheered up by the brightness it gave to the sky. And there were enormous horse chestnut trees everywhere, still damp and fresh from the rain, rocking gently along the sides of the wide avenues like tethered blimps.

The roads were wider here than in the rest of the city. The houses were further apart and the sky felt bigger, so that the scrubbed river light came right down among the houses and the parked cars. She noticed the petals washed into drifts around the storm drains, the men walking home with bundles of Sunday papers, a girl using a credit card to sweep raindrops from the metal table outside a pub. She wanted to remember everything this morning. It was important that it did not become just a day like every other day. You had to do that much.

It was a big house in a quiet side street. No board or anything outside to say what it was. The taxi drove past it by mistake, and then had to drop her on the corner. There was a Kwik-Fit Exhaust place there with a sign which said 'While-U-Wait'. She walked back slowly along the street with her small hold-all, scuffing petals with her toes, watching the continents of damp dwindle on the pavements. Nobody about. There was a smell of roasting meat. On a radio somewhere voices were singing 'Jesus, thou art all compassion', in that bashful, throttled English way.

She stopped at the gate and put down her bag. The house was four storeys tall, red brick, with a glass conservatory on the side. Small panes of blue glass here and there, with a red fleur-de-lys inset. There must have been twelve or fifteen bedrooms in the days when it was a family home.

Could they ever really have been ordinary houses, all these

great brick mansions in the London suburbs? Were there ever enough businessmen and surgeons and barristers to fill them up? Could there really have been enough maids and cooks and nannies to occupy all those attic bedrooms, to answer all those disconnected servants' bells, to stoke those dozens of boarded-up fireplaces? Perhaps they just became straight away what they were now – small hotels and clinics and bed-sits and institutes for this and that.

The front garden had been gravelled over for cars and there were more parking spaces for staff in the back. There was a bell on the front door with a sign saying, 'Day Bell Only', and underneath 'Jour' and 'Tag' and then a squiggle in Arabic. But the door was ajar and she went straight in through a hallway to a pink and grey reception area.

The woman at the desk told her to sit down, and she joined a row of other women, with a few men, sitting on tube-steel chairs. Nobody was talking. A pale blonde girl of about seventeen sat with her mother and father on her right. The girl looked determinedly bright, her father looked stoical and the mother was on the edge of tears, twisting corners of her clothing in her hands. When the father spoke to a passing nurse his accent was Irish.

On her left was an older girl of twenty or so, also with her mother. She had a tousled mane of tawny hair and an air of slightly battered confidence. She wore clown-striped breeches and boots and a suede jacket. The mother wore a Surrey matron's outfit of twinset and pearls and was stroking her daughter's hand, though the daughter looked as if she would have liked to pull it away. Opposite were a couple in their twenties who might have been French. She was very sallow and lumpy-looking, with a bit of a moustache. He looked richer and quite handsome. Next to them sitting on her own was a small Asian girl with a face that was both tremulous and defiant. When their eyes met for a moment, the Asian girl smiled.

She remembered her resolution to remember. The room had been carpeted in small pink and grey diamonds and fitted out with houseplants with St Michael labels. It had been freshly papered in woodchip and painted with magnolia emulsion. Bland modern prints hung on the walls; David Hockney and Glynn Boyd Harte in brushed aluminium frames. Electrical wires had been stapled across the ceiling, and others, coated thickly in new paint, straggled along the skirting boards. A fluorescent light buzzed overhead.

'Catherine Wilson,' said the receptionist, and Rachel almost got up, but the girl in the striped breeches stood first and bent down to give her mother a kiss on the cheek.

There were seven women still waiting now, including herself, and she couldn't help feeling sad. She had decided beforehand not to get all morbid, but she couldn't help thinking it. Eight women. Eight babies-that-weren't-to-be. Eight babies a day; fifty-six babies a week. It must be such a sad place to work, for the nurses and doctors. Even the cleaners must have thought it was sad, cleaning a place that was only there for getting rid of babies.

'Rachel Wilson,' said the receptionist, and she went up to the desk. She gave her the money, £250 in fifties, which she had put in a thick white envelope.

'Is there anyone you would like us to call for you ... afterwards?' said the receptionist.

'No, that's all right.'

The receptionist put a cross in the box on the form in front of her.

'We have to ask you to give us a number to be contacted, in case of emergency,' she said.

'There isn't really anybody,' said Rachel.

'Just a friend or someone,' said the receptionist. 'We have to have somebody.'

She thought for a moment, and then gave Vivien's phone number.

Malcolm phoned Vivien.

'Did you hear about William and Susan?' he asked her.

'I'm going to Uplands tonight to have supper with them,'

said Vivien. She had got out of the bath to answer the phone and was irritably conscious of a certain unrinsed soapiness beneath her arms.

'Oh, right,' said Malcolm, rather disappointed. When his call to Uplands had been answered by Susan she hadn't said anything about everyone else knowing.

'I'm sure it's for the best really, don't you?' he said. 'I mean, Susan was always much brighter than Alec, really. I always thought she and William made a much better couple.'

'Was this all you rang about, Malcolm? I was in the middle of having a bath.'

'I've got some stuff for Rachel.'

'More talcum powder? She's not here, anyway. She's gone to London. Buying herself a motor bike.'

'Where did she get the money?' said Malcolm. 'She told me she was broke.'

'I haven't got the faintest idea.'

'Must have been from Alec, I suppose. Doing his sugar daddy bit.'

'Look, I'm dripping all over the carpet.'

'You should get one of these phones. They're terribly useful.'

'Goodbye, Malcolm.'

A Filipino woman – a nurse, she supposed – in a lemon nylon overall showed her upstairs to the room. At the top of the first flight of stairs the pink and grey carpet gave way to vinyl floor tiles. More dim, pastel prints on the walls. Elaborate plaster ceilings clogged with emulsion paint. Red fire extinguishers. Cast-iron concertina radiators like the flat in Amsterdam. No, stop that.

There were two beds in the room. The Asian girl was sitting on one of them, sniffling. She told Rachel her name was Nita. 'I'm so frighten',' she said. 'Do you think it's gonna be awfuw?'

She told Rachel she came from a Hindu family in Chatham. She spoke in a chirpy Kent cockney, which sounded odd coming from her little dark face. Her parents had come from India in the 1960s. She knew the name of the village they had come from but she couldn't tell Rachel whereabouts it was; north or south, near Delhi or Calcutta or Bombay.

She had four younger brothers. Her mother worked in a clothing factory and from the age of eleven she had done most of the housework, coming home from school every day to cook dinner for seven. 'Never had time to do me homework or nothing.' But she had done quite well at school. She had passed some O levels and got a job in an office in London, operating a word processor, which she had liked.

She also had a boyfriend, an Indian boy she was fond of. But when she was twenty her parents arranged a marriage with the son of her father's friend. Her mother said she could make up her own mind about the boy. So they were introduced and spent half an hour talking together, and then asked if they liked each other. 'I told me mum he was all right, but I liked me boyfriend better, and I din' want to marry this bloke. But they told me I had to. Me mum's a right bitch. She lies all the time.'

Nita had stopped sniffling by now and Rachel helped her to unpack her case. Skirt, jumper, Marks and Spencer underwear, flowered nightie, a Shirley Conran novel, lily-of-the-valley talc, Sony Walkman, a plastic washbag with vintage cars on. 'Pinched that off of him,' she said proudly.

They had got married and she found that her new in-laws had bought an off-licence in Chatham, which she was supposed to run while her husband went out to work. 'I told them I wooden do it, and I carried on with me job in London. But I had to give all the money to me mother-in-law. And all she give me was £30 a week for the train fare and £10 spending money.'

Her father-in-law was a drinker who knocked her mother-in-law about, and she found her new husband drank too. She refused to have sex with him after a while. 'All he wanted from me was sex. He din' want to talk to me or nothing so I wooden have him. He used to hit me and twist my arm and all that but I wooden have him. Then he come home one night, and I woke up and he was on top of me and he wooden stop, and so I got pregnant. D'you want a fag?'

Rachel hadn't smoked a cigarette in years, but she took one anyway. They sat, side by side on Nita's bed, blowing smoke rings. Outside in the corridor a nurse called out a name. There was the rumbling sound of a wheelchair and then the wheeze of a lift.

When Nita knew she was pregnant she told nobody, but began to save the money her mother-in-law gave her for train fares. She dodged the ticket collector on the trains between Chatham and London and waved an out-of-date rail pass at the station barriers. She did that for two months until she had saved enough money for the abortion. Then she ran away from home to stay with an English girl friend in Stratford.

'When this is all over,' she said, 'I'm goin' back to work and sit some A levels.'

Rachel felt cheered up by the terrible story, and Nita seemed brighter for having told her. She asked how come she was there and Rachel tried to tell her. About Toby, who wasn't very nice, and then about William who was nice but had got her pregnant, and then about Alec, who was very nice.

Not nice, nicer, nicest. It sounded like a Latin lesson.

'You din' tell this Alec about coming here?'

'No. He's got his own problems, you see. And he's married. And the fath . . . William, is his friend. I sort of tried to tell him, but I don't think he wanted to hear really.'

It all seemed rather grey and abstract and middle class after Nita's vivid story of forced marriage and beating and rape and fare evasion. Just a lot of people in a muddle really. Rachel could see from the way Nita asked questions before she had finished telling her each part that she was puzzled and a bit bored.

Then they rested for a while on their beds, with Nita reading her Shirley Conran and Rachel listening to the sounds of nurses calling people's names and of wheelchairs rolling to and fro along the corridor to the lift. Someone came for Nita at one o'clock and she wished her good luck, like going into exams.

It was after two when a nurse came for her. Her throat was very dry from not drinking and she was hungry. The nurse was a proper nurse this time, in starched cap and apron. She just rapped out Rachel's name in a sergeant-majorish sort of way, which she quite liked. No phony solicitude. Just doing her job. Eight babies a day. Fifty-six babies a week.

She took off her pyjamas and put on a hospital nightgown and the nurse told her to get into the wheelchair.

'I don't mind walking.'

'It's better if you don't.'

She was wheeled along to the lift, up two floors, and then down corridors to a sort of ante-room full of old red machines with dials like gas meters. Floppy rubber doors with scratched plastic windows led into the operating theatre next door. Another nurse, who was more chatty, told her they had 'a very nice doctor on today and a lovely anaesthetist, very good-looking'. She suddenly felt very cold and tried hard not to shiver. The chatty nurse squeezed her arm.

She didn't get the pre-med injection she had for her tonsils. The anaesthetist just came up and gave her the real injection straight off. He actually said that joke thing, 'You'll just feel a little prick.' He had his hair in a bath hat and a beaky nose and thick glasses. 'You'll feel your feet getting heavy,' he told her, but she didn't. It was just like the shutter on a camera, closing very slowly, right down to a pinprick of light. She could see these tall figures moving about and a lot of green like a garden, and hear the sound of running water.

She was swimming naked, with Alec, in the gravel pits, side by side, watching the clear green water close and break over his white shoulders. Trembling drops and wobbling menisci merging and shattering in the hollows between his shoulder blades. Close and break, close and break. Toby, in

— 193 —

a dressing gown, was following them along the bank in his wheelchair.

'I'd like to meet your father when he's down,' he was shouting.

'My father only rides bicycles to me at night,' Rachel told him. 'He can walk to the lift on his own.'

'Well, I hope you can swim well. The sides are very high. And William lives at the bottom in his old M G.'

'Alec has got his cycling proficiency on a Four-spring Dutch Knick-knack.'

'But it's very cold in a dressing gown,' Toby called, 'and they call him Kemo Sabe the tobacconist.'

But it was all right, because Rachel had looked at Greta Garbo bridges with brown chocolate on her hands and read *Le Monde* turned upside down and Vincent Van Gogh said she only needed £300 for his motor bike.

'He's leaving you now to get Susan the baby oil for the bandstand,' shouted Toby.

And Alec was leaving, swimming far ahead of her, with the clear green water breaking and closing over his shoulders. The droplets and menisci on his white skin trembling and shattering, fusing and forming. Break and close, break and close. But it was only a mini-break, and the water was very cold between her legs and it wouldn't stop because of the off-licence in Chatham, and she shouted out to him, 'I've got the £300 for the water tank because I didn't pay for the tickets.'

But he was swimming further and further away, and the sides were too high to get out Kemo Sabe, and the water tobacconists too cold between her legs. And she wanted to get out of the wheelchair because he didn't like the colour of the *Poseidon Adventure*, where the water came in so cold. Alec, when we sat upon the bridge too far, I hit your nose and I didn't tell you, Alec.

Under the water was an argument for the existence of God, if you drank it slowly with Ryvitas, Alec, so cold and green, eight babies between her legs. To close and break in

Amsterdam, drinking water in the brown café, her throat so dry and full of cold you drank and drowned the water cold. And when you drowned behind, fifty-six a week, the cleaners came and pulled you out and pinched your cheeks because it was so cold they pinched.

'Don't pinch. I've got £300.'

'She's coming round now,' said a woman's voice.

'The water's much too cold to drink.'

'You shall have a drink in a moment, dear. I'll just cover you up now to keep you warm.'

'Pretty little thing,' said another voice. 'These men.'

'I'll be down in a minute,' said Vivien. 'I'm just getting dressed. Make yourself a drink or something.'

Malcolm mixed himself a gin and tonic and turned on Vivien's new Sony TV. He was watching the omnibus *EastEnders* when the phone rang.

'Waverley Clinic here,' said a female voice. 'Message from Catherine Wilson.'

'You mean Rachel Wilson,' said Malcolm. There was a pause and a rustle of paper at the other end.

'Oh, I beg your pardon. Rachel Wilson. Just to say your daughter has come round from the operation and everything's fine.'

'Oh, right. Thank you very much,' said Malcolm.

He sat down and thought for a while. Presently he picked up the phone again and dialled 142 for London directory inquiries.

'Who was that on the phone?' said Vivien later, when she came downstairs, her hair fluffed out from the blow-dryer.

'Just a wrong number,' said Malcolm.

When she woke again, she felt absolutely fine and started trying to get up off the trolley she was lying on.

'God, I don't feel sore or sick or anything. When can I have something to eat?'

Then she felt cold again and started crying. She cried for

half an hour in the recovery room, and the nurse would come and pat her now and then and say things like, 'There, there, best to let it all come out.' She found she was wearing one of these huge, old-fashioned sanitary towels with a loop at either end. When she was at school they called them hammocks for mice.

When she felt better again, a nurse took her to the lavatory and tried to make her pee, because, she said, you mustn't have a full bladder, for some reason. She couldn't go, and so the nurse turned on all the taps, but it still took about half an hour.

Then they finally did have some tea, which was sandwich spread on white sliced bread, with only one cup of tea. The Filipino women who did the cooking were taking away everybody's plates almost before they sat down. She had a sleeping pill in the evening – the first one she'd ever had – and went off straight away, but she was woken up again by someone's buzzer at three o'clock. The nurse didn't come for half an hour and it rang and rang, until everyone on her floor was awake.

Then they woke them at quarter to six and started making the beds straight away, for the next eight babies, she supposed. They went down to breakfast, which was very hardboiled eggs and some toast, which had been sitting there for about half an hour, and one cup of tea. This Arab girl she hadn't spoken to came bouncing into the room, looking very pleased with herself, and said, 'Well, what are you all looking so miserable for. You got what you wanted, didn't you?'

In the black Granada estate car Lofthouse and Green had been waiting since dawn. Lofthouse's head was buried deep in the collar of a quilted green parka coat that made him look fatter than he was, which was not easy. The only parts of him visible above the collar were pebble glasses and a thinning ginger scalp. Green, who was twenty years younger, and slender, was shivering in a t-shirt and denim jacket.

'Four o'clock in the fucking morning the fucking desk

rang me,' he complained. 'Who's going to be getting out of fucking bed at four o'clock in the fucking morning?'

'Give that glass a wipe,' said Lofthouse, just to make him go away for a while. There was a light on now in the ground floor of the house, he noticed. Green took the bundle of J-cloths and plastic spray of de-mist solution and clambered out of the car. As he polished away the dusty ghosts of raindrops and white crusts of bird shit from the windshield, Lofthouse pulled a flattie of Teachers from the parka pocket and took a deep swig. Wiping his lips on his sleeve, he began to assemble the equipment from the scratched aluminium cases on the back seat. Olympus body. Motor drive. 300-mm Canon telephoto. He threaded a tripod mount on to the heavy lens barrel and selected the shortest monopod support in the case.

'Hey, there's a fucking light on over there,' said Green, climbing back inside the car.

'And the Normans have landed,' said Lofthouse.

'Hate these fucking jobs,' said Green, polishing vapour from the inside of the windscreen. 'All fucking night outside fucking Linley's it was last fucking week'.

'Sat outside Fergie's flat eight nights on the trot,' said Lofthouse. 'Ten days at Balmoral in a tent once.'

Green looked critically at the two-foot turret lens. 'You want a catadioptric in this sort of fucking space.'

Lofthouse sniffed. 'They're all right if you're snapping statues. I'd rather have the aperture control.'

They argued companionably about technology, as Lofthouse wedged the monopod into position on the dashboard, and fiddled with the focus ring until he could read the signs next to the door jamb, fifty yards away. 'Day Bell Only', 'Jour' and 'Tag'. He couldn't seem to get the fourth sign in focus, but it was good enough.

'One coming now,' said Green urgently. The motor drive zipped and clicked. Zipped and clicked. It was a tall, blonde girl with clown-striped breeches. She paused at the door, giving him a perfect full face, and as she did so a taxi pulled up. 'And another,' said Green. 'No, never mind, it's a nig-nog.'

The motor drive zipped and clicked, zipped and clicked. 'Shoot everything that moves on these jobs,' said Lofthouse, his pebble lens squeezed tight to the viewfinder. ''Snot my film, and you never know what picture might come in handy one day.' Nita crossed the road in front of the black Granada without a glance and walked off in the direction of Barnes. 'Bet Mister fucking Patel don't know where she's spending the weekend,' said Green.

Six more women emerged from the door in the next fifteen minutes, some getting into taxis, some into private cars. One or two setting off down the street on foot. They all carried small overnight bags. The motor drive zipped and clicked, zipped and clicked. Green loaded a spare camera body with film, but the doorway had become quiet. After another fifteen minutes with no more exits Lofthouse removed the monopod from the dashboard and set down the camera with a sigh.

'You want to do the sub?' he said. He was too old and fat and slow to go doorstepping any more.

The Minox 5X11 subminiature camera was no bigger than a toothbrush holder and could be operated one-handed, with a thumb-slide to advance the film. Green tucked it into the palm of his hand and strolled to the middle of the road. He took two establishing shots of the house, two from the gateway, then two more, closer up, of the door. He paused, listening, in the doorway, then took three shots of the 'Jour' and 'Tag' signs by the day bell. Watching from the car, Lofthouse took another swig from his flattie.

In the hallway Green picked up a handful of brochures from a table and stuffed them inside his denim jacket. The pink and grey reception area was empty except for a nurse, shuffling through a card index at the desk. He got two shots off, the hand with the Minox dangling casually at his side, before she looked up.

'Scuse me, darlin',' he said. 'You wouldn't have change

for a twenty, would you? I got a fare for you outside in the cab, and she ain't got nothing smaller.'

Grumbling, the nurse unlocked a filing cabinet and started rooting through a metal cashbox. Green flipped open the desk register at the last completed page. Holding the camera carefully this time, square over the page, he fired off four shots before the nurse had turned around.

'Hey, what do you think you're doing?'

'Say cheese,' said Green, walking backwards, and fired off three more frames – nurse's uniform, angry face, open register – before he was out of the door and away.

──── CHAPTER FIFTEEN ────

From *The Republican Reader*:

The Royal Yacht (£3 million a year) and the Queen's Flight (£5 million) are paid for by the Ministry of Defence. Upkeep of the Royal Palaces is paid for by the Department of the Environment, State visits overseas by the Foreign Office, while postal services and telephones are provided free of charge by the common carriers.

White ghosts waved handless arms to Alec through the smeary porthole. Brass fly buttons clattered on perforated zinc; trunkless legs turned somersaults through greyish foam.

The Supawash launderette under William's flat was deserted on Saturday night. Hoarse shouts, the chug of reggae and splinter of glasses from the George Robey half a mile away echoed only faintly in the empty street outside. Alec sat alone, reading *Madame Bovary* and sipping steadily from a can of Carlsberg Special Brew. He read a lot these days, from when he woke, at ten or eleven, to late afternoon, when he went to eat at the greasy spoon in Finsbury Park.

After his dinner, of pale eggs and chips, he bought strong lager from Tesco's and read on into the evening. *Bovary*, *Salammbô*, *Trois Contes*, *Bouvard et Pécuchet*, *Bovary* again. He was at the ball in La Vaubyessard now, admiring the coarse provincial aristocracy of Normandy:

Their nonchalant glances reflected the quietude of passions daily gratified: behind their gentleness of manner one could detect that peculiar brutality inculcated by dominance in not over-exacting activities, such as exercise strength and flatter vanity – the handling of thoroughbreds and the pursuit of wantons.

He put the book down with a sigh on the wooden bench, sticky with biological detergent, and rummaged in his pockets for change. This was always the best time to telephone, before the drunks started coming in to fool about and break into the machines. The telephone in William's flat was still not working. He had bought a cheap handset from a market stall, but when he plugged it in found that the line from the exchange was dead. When he looked through the drifts of mail in the front hall, he found six unopened envelopes from the new telephone corporation, Only Connect.

The launderette telephone was Only Connect's latest model: massively constructed, of boiler plate and nickel steel bolts. There was no handset. It was necessary to crouch, like a supplicant at confession, over a heavy metal grid, which acted as both microphone and loudspeaker. It made private conversation impossible, which was another reason for telephoning late at night. He put a £2 coin into the slot.

After six rings a voice came on the line: brisk, Scottish, male. Alec tried his Deep South accent: Burl Ives as Big Daddy in *Cat on a Hot Tin Roof*.

'Hah theyuh. Ah'd lahk ta speak ta Miss Rachel Wilson.'

'Is that you Smith?' said the metal grid.

'Yes.'

'I've told you that my daughter does not wish to speak to you.'

'But look, I only want to . . .'

'And if you continue to make a nuisance of yourself I have to warn you that I will apply to the courts for an injunction to force you to stop this harassment.'

'I . . .'

'Goodnight, Mr Smith,' said the voice, and the grid purred

approvingly. Curious how impotent it made you feel; the lack of a handset to smack down in its cradle. He pressed the coin return button as hard as he could. The liquid crystal display, behind its scratched perspex window, told Alec he had consumed 88p of Only Connect's time but that only complete coins were refundable.

The ghosts in the machine had stopped waving at their porthole. Alec unloaded the heavy, damp coils into a plastic basket, scarred with cigarette burns, and dumped the load into a tumble drier. Some of his clothes had stretched in the wash over the last weeks and others had shrunk in the drier. Shapes were becoming indeterminate, and the colours had run from one to the other, so they were all becoming uniform, launderette-coloured, like his days.

He opened another can of Special Brew. Emma was dancing, still studying the men:

They had the complexion of wealth, that clear white skin which is accentuated by the pallor of porcelain, the shimmer of satin, the finish on handsome furniture, and is maintained at its best by a modest diet of the most exquisite foods . . . The older among them maintained a youthful air, while the young ones revealed a certain maturity.

Alec had egg-and-chip spots on his forehead, he knew, and the beginnings of Special Brew grog blossom on his nose. After twenty minutes he tried the phone again. Ten rings, and a man's voice, not Wilson's.

'Hello, my name is Alec Smith. I wonder if I might speak to Rachel Wilson.'

'You're a cunt, Smith,' said the metal grid.

'I beg your parden. Who is that?'

'A spivvy little counter-jumper. An ageing Trotskyite toss-pot full of half-baked hippie shit.'

'Excuse me, I don't . . .'

'You've really got a fucking cheek, haven't you, cunt?' the grid crackled. 'Get a little girl of nineteen pregnant, buy her a back-street abortion, and then sell her the drugs to top herself with. Now I suppose you want to start getting your droopy little dick into her again.'

There was a commotion in the background at the other end of the line. A woman's voice: 'That's quite enough.' A man: 'I'll call the telephone people, I really . . .'

The Scots voice came back on the line. 'I have warned you, Smith. This number will be changed from tomorrow, and if you make any further attempt to contact my daughter you are going to end up in prison. That is my final word.' The grid purred.

He sat down, trembling a little, on the sticky wooden bench. The tumble drier had finished its cycle, but he sat on, drinking some more, unable to pick up the book at his side, thinking about nothing.

The man, of course, was Wilson, and the woman was her mother, or perhaps one of her sisters. The other, terrible voice – he didn't know what it was doing there; he didn't like to think – but he was almost certain it had belonged to Toby.

He had found her on the Tuesday night, the day the newspaper stories came out. Malcolm's had been first, of course, but most of the other papers got it with their second editions. He was on his way to the tube station at Finsbury Park, going to see that bastard Ellis-Lloyd, when he saw it on the newsstand.

'Back-street Abortion for Minister's Daughter', the headline squealed, and, in smaller type, 'Tutor pays hush money for private clinic'. There was a grainy picture of Rachel, looking lost, standing in the porch of a house, with a small hold-all in her hand. Another picture, superimposed, showed some office stationery: 'Waverley Clinic: Pregnancy Advice and Counselling'. His own name, five paragraphs down, jumped at him from the page.

He bought an armful of papers and walked back to William's flat, the street swaying under his feet. Later he called Vivien from the launderette. Rachel had left the clinic on Monday, she told him. Nobody else had seen her since

Saturday. 'I've just been talking to her parents, in the Vice-Chancellor's office. The V C was quite good really. Rather took my part. But the father was quite out of control and the mother just sat there crying buckets. Didn't you have any idea?'

'No,' said Alec. 'Didn't you?'

He phoned Uplands and got no reply, and then he phoned the house in Islington. Susan answered.

'You've seen the papers?'

'Of course I've seen them,' she said.

'Have either of you heard anything from Rachel?'

'Why on earth should your pregnant teenybopper want to talk to me and William?'

'Why don't you ask William?' said Alec, and there was a reflective pause before she answered.

'William's not here. He's had to go to Amsterdam, on business.'

'Well, that's handy,' said Alec.

Only Malcolm's paper had splashed the story. The other tabloids covered it mostly on the inside pages. The *Telegraph* gave it two paragraphs on page three, leading on Ronald Wilson's denunciation of the gutter press. The *Independent* ignored the story. *The Times* and *Guardian* gave it a diary paragraph.

'Red faces at Prometheus Press,' said the *Guardian*, 'recently acquired publishing subsidiary of Sir Clark Cockburn's Australian-based media empire. The newly knighted Cockburn is said to be hopping mad over reports that the impregnator of the Education Secretary's daughter is none other than Alec Smith, founder of Prometheus, and now a director of Cockburn's U K company. Cockburn is a newly appointed member of the Broadcasting Standards Council, and in his *Who's Who* entry is listed as a patron of Mrs Mary Whitehouse's National Viewers' and Listeners' Association and of the Society for the Protection of the Unborn Child.'

He telephoned Vivien again, where there was no answer, and then Uplands. Still no answer. He called the university and got through to a secretary in the Bursar's office. Mr and Mrs Wilson had left the campus and were on their way home. There was no news of Miss Wilson. He surrendered the Supawash telephone to a Rastafarian with three, tiny, dreadlocked children and went upstairs to William's flat for his car keys.

He drove faster than he had ever driven before down the A2 but it was almost dark when he got to Uplands. There was a concrete mixer outside the garage doors and scaffolding poles were piled beside the house. The hallway had been cleared of debris and there was a powerful stink of creosote, like a cricket pavilion. He went from room to room, switching on the lights.

There was fresh plaster on the damp wall of the kitchen; new window frames were stacked up in the sitting room and master bedroom. Wallpaper stripped off right up the stairwell. In the few days since he had left the house had become orderly, purposeful.

Only his own room had been left untouched. Wine bottles on the floor, a Ryvita packet, ragged science fiction books, and Rachel.

She was lying on the unmade bed, fully dressed. A half-litre of Smirnoff glugged when he pulled back the single sheet and an empty bottle of Nitrazepam rattled on to the floor. A small buff envelope lay crumpled on the bedside table. There was a plastic sachet inside it, empty except for a dusting of white powder.

He shoved her over on to her side and some vomit dribbled from the corner of her mouth. He clawed in her chilly mouth with his fingers and dug out some more. Chocolaty goo; slimy lumps of peanut or pill perhaps. The body was horribly heavy, like a roll of wet carpet. It flopped on to its back and he tried again, wedging it in place with a pillow and panting with the effort.

Her throat was clear so far as he could see, but there

was no sign of breathing at all and she was very cold. He shouted her name, as loudly as he could in her ear, and he thought her eyelashes trembled. He ran downstairs and dialled 999.

It was only the second time in his life he had done it, he realized, and both times on the same telephone.

More hospitals. More smells, uniforms, crashing trolleys. In fiction, he thought, the important things happened in parties, marriages, drawing rooms, hotels, courtrooms, aeroplanes. Places where people met, fell in love, talked and argued. In real life the big events were all in hospitals. Zones of anonymity where people snivelled or whispered, or more often were simply silent. Sitting on benches along scuffed corridor walls. Staring at old magazines.

'What has she had?' asked the cross Indian woman doctor. To his relief she did not seem to recognize Alec. He gave her the sleeping-pill bottle and the plastic sachet. She picked up a grain of powder on a brown, ringed finger and licked it. 'Could be heroin. Is she an addict?'

'No. I think she smoked it sometimes.'

'Addicts smoke it sometimes.'

'She wasn't an addict.'

'Any syringes?'

'No.'

'Where did she get it?'

'I don't know. Somebody at the university probably.'

'Was this the only bag?'

'The only one I could find.'

Through an open door, round the corner of a screen, he could see Rachel's head. The hair was scraped back from her forehead, making it look unfamiliar; white and bony. There was an oxygen mask over her face, a drip taped to her arm. A nurse moved across the doorway, blocking his view.

'Any alcohol?' said the doctor.

'Vodka. About half a bottle.' She scribbled on a clip board.

'How long ago did she take all this?'

'Could have been any time in the last twelve hours. I'm sorry, I really don't know. Do you think she's going to live?'

'Of course she's going to live,' said the doctor irritably. 'It takes a lot more than that to kill you. This stuff is probably mostly talcum powder anyway. She'd have woken up tomorrow morning with a very bad hangover and a stomach ache if you hadn't spoiled her nap.'

'Oh,' said Alec.

'We're going to wash out her stomach and give her a shot of Naloxone to help her breathing. Who's the next of kin?'

'Is that necessary?'

'Of course it's necessary. Heroin is a Schedule 1 drug. The police will have to be informed.'

He gave her Rachel's father's name, and she raised her eyebrows as she scribbled it down.

'You do pick them, don't you, Mr Smith? I told you that you should stick to writing books.'

That was three weeks ago and he hadn't even been able to speak to her. Her parents and a tearful sister were at the hospital the next morning. There had been a conversation, brief and unpleasant. Her mother had cleared the room at Vivien's house. They had driven her back to Wiltshire and they had disappeared into their world.

The newspapers had squealed again, but only briefly. The *Telegraph* had talked of the need to reinforce the Press Council. The *Guardian* ran a feature on the pressures of the new university examinations on undergraduates. The *Mirror* wrote about the gilded offspring of Conservative ministers. Malcolm's paper did an exposé of drug dealing on the campus. *The Times* applauded the government's decision to rationalize the structure of the 1960s universities and to cut back on wasteful spending. The *Sun* ran a profile of Alec under the headline 'Lefty Lothario' and a picture of Rachel, aged about fourteen, in a swimsuit.

'There'll be an election this year,' said Vivien. 'That's why they aren't making more fuss.'

*

The termination of his contract with Prometheus was forwarded to him by Susan. He lost his seat on the board and his equity holdings were frozen, 'pending investigation by our legal advisers'.

'What the fuck do they mean, "investigation"?' he asked Ralph on the phone.

'Well,' Ralph said apologetically, 'they're saying that under your contract you were supposed to have attended a board meeting every month and a weekly directors' conference.'

'So what?'

'Well, you missed quite a few meetings, didn't you?'

'So did half the other directors. So did you. So did Cockburn, for that matter.'

'It was in your contract.'

'So I can't sell my own shares in my own company?'

'You could get a lawyer, Alec.'

'If I can't sell equity, I can't afford a lawyer.'

'The point is they don't want a large tranche of stock on the market just now, with everything being so low. Might bring everyone else's down, you know. You're bound to get it eventually.'

'So who's the new chairman of Prometheus?' said Alec.

'I am,' said Ralph.

He had £1,500 in his current account, £600 outstanding on his Amex card and £850 owing to Visa.

The Audi salesman in St John's Wood shook his head over the drunken front wing and sent him to a greasy forecourt in the Caledonian Road hung with frayed and faded plastic bunting.

'I'll give you two grand for it,' said the dealer.

'It's only three years old,' said Alec.

'Three and a half,' said the dealer. 'Nearly four. And there's not a lot of demand for these big foreign motors when they've done a few miles. Can't get the spares, you see. I'll have to spend at least a grand on that wing. You can take it or leave it.' So he took it.

He bought a bed and a few other bits of furniture for William's flat and a second-hand Kawasaki 250 motor cycle. That left £500.

Dear Alec,

How are you doing, mate? I'm sorry I left the place in a bit of a mess, but I'm sure you're sorting it out. I'd have rung, but the phone still seems to be on the blink. Can't you get someone round to fix it?

Now you've been *chez moi* a few weeks I hope you don't mind if I raise the ticklish subject of rent. I phoned a couple of letting agents to get an idea of a fair price, and talked it over with Susie, and we thought £150 a week would be about right. That would cover the mortgage with a bit left over for repairs and so on.

Hate to ask, you know, mate, but I'm trying to get the business going down here, and I'm sure the groaning coffers of *The Republican Reader* can stand it. The building work on the house is all pretty well finished now, and I'm looking at a tobacconist's in Wincheap as a possible site for a shop.

Susie has decided to take Jonathan and Dora out of Beddington next year and put them into Queens in the town, so they'll be able to come home weekends. Both send their love. I'll drop in and say hello next time I'm in town.

Cheers, William

The two 'mates' spoke of bad conscience and arm-twisting from Susan. Alec tore the letter up into small pieces and dropped it among the cans of Special Brew, in the apple carton that was his kitchen dustbin.

───── CHAPTER SIXTEEN ─────

From *The Republican Reader*:

> Miss Briggs dreamed she was at the Royal Garden Party. As always the Queen was quick to notice her in the crowd, and pushing past the officious and over-protective equerries, made her way through the throng of eagerly waiting subjects to reach Miss Briggs' side.
>
> – Emma Tennant, *Hotel de Dream*

It was Midsummer's Eve.

'Are you sure this is the right place?' said Justice Mainwaring. He peered from the driver's window of the Volvo at the dim outline of a tall house, silhouetted by his headlights against the darkness of a wooded hillside.

'Of course I'm sure,' his wife said. 'I *lived* here for two years, didn't I?'

'It doesn't look as if there's much going on,' said the judge. 'Only two cars. Hardly any lights. I told you we should have phoned before we came.'

'Oh, come on,' said his wife, and stepped out, plump and shapely little legs in black, figured stockings, on to the familiar, gravelled driveway. She could just make out the mass of tree peonies on her left and smell the honeysuckle, beginning to break into blossom, on the roof of the summer house.

At the top of the steps, in the light of the glazed door panels, she brushed wisps of fair hair from her collar and straightened Justice Mainwaring's tie. Muffled rock music filtered through the door. 'See?' she said. 'I told you it was all right.' There was a long pause after she rang the bell, the sound of doors slamming, and someone shouting. A tall, fair man with a lock of hair over his face opened the door. Not Alec.

'William,' she said.

The man looked blankly at the small, plump, middle-aged woman on the doorstep with her handbag and horsy head-scarf. He looked at the grim-faced man behind her, in the black, cashmere overcoat and striped trousers. Somebody's parents? Jehovah's Witnesses? Finally he noticed the small pink hearing aid in her left ear and recognition dawned.

'Daisy Dee.'

The hallway behind him smelled strongly of fresh paint. The judge could make out a new grey stair carpet and a pricy-looking Chippendale card table against the wall. From an open doorway came the roaring babble of a rock music pro-gramme.

'Dora, Jonathan. Turn that bloody television down,' said a voice from the top of the stairs. A crystalline county voice Daisy recognized at once, with a tiny lurch of nervousness. 'Who's that at the door, William?'

Susan's face appeared on the landing at the head of the stairs. Pale, oval, bruised, still beautiful.

'It's Daisy Dee,' said William.

'Hello Susan,' said Daisy, 'we've come to the party.'

'Christ,' said Susan. 'Alec's party.'

The same night Alec rode the Kawasaki out to Wiltshire, a hundred miles without leathers or gauntlets. Her house was a few miles off the M4 on the outskirts of a village: Queen Anne executive with Georgian garage doors and bull's-eye glass in the porchlight. A black Daimler and a lime-green Deux Chevaux in the drive. Lights at the back and upstairs.

He waited for an hour, the Kawasaki parked on the grass verge across the road. He walked up and down. There were few cars on the road. From the house he could hear occasional wafts of television noise. An evening at home with the family. He had been hoping that perhaps she would be going out. That he could intercept her on the bike. He had a letter in his pocket and he thought of putting it through the letter box, but there was no way of knowing she would get it even then.

At ten o'clock a police car cruised slowly by from the direction of the motorway. He bent over the Kawasaki and fiddled aimlessly with an oil feed pipe. The police car cruised on. There was no sign of the Special Branch cowpats. Education Secretaries weren't that much of a target, he supposed. Not yet at any rate. He waited another half-hour, but nobody went in or out of the driveway opposite.

Eventually inspiration struck him. He pulled on his new helmet and lowered the smoked perspex face visor. The doorbell played the first five notes of Loch Lomond and he heard a man's voice above the television. 'I'll get it, darling.' The door opened and Wilson's face, greenish and swollen by the visor, swam into view. 'Delivery for Miss Rachel Wilson,' said Alec.

'Who from?' Even inside the helmet Wilson's voice sounded suspicious. 'Speed Courier,' said Alec.

'I'll take it.'

'Recipient has to sign.'

'Give me your book, then.'

'Sorry. Against regulations.'

Wilson was examining the tweed jacket and corduroy trousers beneath the helmet. 'Who is it, Daddy?' called a voice from inside the house. Rachel's voice. Without thinking Alec stepped forward into the hallway. In the green, underwater light of the visor he could make out fitted carpets everywhere, like his mother's house. Swagged curtains and pelmets. A glass-fronted display cabinet with silver trophies and rosettes.

'What the hell do you think . . .' Wilson had grabbed his elbow, trying to pull him around and Alec pushed him away, harder than he meant to. The front of the display cabinet splintered. 'Ronald,' shouted a woman's voice, and then Rachel again, 'Daddy, what on earth . . .' Frantically Alec rotated his letter box of vision, a disabled tank, seeking the source of the voice in the gloom.

Then a pair of invisible hands seized the helmet and twisted it savagely on his neck. The underwater hallway disappeared from the perspex window and he staggered into something small that went over with a crash. Rachel and the other woman were screaming.

'Get his hands.'

'That bastard Smith.'

'Daddy, don't, he's . . .'

'I've got his legs.'

'My vase.'

'Police.'

'I'll break his bloody . . .'

Two pairs of hands, wrists and ankles, bundled him out of the door and flung him heavily down on the drive. 'You call the police, sir.'

The front door slammed. There was a scuffle of gravel, approaching him quickly. He was scrambling, blindly, to his feet, wrenching at the helmet, when the boot caught him, squarely in the testicles. His lungs emptied with a whoosh and he was on his knees, sobbing for air, when the second boot got him in the kidneys.

Still blind, he reached out, found a trousered leg and pulled hard. He heard a body thump down close to him on the gravel and flung himself across it. Guessing where the face was, he lashed out hard and felt a delicious stab of pain in his knuckles as some part of his attacker's body that was soft and wet and important yielded beneath them. There was a yelp of pain and in the distance the softer yelp of a police siren. He pulled the helmet off, threw it hard as he could in the face of the body on the ground and started running.

'I'll kill you,' called Toby after him. 'You fucking cunt.'

*

A week later the launderette woman told him he had a visitor. A young lady. Very nice. She made a shape in the air with her hands.

He ran up the stairs to the flat, three at a time, and found Vivien, sitting on her suitcase on the landing.

'Oh, it's you.'

'Sorry,' she said, 'I'll try and get some bigger tits.'

They had given her a year's salary, she told him, and a very nice reference. 'Nothing to do with the Rachel business at all, the VC said. Lots of changes going on. Finding a new role for the universities in the twenty-first century. All that bullshit. Actually nearly everybody in the English faculty is going. And the whole of philosophy.'

'What are you going to do?'

'Buy a flat. I got quite a lot out of Malcolm for my house. Then a job. I might do something on the *Bystander*.'

'I'm very sorry,' he said.

'It's not your fault, and I'm not sorry at all. I don't want to teach in a technical college.'

She bought some more furniture for the flat and a cooker and made some curtains on her sewing machine. He started getting up earlier, and drinking less. His egg-and-chip acne faded, and his grog spots. He began to go swimming in the mornings again.

When he told Vivien about William's rent demand she wrote a short note, offering £60 a week, which William accepted. They began going to films together in the afternoons, and art galleries. He discovered that he had always liked spending time with Vivien.

'You have to decide what you're going to do with yourself, you know,' she told him one day.

'Yes.'

'It's much cheaper to start up in publishing these days I'm told. You just get one of these new computers and set up in your own home. I've got three-quarters of a book on Mrs Oscar Wilde you could do.'

'I think you need a bit more than three hundred quid.'

But he started thinking about it anyway, and hanging around the shops in the Tottenham Court Road. He put his name down for a computer course at City University, and began reading obscure magazines with titles like *Desk-Top Publishing* and *Computer Bookmaker*.

Towards the middle of July Alec came home and found Vivien trying on a hat in his shaving mirror. 'I've decided we should go to your royal garden party,' she told him. 'My mother would have a fit if I told her that I'd missed the chance to visit Buckingham Palace.'

And so they went, with Vivien in her Joseph Tricot dress with a black straw hat and Alec in hired tails.

To keep things in proportion, though, they went on the Kawasaki 250, with Alec's top hat on the back carrier and Vivien's arms clasped hot across his stomach. They chugged very slowly down the Mall and twice around the Victoria Memorial. A few passers-by clapped and cheered them, and a Palace parking attendant pasted a permit crossly on the vinyl seat of the motor cycle.

'This is called the Grand Entrance,' said Alec, as they walked across the forecourt, 'and that's the main staircase, which leads up to the Bow Room, and out to the Terrace.'

'I'm deeply impressed. How do you know all this rubbish?'

'*Republican Reader* research,' said Alec. 'Now this is a nice bit of china.' They were surveying the display cabinets in the recesses of the Bow Room.

'The Mecklenburg-Strelitz table service, if I'm not mistaken,' said Vivien. 'Thought to be the finest example of Chelsea porcelain in existence.'

'Now I'm impressed.'

'William told me about it,' said Vivien. 'He said to nick him a teacup if I got the chance.'

*

Out on the Terrace a military band was making preparatory toots and squeaks. Green-striped tea tents were arranged along the south wall of the gardens and the rose beds blazed with July colour. Queen Elizabeth, Silver Lining and Peace. 'Tea first,' said Alec, 'and then we can concentrate properly on being snide about everybody else.'

Tea turned out to be rather nasty iced coffee, with cake covered in aerosol cream. 'The Joe Lyons Black Forest Gateau, if I'm not mistaken,' said Alec. 'Previously thought to exist only at . . .' and then he stopped.

She was only twenty yards away, in a plain white dress with a square scooped neck and a man's panama. She looked very brown, as if she had been abroad, and she was laughing at something her sister just said. Her father and mother were further away, in a group around the Prime Minister. There was no sign of Toby.

'You knew, didn't you?' he said to Vivien.

'Don't stand there gawping,' she told him, and pinched him hard on the backside.

He threaded his way through the crowd towards her, feeling absurd in his top hat and striped trousers. Her sister had begun to walk away towards her father. It was all arranged.

She didn't see him until he was nearly next to her. She didn't really see him then, her eyes following her sister's departing back, her fingers twisting a blade of grass. From the corner of his eye Alec could see her father, looking across, catching sight of him, beginning to move in their direction. He crossed five yards in a stride.

'Hello,' said Alec.

'Hello,' said Rachel.

'Hello,' said the Prince of Wales.

A small phalanx of slender men with wide shoulders, taut waistcoats and glistening shoes had advanced upon them unnoticed from the shrubbery.

'We met at the Frankfurt Book Fair,' said the Prince of Wales.

'Yes, of course,' said Alec. 'And thank you for your invitation. Let me introduce Miss Rachel Wilson' – he hesitated for a moment – 'my fiancée.'

'Delighted,' said the Prince of Wales, taking her hand. Over his shoulder Alec caught a glimpse of Ronald Wilson on the edge of the group, looking red and furious. One of the slender young men had laid a hand upon his arm. It was a gentle, cautionary hand, but it looked quite capable of snapping Wilson's arm like a carrot if its owner thought it necessary.

'Tell me, Mr Smith,' said the Prince of Wales, 'what are you working on at the moment? My father wants to know when the next *Republican Reader* is due.'

'Well, actually,' said Alec, 'I'm launching a new publishing project.' Inspiration seized him. 'It's an inner city publishing project, using new technology, employing young people who have been made redundant by advances elsewhere, and providing training in all basic skills.'

'Sounds absolutely fascinating,' said the Prince of Wales. 'Why don't you come along with us and tell me more about it over tea?'

'I told you he was all right, didn't I?' said Alec, much later.

They were standing on the Terrace of Buckingham Palace, looking down over the lawns where the long shadows of beeches fell, and uniformed servants were clearing away paper plates and sandwich crusts from the cropped turf. The guests had all departed by six. 'I must leave you now,' the Prince had said. 'Children's bathtime. But please look around the gardens. I'll arrange for a car to collect you at seven.'

'I feel bad about abandoning Vivien like that,' said Alec. 'She'll have to get the tube.'

'You know she loves you, don't you?' said Rachel.

The idea struck him with the force of revelation. Vivien loved him. It must be true, because women knew about such things, but it had never crossed his mind.

'And she arranged for us to meet here.'

'She's a very nice person,' said Rachel. 'Nicer than us.'

They wandered around the flamingo lake; admired the black mulberry that had been planted there by James I. They did not speak much.

'Forty acres of central London,' said Alec. 'Just think what it must be worth.'

'Would you really apply for one of those development grants he was talking about, from the Prince's Trust?' Rachel asked.

'Don't see why not,' said Alec.

'He must know how you disapprove of the monarchy and all that.'

'I don't think he approves of it all that much himself,' he said. 'It's just that he happens to *be* it.'

'You should have told me about everything,' said Alec later, when they were standing on the Terrace.

'You should have listened.'

'Yes.'

They were not touching, but they were standing so close that he could feel the warmth of her body through the thin silk of her dress.

'I didn't know you'd been trying to get in touch until that night you came to the house,' she said. 'I was in France with Hattie for a month. I had the most enormous row with Daddy when you'd gone. Did you know that you broke two of Toby's teeth?'

'Good,' said Alec.

'They want me to go to Oxford next year. Daddy thinks he can arrange something.'

'That's not so far from London.'

'No, that's what I thought.'

Now she was there beside him he did not know any more whether he wanted her. Whether he even liked her. Nineteen years old. He thought of driving up and down to visit her at Oxford, getting greyer and more tired. Of the new young friends she would make, and what they would make of Rachel's sugar daddy who had no sugar. Lefty Lothario Alec Smith, who needed injections to get his end up.

By the time she was forty he'd be shuffling around a hospital in his carpet slippers. And he knew hardly anything about her. She slept with people like Toby and William. She took overdoses. Had abortions. Chose Conservative ministers for close relations. What did she read? What did she vote? Could she cook? Would she like his friends? What would his father say? What would his children say?

He thought, nostalgically, about life with Susan, when the children had been small. The family holidays, bucket and spading in Paxos. Driving down the M4 to Gloucestershire, singing songs from *HMS Pinafore*. Reading Roald Dahl to them at bedtime. Sitting up late with Susan over the proofs of the early Prometheus books, a bottle of wine between them.

He thought of the little routine he had established with Vivien in the flat in Finsbury Park. Chaste, orderly, increasingly sober, increasingly purposeful. You could have a sensible life with somebody like Vivien. No more children, of course, but a little house somewhere decent like Camden Town; a modest job; some quiet dinner parties with old friends. Vivien wouldn't expect too much in bed either. They both knew him already, Vivien and Susan. No need to invent yourself anew. No need to become another Alec Smith. No need to try.

Through an archway in the Terrace he could see a Guardsman, his bearskin under his arm and a cigarette in his mouth. He looked about sixteen.

'You remember when the Beatles came here to get their MBEs?' said Alec.

'I wasn't even born then.'

'No. You weren't,' he said sadly. 'They apparently sneaked off to the lavs before their audience with the Queen and had a joint. One of those classic sixties things to do, you know? Pointless, infantile, gesturist.'

'Fun.'

'Exactly.'

He lost his heart again, and slipped an arm around her waist.

'You can't possibly kiss somebody on the Terrace of Buckingham Palace, you know,' said Rachel.

'There were some loos I noticed, back there under the archway.'

She squeezed him back, her hip moulded into his. 'You don't think they might be the Beatles ones, do you?'

'We could always go and see,' said Alec.

He hoped it would be all right this time.